WAR BUDS

Under Attack

JACK HUNT

DIRECT RESPONSE PUBLISHING

ISBN-13: 978-1546687986
ISBN-10: 154668798X

Also By Jack Hunt

The Renegades
The Renegades 2: Aftermath
The Renegades 3: Fortress
The Renegades 4: Colony
The Renegades 5: United
Mavericks: Hunters Moon
Killing Time
State of Panic
State of Shock
State of Decay
Defiant
Phobia
Anxiety
Strain

Dedication

For my family.

Prologue – High Value Target

1987, Eastern Sierra Mountains, California

Thirty Years Ago

Long before the country came under attack, our war began with him. Mack Sheldon was a beast of a man. Aptly nicknamed "The Machine," his six-foot muscular frame towered over us like one of the huge pines that surrounded the small town of Mammoth Lakes. A former Green Beret with more medals to his name than anyone could hope to achieve in a lifetime of service, he embodied everything we wanted to be — courageous, selfless and dangerous. A larger-than-life individual whose crazy feats in the army preceded him, he was the epitome of the all-American hero. The last of a dying breed, and if

I failed to mention him, our account of what took place would be sorely incomplete.

Among his many attributes, Mack had eyes like an eagle. There was very little that you could get past him, and yet that evening in the Eastern Sierra Mountains, that was exactly what we were attempting to do.

He would be our high-value target.

Our job was to locate, secure and extract him.

A seemingly easy task for anyone trained in military tactics, however, that certainly wasn't our group. At fifteen years of age, we were still wet behind the ears, sporting braces on our teeth and having wet dreams about high school cheerleaders.

Still it didn't prevent us from thinking we could achieve the impossible. In our minds, we were unstoppable at that age. The world was our oyster, we could do anything and no amount of persuasion would tell us any different.

That night it was to be our first mission, the first of many we would experience over the course of three years

— years we hoped would mold and shape our future, a future in the United States military.

And though at the time enlistment was nothing more than a dream, if anyone could get us ready it was Mack Sheldon. After many years of service, he had settled into his new life as a mechanic, though rumor had it he was still contracted out by the military and would deploy overseas to protect high-profile individuals. He'd be gone for months at a time and return with insane stories that would make the eyes of folks down at the local bar widen in horror. Others said he was just full of it, and that he was really visiting his sister in Texas.

When he wasn't reeling off some whopper of a tale, he offered to help anyone who wanted to join the military. More specifically, to assist them in passing the rigorous training regime required to become one of the nation's elite. Really, I think he just enjoyed chewing kids out and running them ragged so they would stay out of trouble.

Now at the age of fifteen, my friend and I finally summoned the courage to approach him and ask if he would train us to become Green Berets. I know. Crazy. Truthfully, we really didn't care about being a special operative, we just wanted to get a head start and increase our chances of getting into the military. Hell, at that time we didn't have a clue about what was involved, everything we learned came from watching films. In fact the whole thing had just been a dare. A mad idea concocted from the mind of Chase, my best friend. After watching the movie *Platoon*, he just couldn't shake the image of Charlie Sheen with a M16A1 in his hand. Perhaps like many others who joined the military, he figured life inside was going to be a non-stop thrill ride of blowing shit up and acting all badass. Mack soon dispelled that nonsense.

In all honesty, now as I look back, I'm not sure any of us really knew what we were getting ourselves into, or the impact Mack would have on us thirty years later. My mother would say that everything was in hindsight, that our steps were guided by something bigger than ourselves. I'm not too sure about that. It sounded like bull crap that was spoon-fed to us at church on a Sunday morning. Not that I'm against those of faith, but I've seen a lot of shit in my time that caused me to doubt that we were anything but alone in this world.

However, there is one thing I'm certain about, those years with Mack were some of the best years of my life. A moment in time that would forever remain seared in my mind.

Smeared in camouflage paint, our eight-man recon team lay prone in the dirt with our face masks up. In the darkness, all that might have been seen was a series of blinking eyes peering out from beyond a cluster of trees. We were kitted out in secondhand army fatigues that we'd picked up from some military surplus store in town. Of course the damn things didn't fit, so I had my mother unearth her ancient sewing machine to work its magic.

What a disaster that was.

Mine must have got mixed up with Kai's who was a short ass. My pants were riding up the crack of my ass and every few minutes I had to yank them down to avoid one hell of a wedgie.

There were sixteen of us out that evening in the mountainous region that surrounded our town. An opposing squad of eight was meant to protect the HVT, while ours was supposed to slip in, fuck 'em up, plant demolition charges and then breeze out of there with the prisoner like true medal-of-honor warriors.

Yeah... we hadn't got that far because one thing after another had gone wrong.

"This damn thing is jammed. What a piece of crap," Todd said slamming the palm of his hand against the side of his weapon. Obviously because of our age, Mack couldn't give us real loaded weapons or even ones that fired blanks, so instead he had worked out an arrangement with a buddy to supply him with a whole arsenal of paintball guns. Now back in '87 they weren't as slick as the ones sold today, and there certainly wasn't much to choose from. It was slim pickings; most of the products on the market were modified Sheridans and Nelspots. Still, they did the job and I thought they were pretty damn cool. Todd didn't but then he was a hard guy to please.

"Keep your voice down," I said in a hushed voice.

Mack had hooked us up with several Tippmann SMG-60's. It was pitched as the world's first select-fire paint pellet gun that could fire, semi or fully automatic, 600 rounds per minute. Not that it could hold that many. It was magazine-fed and relied on preloading from the side with bright orange stripper clips that held five .62-caliber paintballs. It would hold a maximum of 60 balls, had a range of 100 feet and could handle up to 450 shots per cylinder. Yep, that sucker was one hell of a weapon in its time. There was only one problem, well two, to be exact. These beauties usually cost three hundred bucks a pop, and there was no way in hell Mack was going to shell out that kind of green for a bunch of pissants that could barely put their pants on the right way around. However, fortunately for him and unfortunately for us, he'd managed to get some for less than thirty bucks because that winning batch he nabbed had a couple of issues, one being the damn things tended to jam and the other was that some of the CO_2 cylinders on the back were leaking due to damaged O-rings.

Todd got up off the ground and started banging the unit on the side of a tree.

"Get down, you idiot, you'll give away our location," I barked.

Marlin grabbed a hold of his jacket and yanked him back.

"Ah who cares, it's not like we stand a chance of getting through their defenses with these pieces of crap." He tossed it and pulled his bag off his back. He fished around inside for a second and that's when I caught sight of a Glock 18.

My eyes widened, I reached over and grabbed him by the collar. "Where the hell did you get that from?"

"My old man's gun cabinet."

"Is it loaded?"

"Of course it is."

"Put that thing away before you kill someone, you moron," Chase Garcia barked.

"But we can use it to our advantage. They aren't going to expect someone to fire a real round at them. One shot of this and they'll get the fuck out of dodge." He pointed the barrel at our heads. I reacted by slamming it to one side only to have it go off. We froze. For a few seconds there was silence as we remained still, hoping that none of us had been shot. After no cries or groans could be heard, Chase lunged forward and started laying into him.

"You dumbass." He dived on top of Todd and start wailing on him. It took three of us to haul him off. Chase wasn't a small guy and even back then he looked as if he was eating for two when he sat down in cafeterias.

"Get off me, you idiot," Todd said while trying to protect his face from Chase's meaty paws. Chase cracked him on the chin and cut his lip open.

At the best of times the two of them had issues with one another but it didn't help that a gun had killed Chase's old man a few years earlier in an argument outside a bar. He hadn't been the same since. Finally Chase managed to wrestle the gun from him, then he pulled the magazine out and tossed it as far as he could.

"Oh for fuck's sake, Chase, now how am I going to find that? My old man is going to go apeshit on me."

"Good," he said dropping the rest of the gun on him, then running a hand over his buzzed blond hair. "I hope he gives you twenty licks of his belt." Marlin and Kai roared with laughter as we watched him walk off to find it. Todd switched on a small flashlight and began sweeping the forest floor while grumbling to himself. Todd Fontane was a complete jackass. A stringy-looking fellow, with less meat on him than a chicken, he dressed in a raggedy old green jacket, like the kind worn by Robert De Niro in *Taxi Driver*. His dark hair was even buzzed at the sides like he was trying to imitate him or his father, we couldn't figure out which one. His old man, Chuck Fontane, was an even bigger lunatic. He was in the habit of getting drunk and giving Todd's mother a shiner. The one time Todd tried to intervene he paid for it dearly. He took a belt to his behind and made sure the buckle struck him multiple times. The kid couldn't sit down for days. He never showed up at school all that week and though we kind of figured what had happened, we never brought it up.

"You guys done jerking each other off?" A barrel-chested kid by the name of Kurt Donahue piped up. Of course, among a group of army wannabes there would always be one dickhead who took everything super serious. It was like they had something to prove. Donahue was "the guy" who would be last to get laid because he was too busy spit polishing his boots and spending every waking hour sniffing the asses of the powers that be. Of course he wouldn't see it that way. He was the kind of freak that would come up with lines like… "if you don't think tactical, you'll get yourself killed" or "I would never do that because I know every fucking rule under the sun and my daddy was a four-star general." As if we gave a shit. Back then it was just fun, we didn't anticipate to find ourselves smack bang in the shit storm of the century, many moons later.

Marlin gave Kurt the bird, and we all moved out

under the cover of darkness. Our first objective was to carry two inflatable boats down to the river and launch in an area across from Banbush Road. From there we would paddle the boats up the river to a bunch of log cabins near Mammoth Mountain. Upon getting close to the location, two swimmer scouts would enter the river and swim near to the primary insertion point and make sure it was all clear. If it was, they would give a red lens signal to the boats, we'd pick up the swimmers and then tie off the boats and haul ass to the secondary insertion point. Now it all made sense when Mack was reeling it off earlier that afternoon, but telling and doing were two different things and our group was full of all types of retards who could fuck it up.

"You sure you know where the hell we are?" Kurt muttered to our buddy Kai. Of course the biggest asshole in our group had been given the position of patrol leader while I'd been made assistant leader. Chase was meant to be a point man while Marlin was the radio guy and good old Todd had volunteered to be the demolition guy along with several others.

We stopped for a second while Kai peered through his Coke bottle glasses at a map. He was down on his knees shining a light over it when Kurt came up and gave him a kick in the ass. "Did you hear me, chink?"

"Yeah, I hear real good and you still as dumb as fuck," Kai said pulling at his own eyes and mocking his own Chinese heritage.

"You cheeky asshole." Kurt went to kick him again but Kai spun around and took out his other leg. Kurt landed on his ass and the rest of us cracked up laughing. Kurt got up scowling, brushed himself off and trudged away threatening to make him pay later. It didn't faze Kai one bit.

Kai Tukami was a small guy but shit on me if he couldn't take down someone twice his size. His family ran a martial arts school in town. It was the only one that offered lessons from a real Chinese Kung Fu master. From the moment he could stand, his father had him doing spinning round houses, and within a matter of eight years Kai had so many gold medals plastered around his bedroom it would put others three times his age to shame. Whether his father's discipline was a good thing was still to be determined, but we couldn't help think he went a little overboard at times.

Anyway, not only was Kai an expert at the way of the fist but he was the only guy who could find humor in some of the lame ass racial remarks made to him by ignorant losers in the town.

Of course his life wasn't too bad. I don't think there was a year that went by that we hadn't seen him with one girl or another hanging off his arms. He was a complete chick magnet and definitely the one who raised the bar of what we thought was possible.

"We're on track. It's north of here."

"Right on, let's go."

As we got closer to the river, the babble of rushing water filled the air. Sweat trickled down my back as we lugged one of the boats down to the water and everyone hopped in and started paddling. Minutes later, only the sound of tree frogs could be heard as we eased our way upstream through pristine waters. Mosquitoes buzzed around our heads and Todd kept slapping his neck and cursing.

Marlin was one of two swimmer scouts that launched over the side and swam ahead to make sure the coast was clear. He was always the strongest swimmer. Seconds turned into minutes and then a red glowing eye flicked on and off in the distance. We paddled in the rest of the way and picked them up and eased down the banks until we reached the insertion point and tied the boats off.

From there it was another two-mile jog through a mosquito-infested forest until the log cabins came into sight. At this point our team of eight was meant to split up. Two guys were to plant the demolition charges while the rest of us moved on to the cabins. Of course it wasn't actual C-4, just simple road flares.

Donahue peered into the darkness.

Mack wasn't loaded with cash so there was only one person on each team that had night vision optics. The rest of us would just have to wing it. Of course Donahue had the optics and was leading the way.

"Now listen up, pussies, I'm taking Nick with me around to the north wing, you guys are to take the south."

"But how the hell do you know where they are keeping him?"

"We don't but our best guess is it's in one of those two northern cabins. Which means you guys are going to watch our backs."

"Don't you think we should stick together?"

"No. We are going to do a two-man room entry, and you four will head over there."

"And what if he's being held in the southern cabins?"

"Then draw them away and we'll circle around and help you out. Shit is about to get real and I don't want you four screwing this up for us."

"What, because you want all the glory?" I muttered.

"Slater, you have a big mouth on you. I'm in charge of this operation and you've been nothing but a pain in my ass since you got here. In fact all five of you have."

"Ah, did we ruin your fun?" Marlin said, the corner of his lip curled up. Donahue looked like he was about to flip his lid when one of the roadside flares ignited. An orange and red glow along with smoke cut into the night.

"That's our signal. Go!"

We split; I led the other three south, towards cabins which had several guards outside. I squeezed the trigger and unloaded several shots at one of the guards from the safety of the tree line while Marlin, Chase and Kai took out the other one. Our confidence was boosted at the thought that they were now two men short, which meant only six remained but the next question was... where were they?

A flurry of shots answered that. Paint splattered against trees around us as we stepped out into the clearing. I tried to make a break for the closest cabin. Kai caught one on the side of the shoulder and let out a groan. Once hit, we'd be out of the mission. It wasn't exactly the most realistic of situations but it was the type of mission he was trying to teach us about, and being as it was our first, he must have known we'd screw it up.

We took cover behind a Jeep and Kai continued to return fire.

"Kai, you're out," some kid named Wendell Clark muttered.

"The fuck I am. It was a shoulder shot."

"But the rules," he repeated.

"There are no rules in war."

"He has a point," Marlin said. I just shrugged and tried to prevent two guys from circling around. In the distance I could see Donahue taking advantage of the fact that we were pinned down. He and Nick were edging their way around the back.

Todd rejoined us and slammed against the back of the jeep.

"Did you see those flares?" He started laughing. "God, this is great."

He then bounced up and unloaded round after round in a spraying fashion before sliding back down. I expected

Donahue to take out the three guys that were preventing us from reaching the building.

"Any second now."

My jaw dropped as Donahue slipped by unnoticed and entered the building but not before flashing me a grin and sticking up his middle finger. He could have easily engaged with the enemy from behind but instead he chose to go for the prize.

"Bastard!" I muttered pulling back from a line of fire. By now the jeep was plastered in splats of paint. If either one of us attempted to make a run for it, we would end up with one in the back or chest. Marlin was on the ground with Wendell, trying to hit them from below the vehicle, while Todd, Kai and I were preventing them from circling around.

"Are you kidding me?" Todd yelled after taking a shot to the head. He sank back down. "Son of a bitch!" A splat of red paint smeared the front of his mask.

"Ah who cares, just keep going," Kai said.

"Don't listen to him," Wendell shouted. "Mack will

have your ass on a platter if you break the rules."

"Screw the rules," I muttered. Donahue wasn't playing by them so neither were we. The rules were pretty clear that we were meant to cover each other's ass, work as a team and if a clear shot was available, take it. He'd had multiple chances to take the enemy out, and instead he chose to be the goddamn hero.

"Let's get in there."

"But we'll be hit. I would strongly advise we don't," Wendell said. The rest of us looked at each other and cracked up laughing and then as if acting as one mind, we burst out from behind the jeep and unloaded as many rounds as we could at them.

Did we get hit? Of course, we got absolutely plastered. But the way I saw it, we were fifteen years of age, these were not real bullets, we had years to learn and I had a beef to pick with Donahue. You see, my trouble with Kurt had started long before we ended up under the tutorage of Mack Sheldon.

Three years earlier my older brother Sam had died

from an IED explosion on his first tour overseas. He was just short of his twenty-first birthday. Though my father hadn't been in the military himself, Sam's decision to enlist had made him proud beyond belief. So when he died, so did my father. He became a shell of a man, given to drinking to deal with the loss.

When I wasn't picking him off the driveway after he'd passed out from an afternoon of drinking, I'd find him absently gazing out the window when I was at home. That was hard, but not as hard as showing up to school a few weeks later. It felt like a million eyes were on me in that first month. Most kids understood but Donahue wasn't like most. While other kids soon forgot, or busied themselves with their own troubles, my brother's death never left the mind of Donahue. I don't know if his home life was shit or he just found joy in the misery of others but it didn't take long for his snarky little comments about how my father had become the town drunk to find their way into classroom banter.

Yep, Donahue was a dick long before he had a reason

to be one. It was as if his only means of communication was to belittle others. So when I burst through the door of the building, you could say that night's operation took a back seat to several years of bottled-up frustration.

Donahue was positioned at the far end of the corridor, firing around the corner, when I came up behind him and shoved him out into what Mack had called the fatal funnel.

The final two opposing team members unleashed hell and emptied their magazines on him and within a matter of seconds, he was covered from head to toe in red paint. The look on his face was priceless. I didn't wait for Donahue to react, I double-timed it around the corner with Kai and squeezed the trigger and fired a burst from the Tippmann SMG-60 into the chest of one of them while Kai took out the other target.

"What the fuck!" Donahue yelled but Marlin got between him and me so that we could complete the mission. The last two guys had been guarding the room with the HVT. We entered and started yelling commands for Mack to get on the ground. He grinned as he saw the state of our fatigues. It was a damn mess. We must have looked like we had stepped out of an oil painting.

Mack got on his face and Todd zip tied him. No sooner had he seized him than Donahue started protesting.

"This is bullshit. Mack, they broke the rules. We were on the same team, dipshit."

He wasn't alone in his whining, several of the opposing team had entered to bitch and complain as well. Meanwhile with grins on our faces we strong-armed Mack out of the building with all the pride of a pack of lions that had captured its prey.

* * *

Later that evening as we all gathered around the campfire, sitting on logs, tension hung in the air. Mack wasn't one to hold his tongue, and he certainly didn't put up with any bullshit but he had little to say after we brought him out of the building. He held off giving us his verdict on how it went until we'd eaten. All the while

Todd, Marlin, Chase, Kai and I became the focus of the others' disdain. If scowls could kill, we were already dead and buried.

Only the sound of wood popping, and murmurs could be heard as the last scraps of food were scraped from metal bowls. As darkness swallowed us and the fire cast shadows on faces, Mack rose to his feet, cleared his throat and spat a wad of phlegm into the fire.

"As you know, with every operation I like to provide a good amount of input but as this was your first, I just wanted to see what you would do without guidance. You see, you learn a lot about a man when you throw him into a hellish situation, and today this didn't even come close to hell. Today was a fuck-up on all fronts. Had this been a real war, you would have all been dead. Every single one of you. So I'm not going to say it was okay or cherry coat this and say you'll get another chance, even though most of you might. That's because in war you don't get a second chance. Nine times out of ten, it's one strike and you are out. Gone. You are coming home in a body bag, and I for one don't enjoy walking up to a buddy's home and telling his wife or parents that their loved one is dead because I was a jackass. Do I make myself clear?"

From across the fire Donahue grinned. Of course he was just waiting for Mack to go ballistic on us. In all honesty I expected nothing less.

"Yes sir," everyone yelled.

"Remember, you came to me to be trained. I'm not here to wipe your asses or mediate between any of you cocksuckers. I'm here to prepare you for the shit storm we call life. For some of you that will mean slogging it out in boot camp and going on to a long career in the U.S. military, for others maybe not. But either way, you will learn to adapt and overcome through adversity. You will learn why people fail in combat and fail at life. You will gain a new outlook, a stronger mind-set and leave ready to conquer the toughest of challenges. No matter what obstacle lays ahead, no matter how high that wall is, you will go over, under and around. You will find a way. The only thing that can stop you, is you!"

You could have heard a pin drop.

He sniffed hard and pulled out a cigar from his top pocket. Everyone watched as he squatted down by the fire and lit it, taking short puffs until the end glowed.

"Now having said that, and without taking anything away from what I've said, as believe me you would all be dead right now, I feel it's necessary to highlight those here who showed grit. They showed something you can't instill in people. You either have it or you don't. Sure, it was a fuck-up and was liable to get you killed in the heat of battle but it's not the actions I'm concerned with right now. That mess can be trained out of them. Thank God for that," he said shaking his head. A few snickers drifted across the group. "It's what they demonstrated here." He tapped his heart with a closed fist. "That's what I'm interested in. Brody Slater, Todd Fontane, Marlin Calder, Kai Takumi and Chase Garcia, stand up."

Donahue frowned at the fact that he'd been excluded. Now, I was fully ready to have Mack chew us out, rip us a new one and humiliate us in front of the rest but that wasn't to be.

"In light of that horrendous display of... whatever the hell that was... I have to ask, why did you continue fighting?"

"Because I wasn't dead," I replied before the others said anything.

Mack smirked and tapped some ash. It drifted down and then was carried by the wind. I reeled off what I felt in the moment. Whether right or wrong, it didn't matter. We were just young guys without training, without understanding and just pumped up by the anticipation of becoming something more than who we were.

"But why did you break the rules of the operation?"

I swallowed hard.

That's when Kai piped up, repeating exactly what he had said on the battlefield. "Because in war there are no rules."

Mack gritted his teeth. "That's not exactly accurate but it does remind me of something old Navy SEAL buddy of mine used to say and it's worth remembering because someday it might save your lives." He snorted again and spat another wad of green shit at the fire before continuing. "In combat, the larger force dictates the rules… and Navy SEALs are always the smaller force. To win you need to break the rules."

"But sir," Donahue said looking even more concerned than when his name hadn't been called to stand.

"Enough, Donahue. The point here is that war is messy. You can go in there with the best training and plan in the world and the whole thing can go sideways. Ultimately when push comes to shove, what determines whether you live or die may come down to a simple decision of what rule you will break or abide by. It doesn't matter if you are a Marine, Ranger, SEAL, Pararescue, Green Beret, or SAS. It doesn't matter what you think is the correct tactical decision. I only have one word of advice on breaking rules. If you are going to break them, do it together!"

With that said he sat back down and even though a few murmurs continued, slowly what he conveyed sank in and all of us learned our first and most valuable lesson that day.

Little did we know that it was one that we would need to remember if we were to survive the coming war.

One – No Respect

2017, Mammoth Lakes, California

Present Day

"Breathe, Brody, breathe!" I said after slamming the phone down. Another argument was brewing. This time the call came in from Hector. It was the same every damn week. Couldn't these morons handle her? I sank into my leather chair, put my earphones back in, took another bite of my bland sandwich before closing my eyes and repeating the mantra.

"I'm in charge of how I feel and today I'm choosing happiness," I said out loud, in unison with the soothing voice of Kelly Laquin, the international best-selling author and motivational speaker.

Another minute passed, and the phone rang again.

Let it ring. Let it ring. They can handle it. It can wait, I told myself as I tried to resume the motivational self-help audio.

"It will be okay. Everything is in your control. It will be okay," I said through gritted teeth. The sound was like fingernails scraping down a chalkboard. An incessant ringing trying to rob my peace and tease me to explode.

"It will be okay," Kelly said. It was easy for her to say from her Hawaiian ocean-view home. What did she know about stress? She obviously had no damn idea about my life.

And then, the sound that I had come to despise ceased.

All was quiet. Perfectly quiet.

I breathed a sigh of relief and managed to crack a partial smile before it started again.

I snapped.

"It will NOT be fucking okay!" I yelled at the top of my voice, yanking my earphones out and tossing my iPhone across the desk. I kicked off my soft slippers and slipped back into the highly polished dress shoes, resenting every second. "I get thirty goddamn minutes a day for my lunch. Is it too much to ask to be able take it without being pestered?"

It was like clockwork. I swear that old coot knew the exact moment I entered the office for lunch. Last week I had been sitting on the shitter when the call came in, the week before that I was in the middle of mountain yoga pose. I nearly fell ass over tit trying to reach the phone that time.

I tugged at the tie, adjusting it, tossed my suit jacket back on and paused for a second in front of the mirror to make sure I didn't have any ham and Swiss stuck between my teeth. I had begun to convince myself that it was life's way of shafting me, as the past two years had been one hellish nightmare after the other.

I'd finalized on my divorce with Theresa.

Got into a car crash that broke my leg and put the insurance through the roof. And I had my Ukrainian landlord riding my ass over rent money. It seemed that he didn't understand the meaning of they don't pay me enough and he thought jacking up the rent to twice the amount was a surefire way to attain the American Dream.

But, it wasn't all bad.

At least that's what I had convinced myself.

I still had my job as store manager at Von's Supermarket and I was damn good at it, even if I did have to put up with the weekly bullshit of Edna Wainright and her fucking coupons.

I ran my tongue over my pearly whites and groaned at the sight of another fleck of gray hair. I touched my receding hairline and gazed at my pasty white skin. Ugh! Getting old sucked. Forty-five years of age and not getting any younger. Where had the years gone? *You were meant for so much more than this.*

I double-timed it out of my office, catching my suit on the door handle and hearing it tear.

"Shit!"

I gazed despondently at the rip and squeezed my fist tight before making a beeline for the checkout.

"Ah, Mr. Slater, just the man I wanted to see."

I was blindsided.

Harold Pimler was a nuisance to society and a royal pain in my ass, second in line of course to Edna. Harold was in the habit of coming in and requesting a specific line of coffee that we never stocked and would never carry as they only sold it in Bermuda. Still, it didn't prevent him from asking multiple times. Either he had the memory of Dory or he just enjoyed pissing me off. My money was on the latter.

"Not now, Harold," I said putting up my palm but wishing I could have flipped him the bird. I expertly slipped through a traffic jam of shopping carts with all the finesse of an Olympic skater. It was Thursday afternoon, which meant all the single mothers in town were out in full force. Every week at Von's there was a different sale but Thursdays had some of the best deals. Mostly on baby food, diapers and contraceptives. I liked to think I was doing my part to cut down on population crowding.

"Hey Brody!"

I turned sharply while continuing to walk backwards to find Erin Davis throwing me her usual fuck-me eyes while ignoring the fact that her two kids were having a pillow fight using bags of marshmallows. The bags burst and white fluffy cubes went everywhere, to which she went from sweet as pie to the girl from *The Exorcist*. "You fucking little brats," she yelled.

"Gotta go," I said, thanking the big man upstairs for that swift act of deliverance.

Realizing her spawns from hell had ruined the moment, she turned and mimicked the global sign for "call me."

Yeah, like I was going to do that. There was more chance of hell freezing over.

Somehow word had got around that I was single. I put it down to my ex telling her loudmouth hairdresser. She was notorious for flapping her gums and spreading rumors, like the one that caused our divorce. I'd go into it but I'm still working through the trauma with Kelly Laquin. Her voice came back to me like an angel on my shoulder. "Accept what is. Let go of what was and have faith in what will be." Personally I preferred my version of it: "Let shit go."

Yeah, in all the rumors swirling around our small town, no one had thought to ask why Theresa was spending all her lunch hours with Carl Stimms, the local butcher. She would have said she was purchasing meat. Oh she was getting meat all right. Cheating bitch. I only wished I'd found out sooner, that was fourteen years of my life down the tube.

I threaded my way around two oldies sporting blue rinses and caught them griping about how the price of bread had gone up, and how their monthly Social Security checks barely covered the essentials. I stopped and fished out of my jacket a couple of "Free for Today Only" vouchers and handed them over. The look on their faces was priceless. It was worth the three bucks.

"Mr. Slater. You are one of the good ones."

"Only to you two," I winked before escaping what would have been a long discussion about how kindness was rare nowadays and how I reminded them of their grandson. I'd had the vouchers made up when I was still living with Theresa and all was well in my world. I kept a tally of the prices of food and paid it off at the end of my shift. It wasn't much, and I didn't do it for everyone but as I didn't contribute to any charities, it made me feel good to know I was helping locals and well, old folks and some of the single moms seemed to appreciate it.

I continued on my way only to find myself doing a tango in the middle of aisle four with several "aisle blockers." They were lower on my list of the most annoying customers. They would stand there gazing absently up at the shelves, looking as though they were suffering from some form of amnesia. Meanwhile their cart would be clogging up both lanes.

I had a good mind to knock some sense into them using a French baguette.

When I finally managed to squeeze my way through, I could see the red light above Hector's checkout blinking and Edna voicing her complaint to several other bystanders. If I didn't deal with it immediately, I was going to have a full-scale shopping war on my hands.

I raised a hand and flashed one of my winning smiles. I hated having to fake it but the alternative would have been unpleasant and I couldn't afford another warning from my district manager. "Mrs. Wainright, what a pleasure to see you again," I said in the most enthusiastic tone I could summon before maneuvering around the checkout to where Hector was standing with his arms folded.

"I wish I could say the same thing."

I raised a finger. "If you'll just give me a second with my employee, I'll have this squared away for you in no time."

She snorted and rolled her eyes. Edna Wainright was in her early sixties. A retiree, she had spent the better part of her life as a beautician, not that anyone could tell as she had a face like someone had set it on fire and put it out with a shovel. The phrase "less is more" obviously didn't register with her. Her hair was a crazy mess, she wore too much makeup and tanned so often that her orange skin made her look like an adult-sized umpa lumpa.

"What appears to be the problem?" I whispered into his ear.

Hector showed me the stack of coupons that she usually brought in. With the amount of coupons that she collected on a weekly basis she could have been a perfect candidate for the *Extreme Couponing* TV show.

"These free coupons aren't valid, Mr. Slater. The register is rejecting them but the expiration date doesn't run out until the end of this week. I tried to explain it to her but she wouldn't listen."

"Let me see."

I took several of them and punched the code into the register, a note came up on the screen that said: INELIGIBLE VALUE CODE FORMAT CODE 832 COUPON. I went through the process of trying another five before I sucked in air between my teeth and cast a glance over to Edna who was scowling at me with pursed lips.

"It's valid. Look at the date," she snapped.

It had recently come to my attention that fake coupons

were circulating in the town. Unlike money which could be verified by holding it up to the light and searching for a holograph of a face or placing it under the cashier's UV light to reveal a thin vertical strip, the process of checking coupons hadn't been as easy for the longest time. However, many of the newer coupons were appearing with a CIC hologram across the top to assist stores. None of these had that.

"Ma'am, where did you obtain these coupons?"

She screwed up her face as if the question was irrelevant. "Does it matter?"

"Humor me."

"From the newspaper."

"And?"

I raised an eyebrow to let her know that I wasn't buying her little game.

"Okay, I bought some of them online. But they are all legit."

I nodded and glanced at the amount on the register. Forty percent of her coupons didn't have the CIC hologram, which meant they were counterfeit.

"I can honor the ones that you got from the newspaper as I'm familiar with the local companies here in town, but unfortunately these major brand coupons that you purchased online I can't accept."

Well, that statement just opened up a whole host of crazy that I was not prepared for, especially since I hadn't had my afternoon coffee and well, quite frankly the town had already filled the quota of crazy for that week.

"This is typical. Absolutely typical. Tell me, Mr. Slater, what is it like working for the Illuminati?"

I coughed hard. "Who?"

"Oh, we're going to play the dumb card, are we?" She jabbed her finger towards Hector who looked as dumbfounded as I did. "I bet you're in on it as well?"

"Listen, Mrs. Wainright."

"No, you listen to me. The war drums are banging louder than ever. Can't you hear them?" She cupped a hand to her ear and moved out into the aisle. Curious shoppers looked on and I began to feel my shirt collar tighten. "My nephew told me this would happen. He made it clear that I had to prepare, and he was right. First America bombs Syria, now Russia and China are denouncing the attack, and if that's not cause for concern we have North Korea looking to launch ballistic nuke missiles at us. Oh but you would deny an old woman her right to prepare. Why? Because you are in on it. Aren't you?"

"What?" I stammered unable to comprehend what the hell she was on about. Sure, I had heard things were heating up over in the east but it had been like that since the cold war. One country threatened another, and another retaliated. It was all just hot air.

She rushed back and grabbed a hold of my name tag. "Where is it?"

I threw my arms up in the air. "Where is what?"

"The eye of the Illuminati. It's on here somewhere. They usually hide it."

"Mrs. Wainright, would you just… just… let go!" I yelled, trying to pry loose her gnarled fingers without breaking them. I took a step back as she paced up and down muttering all manner of absurd things under her breath.

I slowly pulled off the radio from my belt while she continued to stab the air with her finger as if she was giving some speech to the masses.

I cleared my throat and whispered into it, "Security, could you get down to checkout five. One flew over the cuckoo's nest. Repeat. One flew over the cuckoo's nest." That was the code word for that we had a batshit crazy customer and to prepare to take them down.

Of course I could have avoided her outburst by overriding the register but I had all but exhausted my kindness for that week, and crazy, well, I didn't do too well with it.

When our security guard, Augustus Tanbury, shuffled into view, he was still chewing on a candy bar and adjusting his glasses. The kid had to be at least 300 pounds. It was part of the reason we hired him, that and he'd been out of work for over a year. Truth be told, his physical size intimidated people and since employing him, there had been a 22 percent reduction in shoplifting and irate customers. In my book that was money well spent.

When Edna caught sight of him she slammed her hand against the counter.

"Oh really? You are going to throw me out now?"

As Augustus got closer, she started screaming. "Don't you touch me! I'll scream rape!" He hadn't got within a few feet when she hollered "Rape!"

My eyes widened as shoppers turned to see what the commotion was about.

"Mrs. Wainright, please, settle down."

"I will not. Rape! Brutality!"

"Okay, okay. I will override the coupons, just calm down."

I glanced at the amount of three hundred and fifty-two dollars and grimaced. That was going to sting. If I didn't feel it in my own pocket, I was going to end up getting some long lecture on a conference call from the district manager. Either way I was screwed. But having already received a warning after a disgruntled customer filed a false complaint, I was walking a fine line.

I just notched it up to another shafting from the universe.

I tapped in the override code and Hector nervously stepped back in front of the register and began swiping through the rest of her items. She had two shopping carts full of canned goods. Mostly tuna. It looked like she was preparing to feed the five thousand.

"Planning to eat this yourself?" I asked. She stared at me through slit eyes.

"Do I look stupid?" she shot back. I was glad she couldn't read my mind in that moment. God, I disliked that woman.

Several shoppers who were waiting in line had shifted over to another cashier. I glanced at them and though they had witnessed her tirade, it was clear they thought I was to blame. I heard one of them mutter while walking away. "Shame. Shame on you."

Edna clicked her fingers in front of my face. "Are you

listening? You got to snap out of your dream world, young man, and wake up to the reality of what is coming down the pipeline," she said in a condescending manner. "Why do you think I've been coming in here week after week and buying hundreds of dollars of groceries?"

"I just thought you enjoyed tuna," I muttered.

"News alert!" She raised her finger pointing at me and looking around at the rest of the shoppers. "Another clueless American! When are you going to wake up and smell the coffee? We are on the brink of a full-scale war. You mark my words. It might not happen this week, or next month but it's going to happen and when it does, you better be ready."

"That will be four dollars and ten cents," Hector said after making the adjustment.

"Yes!" Edna hollered while fist pumping the air like she'd just hit the lottery. "Now that's what I'm talking about." She reached into her purse and thumbed out five bucks. "And don't you dare shortchange me!"

"Would you like shopping bags, ma'am?" Hector

asked.

Her eyes widened as she stared back at him and placed her hands on her hips. "Well, I'm not going to juggle all this shit out the door, am I?"

"No. Um. Of course not," Hector replied, quickly filling up bags and a few boxes with her items. Meanwhile she stood there with her arms crossed like an overbearing supervisor just waiting for him to screw up. I assisted him just so we could get rid of her. She burned me with a scornful gaze.

"Now Mr. Slater, if you wouldn't mind having one of your employees assist me in taking out my groceries, that would be kind."

I smiled politely. "Would you like me to fucking eat them as well?" I muttered under my breath.

"What was that?" she said.

"Oh nothing."

I motioned to Augustus, and Nancy who was just about to take over on checkout six. All three of us loaded up the carts full of bags and wheeled them out. Of course

I got the one with the wonky wheel. Every time it got stuck, Edna would crack some joke about how she would hate to see me drive.

Outside I slammed the trunk closed, and we stepped out of the way.

"Thanks, guys," I said to the other two before they strolled back inside. As I stood in the parking lot, a warm summer breeze blew against my face. I watched her drive away and I couldn't help be reminded of Mack Sheldon. He'd always harped on about preparation for the worst-case scenario. It had been a while since I'd dropped in on him. Several months to be exact. So much had changed in thirty years. The struggle and busyness of daily living had got in the way. Heck, I hadn't been out with the guys in years. They were all working different jobs and like most friends I grew up with, we all went in different directions. A couple of them I still saw when I was running an errand in town but beyond a nod or a wave that was about it. I stuck my hands in my pockets and wondered what had happened to us? We'd all aspired to join the military and yet from what I could see, none of us had enlisted.

"That was very kind what you did," a female voice said from behind me. I twisted to see a dark-haired beauty. I squinted as the glare of the sun blocked my view. *Is that...?* I couldn't believe it. Jen? We'd once dated back in high school, it wasn't serious and it didn't last long but she was always sweet. Looking back, I think it was me who screwed it up. She was shy, and like any testosterone-fueled guy, I only had one thing on the mind back then.

I shifted from one foot to the next and squinted. "Jen Lawson?"

"I know I look old, don't say it."

She smiled while juggling five grocery bags and then extended a hand. I shook it while soaking in the sight of a ghost from the past.

"Brody Slater," she said slowly. "It's been a long time."

I inhaled deeply. "That it has."

Old? She was still as gorgeous as ever. In fact she actually looked better now. My eyes drifted to her hand that still had a grasp on her bags. There was no wedding band. *Um, promising,* I thought. I figured someone of her caliber would have a boyfriend. She was the kind of woman that any man would have been proud to introduce to the family.

"Von's Supermarket? Huh!" She gazed back at the building like it was some mental hospital for the insane. Which of course wasn't far from the truth. "I would never have thought you would have ended up here."

I placed two hands on my lower back and arched a little feeling the tension of carrying all that tuna. "Yeah, me too."

"Weren't you going to join the Marines or become some Green Beret or something?"

I laughed and then felt completely stupid. It seemed ridiculous now, like an old schoolboy's dream, but she was right. At the time that was all I wanted to do, and perhaps I would have if things hadn't gone the way they had.

"Yeah. Never happened."

An awkward moment.

Then it must have dawned on her what she'd said.

"Oh, too bad. I didn't mean… Um." Another pause. "At least you're working, right?"

"Yeah, store manager. Eleven years." I nodded. "It pays benefits."

It pays benefits? What a dumb thing to say. I chided myself inwardly.

She made a face with her lips as she considered my words. I cleared my throat and shifted the topic from the awkwardness. "Can I give you a hand with those?"

"Oh, no, it's fine, I can do it, it's just over there."

"Please. I insist."

The corner of her mouth curled. "Okay." She handed off a few of the bags and I walked her back to her vehicle. We only took about five steps.

"Like I said, it was just over there."

She chuckled and once again I felt like an idiot.

I glanced at the black Escalade like I was some connoisseur of motor vehicles.

"Nice ride."

"Oh this." I expected her to tell me it was her boyfriend's. She was probably dating some professional snowboarder or millionaire entrepreneur. "Thanks." She never did divulge whose it was, and I wasn't going to pry.

"So, you visiting family?" I asked.

"Actually just moved back to the area because my mother has been pretty sick."

I frowned. "Sorry to hear that."

We were all getting to a worrying age where our parents were in their late sixties or early seventies. Mine were still alive but both of them had relocated to Florida and I kind of figured that my days of seeing them in good health were numbered.

"I was living out in San Francisco working as a nurse."

"Ah, that's good. Nice place."

"Yeah, paid the bills."

She unlocked the trunk, and we loaded the grocery bags in and she pushed up her aviator shades and flashed those forest green eyes that had once caught my attention so many years ago. For a few seconds I felt like I was standing in high school asking her to go out with me. I noticed now that she had a few lines around her eyes, not many, just a few.

"So are you back permanently?"

"At least for now."

I wanted to ask if she was dating someone, or if she had kids. Most people I knew that still lived in the area had two or more of their own. I had one, a daughter, though my relationship with her was strained because of Theresa. She had practically turned Ava against me and made up some bullshit reason why I wouldn't see her. The truth was she had full custody because her brother was a lawyer. I guess he knew how to pull a few strings.

A few more seconds passed, and I was fully expecting the moment to end as quickly as it had begun and I would return to the hell that I had come to know as my employment, and she would disappear, nothing more than a beautiful reminder of what once was. Instead, she said, "We should go for a drink sometime."

I didn't say anything. Where had the shy girl

disappeared to? My tongue stuck to the roof of my mouth. I swallowed hard and wanted to ask her to run that by me again but instead I nodded.

"Just a drink. It's been a rough couple of months and I could use a break. That's if you're available."

I nodded like a bobblehead. "Yeah, yeah, that sounds good."

I assumed she was just being polite, and that it was nothing more than a conversation closer. A way to put an end to an awkward exchange, which had me second-guessing everything I'd said.

"Well, I should be getting back to work." I thumbed over my shoulder

"So how's tonight sound?" she shot back.

"What?"

Her eyes widened. "Tonight. The drink?" she said in a manner as if I had forgotten.

I shook my finger out in front of me. "Tonight. Um. I actually. Well."

"Or another night, whatever is good for you."

She shifted her weight in a way that showed off her trim figure.

"No, yeah, tonight… I think is good. Just let me check my schedule."

I flipped over my empty palm and swiped at it and she grinned. "Yep, looks like I can push back that prostate exam to Friday."

She let out a chuckle, and I smiled. "Well, I'll see you tonight."

I turned to walk away, and she spoke again, "Brody."

"Yeah?"

"Don't you need my number?"

"Oh right. Shoot!" Flustered, I ran a hand through my hair and took her number and promised to call her around seven. She grinned as she walked over to the driver's side and I slowly ambled away, casting a glance over my shoulder every few seconds until she left the lot.

As I passed by the store window, I adjusted my tie and straightened the name tag that Edna had almost torn off. I flashed my teeth to double-check that I didn't have ham and Swiss between them. I coughed into my hand. Breath was fine. "A few gray hairs. I can handle that. You've still got it, my son, you've still got it!" I smiled at the reflection and then realized that several of the staff were staring, so I shuffled back in to finish the rest of my shift.

Yeah, all in all, not a bad day.

But life had a wicked sense of humor.

And I was about to find out how twisted it could be.

Two - Funeral

24 Hours Until Blackout

Mack Sheldon's death blindsided us all, and yet as I look back now I wonder if it wasn't Mack's way of bringing us all together again. One final send-off that would attempt to steer our lives in a new direction, or at least remind us of who we were before the problems and challenges of responsibility had drained us dry.

When I received the call from his daughter Bridget, it was on my day off. Jen had taken the call. A month had passed since that offer to go for a drink, and we'd become close friends. I figured that perhaps the second time around could be the trick though I was still unsure.

Anyway, Mack's funeral was to be held at the Lutheran church off Meridian Boulevard. Bridget had made it clear that her father wanted all five of us to be there, a task that wasn't going to be easy being as we hadn't kept in touch. She asked if I had the phone numbers of the other guys. I knew Marlin's as he ran some fitness boot camp in town called Soldiers of Fitness, and Kai's as he worked for a company that offered helicopter tours but the others I hadn't seen in several years for one reason or another. I assured her that I would look into it, starting by speaking with Todd's mother. Chase, well, that would have to be done through social media. She left it open if I wanted to say anything on the day; I said I would but then after setting the phone down; I began to have doubts. What if I couldn't speak? What if I said the wrong thing? I hated funerals. I was uncomfortable with seeing people cry. The last one I attended was my grandmother's and the one before that was for my brother Sam. That one was forever burned in my memory. Others I had been invited to would have been so somber and downright depressing; I couldn't bring myself to show up. Did anyone care if you said anything? Would they remember? Most would hit the bar straight after and swap stories about the good days, regardless of whether the deceased was a prick or not.

To agree to speak just seemed like the thing to do at the time, like agreeing to make a toast at a wedding, or saying yes to help someone move. You didn't really want to, and you hoped something came up to prevent you from being able to follow through. Either way, it was going to be tough.

* * *

Jen offered to go with me even though I tried to talk her out of it. It wasn't that I was ungrateful for her company but it just didn't make for a great date. Then of course there was the fact that I didn't know if the other guys would show up and if they did what they would say. From what I could recall they weren't exactly the most tactful individuals.

That morning a long line of people gathered outside the church building. It was nearly eleven and the sky was clear. A harsh sun beat down on the crowd as I sat inside the Escalade scanning the crowd for anyone I knew. Who were all these people? A few older guys were dressed in suits sporting military medals. No doubt, old buddies from the past. A teary-eyed Bridget was there with Candice, Mack's third wife and a woman who was twenty years younger than him.

"You recognize anyone?" Jen asked.

"A few."

Five more minutes passed until a Jeep came roaring into the parking lot and swerved nearly hitting a few vehicles in the process. It was Marlin. Mack would have been proud. At least one of us had turned out looking the part.

"I just want to say right now that I'm sorry for dragging you along to this," I muttered to Jen.

"You didn't drag me, I agreed."

"Exactly."

"Come on, let's go," she said. I pushed out of the vehicle and caught Marlin's eye. He grinned and yelled loudly.

"Slater. Masterbater," he said it in such a way that it

sounded like he was dropping a line from a rap song.

I wished the earth could have opened and swallowed me whole in that moment. It was something he used to say when we were kids after he stumbled across my elder brother's collection of porno mags. I thought he had grown out of it, obviously not.

Several people turned their heads and frowned in disgust as Marlin made his way over with his hot-looking girlfriend. She was plastered all over his advertising dotted around the town. Her curvy figure had caused such a stir that a few town council members had been in contact with Marlin to have him change it.

"Marlin Calder, always the wiseass."

"But always in first," he said jabbing me in the gut then grinning. "Wow, Slater, time to start working those abs. You should sign up to my boot camp, Amanda here will give you one hell of a workout, won't you, hon?" He turned to his blond, blue-eyed girlfriend who was squeezed into a body-hugging dress. "Oh you haven't met? Amanda, this is Brody Slater. Brody, Amanda

Austin."

I extended my hand, and she leaned in to give some kind of awkward hug. I was mindful of the fact that her breasts were almost popping out of her outfit. It wasn't exactly funeral attire but at least it was black, and I didn't imagine anyone would complain.

"And look at you." I gripped him by the bicep and it was as hard as rock. "Still got that poster of Arnie on your wall?"

"He does," Amanda said before turning to greet Jen.

Marlin was quick to set the record straight. "It's in a frame and in my office."

"Closet?"

"No, on the wall!" he said before going red, which was tricky to see being as he was African American.

Marlin had always had a fascination with Arnold Schwarzenegger. We used to joke it was his man crush. When we stayed over at his home as kids he had a ton of war posters plastered over his walls but in his closet there was only one — it was of Arnie from the 1985 movie

Commando. It was a completely badass image of him holding a grenade and knife but a little odd to be found on the back door of his closet. Todd said it was his shrine and that he probably locked himself inside and jerked off to it. Childish but funny at the time.

He leaned in close and whispered. "So what's the deal with Jen Lawson? Man, did she turn out okay." He got real quiet. "She, uh…"

"Don't even say it."

He leaned in closer. "Do you know Theresa and Carl Stimms came out to one of the boot camps a few months back?"

"I don't keep up with what she does."

"I sent her on her way."

"You refused to train her?"

"Of course, bros before hoes, right?"

I nodded just as the sound of a roaring motorcycle shook the earth. "Todd," we both said in unison before even turning to see him roll in. Todd Fontane hadn't changed, except he'd graduated to a larger military-style green jacket, and was now wearing a red bandanna around his skull. Gone was the '80s rock-star hair and in its place was a shiny bald head. He was sporting aviator glasses, had a cigarette hanging out the corner of his mouth and was wearing leather-studded gloves. It truly was a sight to behold. We all figured he would have rented a suit or at least had one in his closet. Nope. Here he was in torn jeans and a Metallica T-shirt with the words Death Magnetic in bold lettering. He revved the engine over and over as he backed into a spot. It literally sounded as if he had no exhaust pipe. The fucking thing was kicking out more fumes than an industrial factory.

He killed the engine, pulled off the glasses and got off the bike with a big grin on his face. "Wassup donkey dicks!" He strolled over like a rock star who had lost his following. He gazed around at the crowd. "Bollocks to this funeral. What a turnout of wankers."

Todd was in the habit of moving back and forth between an American accent and a ridiculous British one. When we were kids, he was always calling things the dog's bollocks and saying aye mate and calling us all blokes or geezers. It was amusing when we were twelve but disturbing now. He came over and hugged it out with Marlin.

"Calder, I see you're still popping steroids. Has that shrunk your junk yet?"

Marlin snorted and shook his head.

"And Slater. M..."

I put up my finger. "Don't even say it. Marlin's already beat you to the punch."

He jabbed the air and frowned. "Bugger!" Then he leaned in and whispered. "Which reminds me, whatever happened to those mags?"

"I donated them to the Salvation Army."

He grinned, and I feigned a laugh.

"So where's Theresa?" he asked looking around.

I ran a hand over my mouth and was about to tell him when he burst out laughing. "Shit, I nearly had you there. Of course I know about her screwing Stimms. Hell, half the town does. Damn that has got to hurt." He stared at me for a second before continuing, "You think he had a bigger dick?"

Marlin gave me the look, the one that we always passed between us when Todd talked like that. Then Jen came over and gestured that she was going into the church. Todd's eyes widened as he followed her ass as she walked off.

"Oh now that's got revenge sex written all over it. Nice work, Slater! Damn and I thought you were batting for the other team."

And there it was, the rumor that my bitch of an ex had started to deflect all the attention away from her infidelity. Of course it wasn't true, and hell, I didn't have anything against gays, some of my best customers were interior designers but I thought everyone had pretty much forgotten. Obviously not.

"No, I'm…"

I began to explain but trailed off thinking it was pointless. Everything I had ever said to him flew over his head; I didn't expect that had changed now that he was older.

Right then a Chrysler minivan came rolling in and we all caught sight of Chase Garcia riding shotgun. His wife and childhood sweetheart, Tiffany, was driving. They pulled up and Chase hopped out and rushed around to the other side and opened her door. He then proceeded to release two girls and one boy who looked to be an older teen. He reached in and pulled out a fourth kid, which was an infant. Over one shoulder he had a baby bag and with the other arm he was carrying the car seat. Tiffany was yelling orders.

"Don't forget the extra diapers, or the rash cream."

"Didn't you put them in the bag?" he asked.

"You were supposed to do that while I was feeding the baby."

"Can't you reach in?"

"With this belly?"

"But I thought…"

"Are we going to do this now? Huh? Cause I will get back in and drive us home."

"No. No. It's okay. I'll get it."

"Are you sure? Because I'm not going to put up with any more of your shit, Chase!"

"I understand. Don't worry," he said in a pathetic voice.

She scowled at him and he raised a hand to motion that he had it under control as she charged off after their other kids.

We all stood slack-jawed and with our eyes wide open. The great Chase Garcia had been reduced to a groveling, baby-carrying, subordinate yes-man. It was a pitiful sight. Not the part about carrying a baby of course but the rest, well, it was clear who wore the pants in that family.

"Oh hey guys!" he said as he slammed the door shut with his foot and waddled over. Gone was the fit, muscular guy we knew when we were fifteen. Before us now was someone who crested two hundred and forty pounds and at his height and age that had to be a tough pill to swallow. In place of his cropped hair was a more sporty, modern-day quiff, and he was wearing khakis, boating shoes and some cream-colored suit jacket that would have made any father of an Ivy League graduate proud.

"You traded in the Jeep for a wiener mobile?" I said with a frown. Chase turned and tried to gesture towards the vehicle that had stripped him of what little masculinity he had left.

"Ah yeah, with the kids and all, Tiffany said it was time."

"Does Tiffany carry your balls as well?" Marlin said before jabbing him in the shoulder. He let out a chuckle, but it was clear he was embarrassed. His eyes fell upon Todd and he looked as if he was having the same reaction we did.

"I thought you would have rolled up in a squad car. Last I heard you were going for the police, did you get in?" Marlin asked.

"No, I'm still stuck in security hell as a TSA agent down at the airport," Chase replied.

"Shit! Well at least you don't have to pay to feel up the

ladies now," Todd said before going to fist pump Chase, who just left him hanging. Back when we were thirteen, Chase had paid some senior at our school to feel her breasts. It had started as a dare but when he got the courage to go and ask, she shot him down, then as he turned to walk away, she changed her tune and told him he could for five bucks. It was the craziest shit we'd ever seen. Both of them walked away with smiles on their faces and another moment fell into the history of the strange and absurd.

"Chase!" the voice of Tiffany snapped. She was standing in the doorway with a hand on her hip looking super pissed.

"Look, I'll catch up with you guys later, okay?"

I patted him on the back and he waddled off liked a dog that was still recovering from being freshly neutered.

Marlin shrugged. "Well, some things change I guess."

"And some things don't," I said as there was a rush of wind and rotors thumped overhead. Above us loomed a helicopter with the words Skytime Tours plastered across the side.

"Is that?" Todd asked loudly.

I nodded. "Yep. Kai."

Older women wearing huge hats grabbed a hold of them as a strong gust blew anything that wasn't attached across the ground like tumbleweed. Kai was about to land the damn thing in the middle of the parking lot. Several people made a beeline for the church to get out from the plume of dust that was being kicked up. I raised a forearm to guard my eyes, and we all kept our distance as the cherry-red Robinson R66 Turbine helicopter landed.

The low whoosh of rotors soon slowed as he killed the engine.

Kai hopped out wearing aviator sunglasses, a Hawaiian shirt, shorts and a pair of flip-flops. I could tell Todd didn't feel so out of place now. Staying low, two women in cut-off jean shorts and bikini bras looped their arms around Kai as he came over with a smile a mile wide.

"How the hell does he do it?" I asked.

"Some guys are just well endowed," Todd muttered.

"Hey, at least one of them isn't your Theresa. Could you imagine that?" He chuckled, but I didn't even want to go there.

Kai slipped out from the grasp of the hotties and looked us up and down with a look of confusion.

"Crap, did I get the wrong time? I thought this was the after-party." He started laughing and then lunged forward to hug each of us. "Guys, meet Misty and Kristy."

"Ah, taking the tour?" Marlin asked.

He thumbed towards them. "No, these are my ladies."

"Of course they are," I said as if it was obvious.

All three of us stood there still trying to process again how he managed to lure in such stunners. It had always been a mystery. On the surface he wasn't exactly what women might have considered eye candy, he was the shortest of us, and he had this thing that he did with his shoulder that made him look like he had a nervous tic. Still the ladies loved him.

"You going for the whole Magnum PI look?" I asked noting his facial hair.

Todd snorted. "Magnum? More like Higgins."

"Hey, I'll have you know it took me four months to grow this out," he said running his fingers over it. When we were teenagers, he was a late bloomer. "Besides, the ladies love it, don't you?"

They pawed his face and swapped mouth fluid before he patted them on the ass and headed on into the church. I glanced at the helicopter taking up a large portion of the parking lot. It was already causing several latecomers to get out of their cars and look around for the owner. I smiled and shook my head.

* * *

It was an odd funeral to say the least. Draped either side of the coffin were two large American flags. They literally went from the ceiling to the ground. Either side of that were two huge potted plants. Instead of flowers they contained several AR-15's. In fact there wasn't a flower in sight. At the bottom of the memorial pamphlet that contained the agenda for the funeral, it advised people that Mack wasn't fond of wasting money and had instructed his daughter to tell people to donate to the NRA, of which he was a strong advocate and member. Everyone shuffled in and found a spot on the hard seats and waited patiently for the service to begin. Background music played softly for several minutes only to change to the Peanuts theme song from Charlie Brown. A few heads turned as if searching for whoever was in charge of the music. Surely there had been a mistake? A couple ahead of us stifled a laugh. A few more awkward minutes and someone got up and disappeared out back to find out who was in charge. Meanwhile the song had us all in stitches. All five of us glanced at each other like we were still fifteen years of age and had been dragged into a church and told to behave. Mack had always had a good sense of humor; I figured he would have found it amusing.

I turned to my right to take in the sight of those in attendance. A few smiled back, folks that frequented the store. I was about to speak with Jen when I caught sight of Kurt Donahue. I hadn't seen him since I was twenty-one. The last I heard, he'd moved away to join the Marines. Did he get in? If his trim haircut and strapping build were anything to go by, I assumed he did. Beside him were a young Asian woman and two kids. He glanced around and we caught each other's eye. His lip curled up, and he pointed a finger at me and made a gesture as if he was shooting a gun.

Back at yah, dickwad, I thought. I'd never liked the guy. Too serious. Always trying to prove himself. It was if he thought the world hung on his every word. The kind of guy that thought he was educating every person he met. Little did he know he was just making himself look like an asshole.

Once the service finally got underway, the pastor mumbled his way through a series of cards in front of him, no doubt the same ones he used for every funeral. He probably just swapped out the name and said the same platitudes. That was the thing about funerals, it didn't matter how the person lived. When they died, they could do no wrong. Though in our eyes, Mack couldn't.

He didn't open up to just anyone. Most of those that trained with him soon forgot him, except a small group that included us. Maybe that's why he'd asked his daughter to have us all attend. We were a motley crew and though our lives hadn't exactly worked out the way we envisioned when we young, when it came to Mack, we all showed up.

"We are gathered here to pay tribute to a soldier, a brother, a husband, a father and a friend, Mack Sheldon. Not only have people come from far and wide, and this community has gathered, but also many veterans have come to show their respect. Veterans that stood beside him in the heat of battle and knew him better than some would ever know. We are here to show our love and support for Mack's precious family. Not only do we feel the sense of loss but also our hearts are drawn to them and will continue to be with them over the coming months. A few days after Mack passed on, his daughter Bridget told me that there were only a handful of people who he'd wish to say a few words to pay tribute. So I would like to invite Brody Slater to come up."

I swallowed hard, squeezed out of the pew and fished into my jacket pocket for a scrap of paper that had a few notes on it. I say a few as I never ended up finishing it. I must have torn up eight pieces of paper before deciding to wing it.

As I turned to face the crowd of people, my mind went blank.

"What can I say about Mack that would add one iota to the life he lived? I tried to jot a few things down but I couldn't do it." I turned the paper and showed the folks a few lines of illegible text. "Here was a guy that squeezed out every last drop from life. He drained the well dry through a life well lived. He gave more than he took that's for sure. He didn't make excuses, and he wasn't one for backing down from a challenge — even if it meant attempting to train a ragtag group of fifteen-year-olds." Smiles spread throughout the church. "I have to admit, even though I saw him fairly frequently, I wished I had spent more time with him, but like everyone, I got busy living and distracted." I inhaled deeply. "Then again, I think we all say that when we lose someone close, right? The fact is we always think we never said enough, did enough or spent enough time and it's only after that we truly realize how much a person mattered and meant to us by the enormity of the vacuum they left behind. And I think we would all agree that Mack left one hell of a gap." I sniffled. "Most of you in the town know Mack from the large number of kids he helped. Those who went on to become jarheads, and others who made it into the Special Forces, but what you might not know is what he did for those who didn't." I stared out at the other four. Chase's head dropped a little. It was safe to say that each of us felt the pang of regret for not pursuing our dream for one reason or another. I smiled. "I remember waltzing up to his house in 1987. Chase Garcia dared me to knock on his door and ask him to train us." I let out a chuckle and a glimmer of light came back into the eyes of Chase. Light that perhaps had been dimmed by the years. "Man, I don't think I was ever as nervous as I was that day. My legs were shaking, and I can still remember my mouth going dry when he opened that door. Fortunately he agreed. Oh he busted our chops and put us through the wringer but through it all, we came out of it stronger, I think." I shook the piece of paper in my hand. "And though I never made it into the military, it didn't matter to him. There was me thinking I had let him down, let myself down, but it was like water off a duck's back to Mack. Nothing fazed him. Perhaps that's why he was such a good soldier." I breathed in deeply. "But you know what he said? Brody, life is short, smile while you still have good teeth." Chuckles turned into laughter "Here was I thinking he was going to drop some profound lesson about regret and he said that. And yet for those of us who were privileged to have known him, we know that was Mack. Unpredictable and kindhearted. And if I'm honest, those three years were the best years of my life. So… here's to you, my friend." I turned and gave a salute toward his coffin. "Godspeed."

After a few more family and friends spoke, surprisingly

enough Todd came up and was handed a Fender electric guitar. Someone wheeled out a small 15-watt amp, and he plugged in. The damn thing kicked out some serious feedback. It was so loud; I thought my ears were going to bleed. We sat there wondering what the hell he was going to do.

Todd coughed and mumbled into the mic. "This was a favorite of Mack's."

"Oh God!" Marlin said planting his face in an open palm.

And just like that he started playing a rendition of "While My Guitar Gently Weeps." I didn't know whether to laugh or cry. Chase turned to me and muttered, "Did you know he could play?"

I shrugged.

I mean we had seen him perform air guitar on a weekly basis when we were kids but from what I could remember he couldn't play one lick and now, here he was, crunching out chords and whipping up and down the fretboard like he was Jimi Hendrix. However, he was no Hendrix. It was only made more painful when he opened his mouth and croaked out the lyrics. It was like listening to someone choking on marbles. An old lady ahead of me took off her hearing aid while a few others slipped out.

Once the assault on our senses was over, those of us who had managed to survive began to stream out of the building to head over to Mack's home for drinks and finger food. Bridget made a point of pulling us aside and reminding us that her father had wanted to give us something.

"You are going to stick around?"

"Of course. We wouldn't miss it."

"Good, as he was pretty adamant about this."

As she wandered back to her husband, I pondered what could have meant so much to him that he'd made a point to make sure his daughter didn't forget.

Three – The Gift

For a man who adored the outdoors, Mack chose to live in a regular home in the suburbs so he could be close to his daughter. The longer I knew him the more I saw another side to him; one that went beyond guns, military jargon and male bravado. And yet for all the time we spent with him, there was always more to discover. Just like one of those Russian matryoshka dolls, the moment I thought I had him figured out, he would unveil another side to him. Today was no exception.

The three-bedroom home was in a neighborhood called Crestwood Hills on the west side. They were a close-knit community that was known for throwing block parties and watching out for each other. It was an up-and-coming development that was making a name for itself due to some of the well-to-do folks who built homes in the area.

That day, three hundred people crammed into every

corner of his property. It was like Black Friday at Wal-Mart. Elbows and knees everywhere, people stumbling over each other and saying excuse me every damn second. The four of us nudged our way through the crowd searching for Kai while gorging on finger foods.

"Damn, you think Ms. Parnell could stuff any more of those deviled eggs into her mouth?" Marlin said.

Parnell ran a yoga business in town for the overweight. She was like the female version of Richard Simmons. Eccentric but always smiling and ready with a kind word. Marlin was just pissed off because the two of them had been competing for business for years. The strange thing was even though she was toned, everyone knew that was because she threw up most of what she would eat. Of course she wouldn't admit she had an eating disorder. It was the tantra yoga, she'd say. She'd even convinced me and anyone who she could corner into taking a few classes. *It will ease your stress.* I had to admit, it worked wonders when I remembered to do it.

"You still going out to her sessions?" Chase asked with

a smirk on his face. "Better question, are you still wearing those pants?" He chuckled. I never replied. The last time we had seen each other, he had happened to be passing by her place of business with Tiffany and the kids. He had to cover their eyes. It was the second class I had taken and Parnell had convinced me to wear these tight yoga pants until I realized they were for her benefit not mine. Not long after that I opted for the online version and squeezed in ten minutes every other day.

Yep, twenty-two overweight folks squeezed into tight pants doing downward dog with their asses facing the window, wasn't a pretty sight and certainly not a good advertisement.

Outside the sky was a bright blue, not a cloud in sight. Bridget had created a minibar off to the side and folks were milling around drinking and talking about anything but Mack. It was always the same shitty questions. How's your mother? What do you do for a living? Are you still working at…? And then they would wait for me to fill in the name of the grocery store to avoid embarrassing themselves.

After grabbing a few brewskies, we stood around in a cluster beneath an old oak tree observing the steady flow of people. We eventually spotted Kai hovering around a food table where both girls were taking turns feeding him grapes.

"You think it will last?" Todd asked

"No," Marlin said. "I bet you ten bucks by the end of the week one of them will be ditched, and then the other will be gone within the month."

As insane as it sounded, it was true. Kai was a perfectionist when it came to women. Though he had all manner of women throwing themselves at him, he didn't know a good thing when he had it. He was always searching for the Holy Grail, the perfect woman, and never content with the one he had.

"How does he do it?" Chase muttered. "I would give my right nut to get that kind of attention from Tiffany."

Todd tapped him on the arm. "You do. It comes in the form of a yearly blowjob,"

I nearly spat out my drink as Chase nodded. "Sad part is, it's true, and even then it's only on my birthday."

"Ah, married life," Marlin said. "There really should be a disclaimer at the bottom of every marriage certificate that says, I do solemnly swear that I know not of any lawful impediment as to why I can't put out once a week."

"Here, here." We grunted and clinked our bottles together.

"What do you know about marriage?" Chase asked Marlin. "You're here with one of the hottest women in town and yet you still haven't put a ring on that finger."

He took a gulp of his drink.

"And it will stay that way," he said gasping as he took a swig from his bottle. "Commitment. It's bad mojo. Just look at you guys. Theresa cheated on Brody. Tiffany has made you her man bitch. Marriage is a death sentence. Once you put a ring on that, you might as well lop off your manhood as that shit is going to spend the majority of its time as limp as a turkey's wattle."

"Come on, guys, is that what relationships have become to you? Nothing more than sex?" Todd asked.

All three of us started laughing. "Says the guy who's turning women away at his door."

"Yeah, what is the deal with you, Todd? Are you even getting any ass?" Marlin asked.

"Listen up, I get plenty of ass—"

"I bet you do, how much is that subscription to All Ass website going for nowadays?" Marlin snorted.

"That's right, yuk it up! Unlike you fools I actually take the time to appreciate and respect my ladies."

"Oh I bet you do. Do you use a foot pump or an automatic to inflate them?"

We all cracked up laughing.

"Screw you. I can't help it if you don't know how to treat a woman."

I took a step back. Oh this was priceless. Here was a guy handing out relationship advice and I hadn't yet seen him out and about with any woman besides his mother.

"All right, Casanova, then tell us one woman that you

have been out with in the past year?" Chase chimed in. We all waited with bated breath for an answer.

He began mumbling and Chase told him to speak up. "Well, you know, there's that one who works down at the library." He scratched the back of his neck and cleared his throat. "And you know… the dark-haired girl from…"

"Loserville," we all said in unison before clinking our bottles.

"Whatever, man. I'm going to have a cigarette. Assholes." Todd wandered off and even though it was funny to jerk his chain, I couldn't help wonder. Being single at our age wasn't easy. It was easier to lie. Married or not, relationships were tough. We all suffered in one way or another. Chase treated relationships like they were going to end tomorrow, so he never really had the balls to speak up, and every girl he'd dated in the past had walked out on him. Todd pined over girls to the point that he became claustrophobic or creepy. Marlin, well, he avoided commitment, so he kept ladies at arm's length. I hadn't really figured out what my issue was. If I even had one?

My eyes drifted over to Jen who was busy conversing with a group of old-timers.

It didn't matter whether someone was dating, married or divorced, if most were honest, the fact that any relationship survived was a miracle. Slapping two people from different backgrounds together was a recipe for disaster, how could it not be? I still had the relationships self-help audio from Kelly Laquin sitting in my car, in the same spot since purchasing it. I just couldn't bring myself to crack it open.

Jen came over with Mrs. Tomah. She'd been one of our sixth-grade teachers eons ago.

"Boys, how lovely to see you all. Haven't you grown up!"

I tucked in my shirt, feeling self-conscious. She had a way of making you stand to attention even though she was now retired.

"Jen was just telling me you are dating. That's good news, Brody, because I thought—"

I jumped in before she could finish.

"Dating? I wouldn't call it that. Just good friends, right?" I said nodding and then taking another sip of my beer. Jen frowned, and I had a feeling I'd put my foot in my mouth. Truth was I really didn't know what to make of our relationship. It was still early days, and I certainly wasn't ready to slap a label on it.

"Brody, can I steal you guys away?" Bridget hollered from across the way. What a relief. By the glare that Jen was giving me, I was beginning to think that I was going to have to clarify my response to Mrs. Tomah. Instead, my hand shot up, and I gave a nod. "We'll be right with you. Sorry, gotta go. Something to do with Mack and whatnot. Chat later?" I leaned in to kiss Jen and she turned her cheek. Marlin snorted. Great, now I was going to have to listen to him drone on about how he was right.

* * *

Once we managed to pull Kai away and find Todd, Bridget led us out into the garage and closed the door behind her. Before us was Mack's spruce-tip green, 1976 AMC Jeep Cherokee Chief SJ four-wheel drive. He was super particular about how good it was on gas and the fact that with it being American made, parts were easy to come by. He'd bought it brand-new and treated it with tender love and care ever since. The damn thing was in immaculate condition.

"How are you holding up?" Chase asked Bridget who looked a little flustered.

"No disrespect to my father but I'll be glad when it's over. I never knew how much work was involved in a funeral. I still have to go through all his belongings and figure out what to keep and what to give away. Which brings me to this."

She crossed the garage and pulled out a drawer from a dresser that Mack had been using to store all his documents related to his business.

"Here we go," she said, turning and handing me a sealed envelope. It had some weight to it. "Now he was pretty clear. You are to follow his instructions to the letter. He didn't want to hear excuses and most of all, he didn't want you all to fight about it. It was his one last request." We glanced at each other a little confused. "Well, I'll leave you to it."

She exited, and we crowded around.

"Well, open it up," Todd said, coaxing me to get on with it.

I flipped it over and ran a thumb along the seal. Inside were a piece of folded paper and a set of keys. I pulled out the letter and began to read.

Hello boys!

I'm hoping your all here. If not, then you can be damn sure I will come back and haunt your asses. Now you're probably wondering why I gave my daughter explicit instructions. Here's the thing, I never wrote out a will. Couldn't be done with it. I already told my daughter in advance what she could have and had already transferred what little money I had left into her account. So if you were thinking I was going to bestow upon you all my millions, dream on, cocksuckers!

Nope. Instead, I have something far better for you guys.

One last mission. That's right, I know you aren't fifteen anymore but I've kept my eye on each of you over the last thirty years and I've held my tongue regarding the life choices you ladies have made because quite frankly you don't need someone to hold your hand or wipe your ass. That's because I know that someday what I instilled in you will serve you when you're ready to man up and grow a pair.

Until then, it's time you served your country.

How? Well, you didn't enlist, so I thought what better way to give back than to have you serve someone who did — me! *That's right, numbnuts. Even in death I'm going to have you limp dicks breaking a sweat. You're going to lug a load, hike on dirt paths and camp out in nature. But before you start thinking about packing those tighty whities, I want to make something crystal-clear.*

There are to be no excuses. I'm talking about you, Brody. That damn job of yours can just wait. It will still be there when you get back. And Marlin, put the goddamn weights down and start carrying some real weight. The stuff that life is made of. And Todd, wipe that damn smirk off your face. If anyone needs slapping around the side of the head, it's you. It's time to crawl out of your mother's basement and take some responsibility. You can't blame your old man all your life. And Chase, Tiffany is a strong woman, she can handle the home for a few days. Don't you hem and haw, boy, I might not be there to give you a swift kick to the nuts but I can damn sure tell Marlin to do it. That is if he can find them. And finally, Kai, enough with eating pussy before you become one.

With that said, you're going to Devils Postpile National Monument.

Why? Because that's where I want to be buried. That's right, you are going to take my ashes and scatter them in the place I most loved to be, up in the mountains, where we used to train. Three days. That's all.

Now, you're going to need to prepare for a long hike, as Kermit isn't going to get you all the way there. And I swear if you get one scratch on my baby, I'm going to torment you all in the afterlife with an eternity of hiking.

We all turned our heads and looked at the green Jeep. I glanced at the keys in my hand. Kermit was the name he'd bestowed upon his ride. In life he wouldn't let anyone get near that thing, we figured he would be buried in it but that wasn't to be.

Now everything you need has already been packed in the back. That's right, I kind of figured you might groan at the overwhelming prospect of having to gather together what you need for this trip, so I did it for you. All you need to do is jump in and go.

Life is not waiting for you, boys, so you better start living. And one last thing...

Don't fuck this up!

Always watching,

Mack Sheldon

P.S. Scatter the majority of my ashes over Rainbow Falls.

P.P.S. Keep Todd back from the edge, unless he's wearing water wings.

I folded up the paper as Marlin took the keys from my hand, walked over to the back of the truck and popped it open. We all gathered around the rear and stared inside. There were some of Mack's old military fatigues, several tents rolled up, blankets, packed backpacks, rifles, shotguns and handguns with several boxes of ammo.

We stood there for a few minutes, nodding slowly just soaking in his message before the excuses started to roll in from all of us.

"I need to talk to Tiffany, this isn't going to fly."

"Three days without pussy? I'll go into withdrawal."

"Does that mean I have to skip leg day this week?"

"I don't sleep in my mom's basement. I swear. But let me send her a quick text."

"Von's district manager is going to lose his shit. Do I have enough vacation time?"

Four - Rules of The Road

12 Hours Until Blackout

The day darkness would fall over the nation, we had already embarked on our journey into the wild. Chase had been the last one we'd collected early that morning. We'd left at the break of dawn before the sun would bake us alive. Though each of us had a few things to square away before we could leave for what would be a three-day trek, it would be safe to say that Chase won the award for bravery.

Tiffany had fought him tooth and nail, right up until we picked him up. And yet I think he was stronger for it. I'm pretty sure I caught a glimpse of the old Chase as he told Tiffany to put a sock in it and then loaded a few items into the back of the Jeep. It was a stark contrast to the man we'd seen juggling baby gear at the funeral.

Devils Postpile National Monument was located forty-three minutes from Mammoth Lakes. As the Jeep weaved its way west on Highway 203, the natural beauty of the region we called home spread out before us. Looming over tall pines in the distance was Mammoth Mountain, a young volcano that was now home to the Mammoth Mountain Ski Area, the highest ski resort in California. Every year we'd visited the place as kids, to ski, snowboard or snowmobile in the winter months, or we'd mountain bike up in the summer to take in the summit view of the Long Valley Caldera, which was located to the east, while the Sierra peaks hedged us in on the west, north and south sides.

"I still can't wrap my head around why he wants us and not his daughter to scatter his ashes," Todd said smoking a cigarette and blowing out the rear window. I glanced at the urn that she'd given me, resting in the coffee holder.

"It's not all his ashes. We got half, she got half."

"I'm not sure I would like that," Kai muttered in the

back.

"Why not? It doesn't matter. Once you're dead, you're dead."

"I'll remember you said that when I feed your ashes to the pigs," Todd said as he put his feet up on the center console.

Chase nudged his boots. "Dude, get your feet down."

"Or what? Is Machine here to stop me?"

"He's always watching," I said.

Todd chuckled. "Slater, you are too much. You still believe all that mumbo jumbo after all this time?" He then reached up and yanked the earphone out of my right ear. I was listening to Kelly Laquin's latest release called "The 10 Secrets of Inner Peace." Todd stuck it in his ear and then started laughing. "What's the deal with this self-help bullshit?"

I kept one hand on the wheel as I pulled the earphone back. "It's not bullshit."

"Oh no?"

"It works."

"The only thing that works is all that marketing shite. Do you honestly think for one minute that sitting like a pretzel and chanting is going to make you more peaceful?" He roared with laughter. "You can bet the second those self-help chumps rise from their time of becoming one with the universe that all it would take was for them to stub their toe and they would fill the air with cursing. They've got it all wrong."

I rolled my eyes. "Here we go again, and let me guess, you have it all figured out."

"You bet your ass I do and I don't need twenty steps to being a nutcase to get my chill on."

"No, you just have beer and weed," Marlin said casting a glance over. Todd looked down at what he was doing. I gazed at my rearview mirror just in time to see Todd snatch out of Marlin's hands his iPad. "Work. Now what did the Machine tell you about those weights?"

"I have to schedule in a few clients."

"Do it when you get back."

"Give it back, Todd," he said politely holding his hand

out. Todd tossed it up front where Chase was.

"Damn, you're such a child. No wonder you still live with your mother."

Chase handed back the iPad and Marlin continued working away. He wasn't the only one still attached to his technology. Kai was talking away to some customer on his Bluetooth headset. It was something about a package deal he was offering for families of four. The fact was our lives had become so hard-wired into what we did for a living that it was hard to switch off. Even as I drove up through the expanse of the valley and was surrounded by crystal-clear mountain lakes and boundless opportunities for adventure, my mind was still preoccupied by all the paperwork that was sitting in my office. By the time I returned I knew there would be hundreds of e-mails to wade through. The thought of it was enough to give me a panic attack. I literally could feel my chest becoming heavy. It never used to be that way. When I was a kid, every day felt light. Of course I was plagued by the common pitfalls and challenges of teenage life but something was different back then. Perhaps it was the lack of responsibility.

"Check this out," Chase said reaching under the seat and pulling out a cardboard box full of tapes. He flipped the lid, and I glanced over.

"Well look at that, he still has those?"

Mack had recorded himself reeling off rules for survival and preparedness. They were short snippets, stuff that could have been used on a flash card. It was mostly stuff he'd learned after he was in the military, though every year he kept adding to it. He'd then hand out a tape to each of us and tell us to listen and to be ready to give an example when we saw him next. While he was big on being practical, he liked to make sure we had a healthy dose of theory. Instead of just telling us how to survive, he showed us. That's why our trips into the wilderness were such a big deal to him. He wanted to see what had sunk into our thick skulls.

"The better question is, did you actually listen to them?" Todd asked reaching between the seats and grabbing one of the tapes. I shot him a glance, and he chuckled. "Don't even answer, Slater, we all know this was like your personal stash of crack cocaine."

He wasn't far wrong. I was intrigued by it. Here was a guy pouring out his guts on how to survive under the worst conditions, who wouldn't have wanted to listen to that?

"Skills vs. Supplies," Todd said as he glanced at the title jotted along the cassette spine.

I snorted. "Oh I remember that one. Stick it in."

"Don't," Todd said tossing it back to Chase. "If you want to torment us with more of his drivel, at least give us the condensed version."

Chase grinned and held it up. "Yeah, come on, let's see how well you know your shit, Slater."

"Skills vs. Supplies. Pretty simple. The rule went something like this. You can have all manner of supplies, first-aid kits, purified water tablets and freeze-dried food but if you don't know how to find and hunt for food in the wilderness or you lack the ability to patch up a serious wound, it doesn't matter how well you stock up, you are screwed. Skills trump supplies every time."

"Not every time," Todd shot back. "Look at Carl Stimms, he obviously had both in equal measure. Which does raise the question—"

"Don't say it!" I said before asking Chase to move on to the next. Fucking guy was always going on about how Carl Stimms had lured my wife away with some unique ability in the sack.

Chase nodded. "All right, how about this one?"

He pulled out another tape and reeled off the tag on the side which read, Seed or Plead?

"Come on, Chase, you must have a harder one than that. The title pretty much gives it away."

"Isn't this one about sowing your wild oats?" Kai chimed in, finally joining the conversation and taking time out from talking on the phone.

"Kai, only you could think that's what it was referring to," Marlin muttered still gazing down at his iPad.

"Well?"

"No, it was all about making sure you had stocked up on seeds. Food might become scarce but if you could sow seeds, you wouldn't go hungry. Failure to do so would mean pleading for food. And that's never a position you want to be in."

I tapped the steering wheel, finding it amusing that I could remember. It had been close to thirty years since he'd handed them out and graded us like we were students in his school of survival.

"Okay, smart-ass, what about this one?" He flashed the spine. "The Battle of The Mind" was scrawled across the side in black ink with the word battle underlined.

"What will you do when looters start ransacking stores and homes because they're desperate? What do you do when they show up at your door asking for food, shelter or to use your vehicle because it's the only one that didn't get fried in an EMP? Staying level-headed and being prepared to make tough decisions will be what gets you through when others are desperate. Every battle begins in the mind."

Chase closed the lid. "I'm not even going to bother with the rest. You really did do your homework, didn't you?"

I shrugged.

"Mack Sheldon was his self-help guru long before Kelly Laquin," Marlin muttered before putting his iPad down. He wasn't wrong. At fifteen I felt like I was drifting along without any sense of direction. After losing my brother, and watching my parents struggle to get out of bed in the morning, it was hard not to fall into the same pit of despair. I swear if it weren't for Mack I would have lost my mind. He gave me something to focus on; something to aspire to, even if nothing came of it later in life. Each of us had our reasons why it didn't work out, and yet none of us had discussed it. It was like working on the same project but never having it see the light of day. I wasn't going to bring it up and I kind of figured the others wouldn't, being as they were in the same boat. Instead we each went in different directions and notched it up to getting distracted but that wasn't it. Not really.

When we finally made it to the Devils Postpile parking lot, the sun was up. The lot itself was empty, but we knew it would soon fill up with hikers and mountain bikers looking to explore the pristine mountain scenery. It brought back fond memories as we stepped out and breathed in the aroma of pine and fir trees. An eagle flew overhead, and I wondered if it was Mack looking down on us. I'd heard all manner of stories from people whose friends and loved ones had passed. Some believed that they returned in the form of animals to watch over those left behind, Todd would have said it was just bullshit made up by the weak of mind.

"Why are we parking here? We can take Minaret Summit Road and be at Rainbow Falls in less than ten minutes. If we walk, it will take an hour."

"Because it's what he wanted."

"He didn't say anything about that."

I fished around in my jacket for the letter he'd left for us. Inside was one extra piece of paper. I hadn't read it in the garage as it was just a small hand-drawn map on one side, and a list of points that he wanted us to carry his ashes to before finally making it to Rainbow Falls and scattering them. I flashed it and Todd groaned.

"Instead of moaning, give me a hand getting the gear out of the back," Chase said.

Kai came up alongside me and snatched the map out of my hand. "Come on, man, some of these locations are going to take forever to reach. I should have brought my helicopter, we could have done it all within a matter of hours and dumped his ashes all over the landscape. At this rate we are going to be lucky to make it back in three days."

Marlin took it from Kai, with a concerned expression on his face. "Screw that, I say we do Devils Postpile and Rainbow Falls and head out later this evening."

"What is up with you guys?" I turned and looked at them. "Sure, we all have lives to get back to but we're doing this for Mack."

"Mack is gone, Brody. As much I liked the old man, he's not the one paying to keep the lights on in my business, and this little venture is going to eat into my profits — big time! I've already had to turn away six clients, and you can guess where they'll go." He began walking to the rear of the Jeep only to turn back and point his finger at me. "And before you harp on at us, you're exactly the same. Hell, we haven't gone out for a beer in years. Why? Oh that's right, you were working all the time. Just like me."

I stood there gazing at them in astonishment. Were these the same guys I grew up with? They would have come up with any amount of excuses to avoid doing work, now they were biting at the bit to get back to the grind.

"Sure, I'm no different but this is about doing something for someone who poured his life into us — for no payment I might add. It wasn't a business to him, it was more than that — and maybe if we stick around and trek to the sights he wanted us to visit, perhaps we'll discover something that's been lost."

"Like Chase's balls?" Todd and Marlin started

laughing and both of them fist pumped before dragging out the gear. I shook my head and didn't even bother responding. Perhaps cutting short the trip was a good idea. Maybe Mack was wrong selecting us to scatter his ashes. Kai was back on his Bluetooth yakking away to another customer, had Mack been there he would have ripped it off his ear and stomped on the damn thing.

Once we unloaded the backpacks, Marlin wanted to leave the three rifles and two shotguns covered up inside the vehicle but I insisted that we take them. In all the years we'd visited the place we'd yet to see anyone attempt to break in, but that didn't mean it wouldn't happen. Sure we could have left them in the garage but Mack was the kind of guy that was never too far from his weapon. He believed in his right to bear arms and as long as he wasn't breaking the law he did. Besides, the National Parks had come a long way over the years regarding carrying weapons. At one time they wouldn't have allowed it but now anyone with a permit could carry an unloaded firearm in the National Parks, and keep a loaded firearm in a campsite, tent or trailer. That's not to say it was required, or that folks didn't ignore the law and use their weapons to take potshots at mountain lions, bears and rattlesnakes prior to the law being changed. At the end of the day park rangers wouldn't go to all the trouble of hiking for miles just to tell some idiot to stop firing at beer cans.

I yanked the straps on my backpack and adjusted it for comfort. "You ready?"

Besides Chase, the other three grunted and started heading towards the trailhead.

Five – Darkness Falls

We spent the better part of the morning hiking to Devils Postpile and winding down the San Joaquin River to Rainbow Falls before we stopped for lunch. It worked out to be less than five miles, and took us close to three hours because Todd drank a shitload of beer and kept stopping to take a leak which slowed everything down. After spending a short time taking in the view from Devils Postpile, we hiked across to Red's Meadow, then down to Rainbow Falls.

It was a little after nine in the morning when we arrived. By now the sun was beating down, and the trails were starting to fill with other hikers, a few runners and several mountain bikers. The rush of the water as it plunged over the 101-foot drop to the turbulent waters below filled the air with mist as I dropped my backpack on the ground and swung my legs over the edge of the cliff. I leaned back and wiped sweat from my brow as we took in the spectacular sight.

"Seems strange being here without him," Chase said

"Peaceful though. I can kind of see why he chose this spot."

"You got the map there?"

I pulled it out and handed it to him.

We cracked open a beer and perched on the edge soaking it all in.

"John Muir Trail, Minaret Lake, Beck Lake, Minaret Falls, Fish Creek, Fern Lake and Iron Mountain. Three days of hiking and camping. Why these places? Some of these spots we didn't even train in."

"He did," I said staring out.

Chase tossed me a confused expression. "What are you on about?"

I leaned back, propping myself against a rock. "Bridget told me Candice took him to these locations. She said her father learned more about women and life in those camping trips with her than he ever did in his time in the military."

Chase snorted. "I should have figured this wasn't about us."

"Oh it is."

Again he looked confused. I looked his way and pushed up my sunglasses. "Don't you get it, even when he was training us as kids he was always harping on about life being more than a career. He said it made up such a short period in a person's life. Like the mortar between the bricks of a house. The stuff that held life together was the relationships. Family. Friends. Not how many medals a person had pinned on their chest. That's why he didn't come down on us when none of us enlisted."

Chase looked as if he was about to say something but instead he returning to gazing out at the view.

"So who's going to do it?" Marlin asked looking over to the urn.

"Hand it over, I'll do it," I replied.

Marlin picked it up and handed it to Kai, who passed it down to Chase before giving it to Todd. "Here you go, Slater." As he turned to hand it to me, the cigarette dropped from the corner of his mouth into his lap. It was like watching a disaster in slow motion. The urn slipped out of his hand, my eyes widened as I went to grab it. The tips of my fingers touched it but it was just out of reach. I lost my footing and slipped over the side of the cliff while at the same time the urn disappeared into the mass of water below. Loose rock fell away as my hands raked at the stone trying to grab anything. Fortunately my hand clasped on to a protruding outcropping and I found myself dangling.

"Brody!" Marlin hollered.

I croaked back a reply. "I'm here."

"Hold on, buddy. We'll have you up in a second," Chase yelled before barking orders for someone to check the bags for some rope.

My fingers burned, and the muscles in my arms felt like they had torn.

"Shit! Shit!" I could hear Todd yelling at the top of his voice. It wasn't but twenty seconds before they tossed over a yellow rope and it slapped against the side of my arm.

"You better have the other end," I hollered back as I reached for it and held on to it for dear life. Slowly they reeled me in. When I made it back to the top, I collapsed on the ground to catch my breath. It still felt like my heart was in my throat. Meanwhile the other three were yelling at Todd for having drunk too much.

"How the hell did you do that?" Kai asked almost dumbfounded by it.

"It was the cigarette."

"Which you could barely keep in your mouth."

"I'm sorry, it was a mistake."

"A mistake? That's the story of your life, Todd," Chase barked.

"Oh and you're so damn perfect with your perfect minivan and your perfect little family. At least I'm not living under someone's thumb."

"No, you're just leeching off your mother."

"Shut up," I said, but no one was paying attention, they were too busy blaming him.

"How the hell are we meant to scatter his ashes now?" Kai asked.

Todd shrugged. "He wanted them here, I don't see the problem."

"Oh you never see the problem. That's because you're too busy navel gazing."

"Yeah well at least I've been in a relationship longer than you have."

"What's that supposed to mean?" Kai said getting confrontational.

"Now who's navel gazing?" Todd shot back. Kai shook his head and walked away.

"Look, he'll travel downstream. He'll be all over the place. That's what he wanted. Right?"

"You're such a dumbass," Marlin said to Todd.

"Screw you Marlin, you think you're such hot shit. You're no better than me."

"Really? The last time I checked I have a job. What the hell do you do? Oh that's right, you collect a check from the government."

Todd slammed his open palms against Marlin's chest, shoving him back.

Chase tried to intervene and Todd swung at him. Thankfully it missed and he landed on his ass.

"Would you all shut up!" I raised my voice even louder. I rose to my feet and brushed myself off. "Just stop it." Part of me wanted to go nuclear on his ass for screwing up what was meant to be a sacred ritual of scattering Mack's ashes in various spots but instead I took a second to calm myself. "Breathe, Brody, breathe. Serenity now."

Todd stared at me as if preparing for the worst but I just shook my head and grabbed up my bag. "Let's go."

"Are we going home?" Todd asked.

Marlin kicked some loose rocks into the water below. "Of course we are, there isn't much point being out here now. Thanks to you."

Again they started going at it, and I managed make it a few feet before I couldn't handle it. Kelly Laquin was going to have to remain on pause while I unleashed my dark side. I threw my backpack down and grabbed hold of both of them.

"One thing, one goddamn thing, that's all he wanted us to do and we couldn't even fucking do that. And now you want to quit?" I stared at them both before pain shot up my arm. I shook it out, then noticed a bloody gash down the side of my forearm. "Shit!" My voice echoed, and a flock of mountain bluebirds and western tanagers broke from the trees. I returned to where my backpack lay and hauled it over my shoulder.

"Brody," Chase called out. "We should stop."

"No, I'm finishing this damn hike, at least we can do that."

I started making my way down. It took them a while to catch up. The rest of the afternoon was spent hiking to four more of the seven locations before I could tell the others weren't enjoying themselves. I'd pretty much spent the following hours leading the way and what should have been filled with conversation about our lives was spent in silence. Eventually I stopped near the water's edge of Fern

Lake. It was a gorgeous spot. We'd only seen two other people on the way in. When they appeared through the trees, Kai was ahead; he made his way over and took a hold of my arm.

"Listen, we've been talking. We're going to cut this short."

I snorted. "Really? One screw-up and you're calling it a day. I would have loved to hear what Mack would have said."

"Mack's gone, Brody," Marlin said as he made his way over. "And so are we. I've got a business to get back to, so does Kai."

"But we were gonna pitch camp here for the night. It'll be dark soon."

I looked over at Todd and knew straightaway when he dipped his chin that I wasn't going to get his support. Chase scratched the back of his head. "Buddy, I'm all for traipsing around the outback but I'm a realist and those days are over. They were fun while they lasted but..." he trailed off and then sighed. "I'm going back with them, and I think you should come too."

I fished into my jeans. "Oh yeah? Well I'm the one with the keys."

"And I've got twenty pounds on you, Slater," Marlin shot back. "I will beat you to your knees if you don't hand those over."

"Oh you want them?" I clutched them hard and threatened to toss them into the pristine waters.

"Don't you dare," Kai yelled. I shook my head and paused for a second before throwing them at Marlin. I grabbed up my backpack and started trekking out. The keys landed a few feet from him and he went to retrieve them. We'd come all this way and not only screwed up the important task of spreading Mack's ashes but we hadn't even completed what he wanted us to do. Whatever the hell that was, I could only imagine.

"To hell with you assholes," I said as I brushed past Chase. I was starting to realize why we had gone our separate ways, and why none of us had ended up in the military. As when it came down to it, none of us were ready to push through discomfort, or face the hard stuff that Mack knew would shape us.

To make matters worse, on the way back dark clouds began to form across the sky, and the distant sound of thunder threatened. The sun was soon swallowed by the horizon as mosquitoes buzzed around my head. Within fifty minutes the sky opened up and a heavy downpour turned the earth beneath our boots into a mini-stream. Every few minutes sheet lightning would illuminate the atmosphere, followed by cracks of thunder and fork lightning that webbed across the sky. The humidity of the day wrapped itself around me like a blanket making the final stretch back that much harder.

Hours earlier we'd been surrounded by nothing but tranquil beauty and now it was as if evil itself had descended as darkness squeezed itself into every nook and cranny.

The continual clap of thunder was enough to unnerve anyone, but it was the explosive clap of unusual thunder next that made each of us drop as if the sky was about to fall on us. Like a bomb erupting high in the atmosphere, it shook the earth. In that instant a brilliant flash lit up the sky, then faded out.

"Holy shit!" Todd hollered. "The gods are seriously pissed."

"Nope, that's just Mack," I muttered in jest. In all seriousness though, it sure as hell didn't sound like thunder.

* * *

By the time we made it back to the Jeep, it was dark and pretty much all the other visitors had left for the day. There were only a couple of SUVs remaining. We loaded our gear into the back without saying a word to one another. Forty-three minutes. That's all it would take for us to get back to town. I could handle that. We had already endured each other's company for most of the day. By tomorrow morning this would all be just a vague, unpleasant memory. We'd return to our mundane lives and no doubt lose touch with one another as we had before. I would of course lie to Bridget and tell her that it all went off without a hitch and the scattering of her father's ashes had been nothing but a touching moment filled with heartfelt words. I sure as hell wasn't going to tell her what really happened. Marlin would drive back while I rode in the rear with Kai and Todd who were on either side. Chase sat up front. Within minutes of being in the vehicle he was on the phone trying to get hold of Tiffany.

"Anyone else got a phone on them? Mine appears to have given up the ghost."

"Use mine," Kai said pulling out his Bluetooth and phone and handing it to him.

The Jeep rumbled to life, and we pulled out. One other couple was standing by their vehicle looking concerned. I just assumed they were waiting on some stragglers who had fallen behind. It was common to find hikers taking a break while others continued on and then the rest of the group would catch up later. As we veered out of the lot, Chase handed the phone back to Kai. "It's not working."

"What?"

Kai began fiddling around with it. "What the hell?"

"Try mine," Marlin said but Chase was already one step ahead. "It's fried."

"Well this trip is just going fucking perfect," Marlin said, his eyes darting to the rearview mirror and glaring at me. I pulled out my own phone and gave it a try. No luck. My stomach churned within me at the thought that perhaps that eruption was something more than just thunder.

Mack's multiple warnings echoed in my mind as we hauled ass back toward Mammoth Lakes but only one stuck out — an electromagnetic pulse caused by either a high-altitude atomic blast or a solar flare.

Six – Blackout

The nearer we got to town, the clearer it became that we weren't the only ones experiencing problems. Littered along the highway were several abandoned vehicles while others had occupants inside. Several motorists had their hoods up and were shining flashlights into them as if hoping to fix their stalled vehicle. A single truck had drifted to a standstill off to the side of the road and the owner was out yelling at her husband as if he was somehow to blame.

"I'm starting to think we aren't in Kansas anymore," Kai said peering out the window. It must have looked strange to see a Jeep passing by inoperable vehicles. A pregnant woman in the distance stuck out her hand and Marlin weaved around her.

"What are you doing?" Chase asked grabbing hold of Marlin's arm.

"Haven't you heard? You shouldn't stop for

hitchhikers," he muttered.

"But she's pregnant. Stop the vehicle, dumbass," I said.

"But…"

"Stop the vehicle."

The Jeep came to a halt and idled as the woman struggled to catch up. I glanced out the back window and then realized that she wasn't alone. Four other motorists followed her after she waved them over. We brought our windows down as the woman came shuffling up, gripping her stomach and out of breath.

"Thank you. Would you have a phone by any chance?"

"Actually ours aren't working," I said, my eyes drifting over to her friends as they caught up.

"Perhaps they can get her there."

"Where?"

"To the hospital. We were on our way. My wife is having contractions and our damn vehicle stalled. I can't get any reception on the phone otherwise I'd call a friend. I'm not sure what the hell is going on, but it seems as though everyone has the same problem, except you."

He stepped back and his eyes glazed over the vehicle as if trying to figure out why ours hadn't been affected by the mysterious outage. The fact was it was manufactured before vehicles started having computer chips. Before 1980 almost all vehicles were mechanical and pneumatic whereas modern vehicles relied heavily on computer chips to control the fuel injection and other essentials. In all honesty I don't think Mack was thinking about that when he bought a 1976 Jeep but he sure as hell must have taken it into consideration later on when it started having issues and he could have just sold it and bought another. Mack was the kind of man that didn't leave any stone unturned. Every decision he made, he made it for a reason. It was crazy to think that manufactures hadn't thought about the complications that might arise from a powerful, sudden burst of electromagnetic energy. If the phones were fried, so were the chips in their vehicles. I wanted to tell them but chances were it would only create further panic. And with so many motorists shit out of luck, it wouldn't have been smart to mention we'd just been hit by a solar flare or a nuke had exploded in the atmosphere, as we really didn't know for sure. The thought of radiation passed through my mind. What if it was a nuke? How long would it be before we would begin to feel the effects of radiation?

"Well do you think you could give us a boost?"

Todd snorted as if finding something amusing.

"We don't have cables," I said at the same time that Chase said, "Sure."

The man's eyes bounced between the two of us. I quickly answered before Chase could speak any further. "What he means is that we could, but it isn't going to help."

The man shrugged. "How do you know unless we try?"

"Look, we're in a bit of a hurry, we'd like to help but eh…" I gazed at Marlin who had swiveled in his seat.

"Well can we get a ride into town?"

"There's really not much room in the back," Marlin

said.

"Then just my wife? She's going to have a baby."

The woman groaned and was holding her enlarged stomach. Memories of Theresa giving birth to Ava came back to me. We'd arrived early at the hospital and been sent home because the nurse didn't think she was going to give birth for a least another day. They should have fired her because within a matter of three hours Ava's head was already starting to come out. It was for that reason only that I hopped out and went around to the rear and made some room for the woman. Chances were there wasn't going to be any equipment working at the hospital but I would have felt like a complete jerk if she'd ended up having the baby on the side of the road. The father assisted his wife into the back and she squeezed in between the shitload of gear before I closed the tailgate. She clung to her husband's hand, he reassured her that everything would be okay and that he would start making his way into town.

"It'll take us twenty minutes or so. I'll be there."

As I went to get back in, the man grabbed me by the shoulder and used both hands to shake my hand. "Thank you for this."

"Sure. Okay."

I eyed the others before getting in and we pulled away. If the power grid was down, had it gone out only in the state? Or worse — across the entire nation? Troubled thoughts plagued my mind as we drove the final stretch of highway into town. Confusion would be common in the early stage of an EMP. Society had become so reliant upon the grid that people would assume it would come back on within a matter of hours. Eventually that confusion would turn to panic as hours turned into days and food supplies in fridges started expiring, and then desperation would set in. Residents would set about stocking up what they could but by that point it would be too late. The smart ones, or those that had been called paranoid prior to the outage, would have already stocked up, and replenished supplies of food and water in the first few hours. Shelves in stores would empty, and would remain that way, as trucks that would have brought in more goods wouldn't arrive.

That would be the start, and then the water would stop running. Sure, we lived in a region rich with streams and rivers but most wouldn't think to fill up their bathtub with as much water as possible, and others wouldn't know how to filter water beyond filling up a jug they had purchased from their local Wal-Mart.

How long would it take until people started acting erratic? Hell, people couldn't control themselves on Black Friday, never mind an EMP. The fact was, there was no telling how folks would respond. It could take weeks before people resorted to violence, but the reality was, no one really knew what anyone was capable of doing until they were pushed into a corner and right now as far I could tell, our little nook of the nation was on the precipice and it wouldn't take much to push it over.

"This is not good," Marlin said tapping the wheel as the Jeep continued to thread its way around more stranded vehicles.

"What, for your business or in general?" Chase said, quick to get a jab in after all the ones Marlin had. As we came over a rise in the road that led down into Main Street, my eyes widened. Seeing the entire town plunged into darkness was beyond unusual, it was downright terrifying.

Seven – Family First

Upon arriving at the hospital, Marlin swerved up to the entrance, and I hopped out. The woman in the back was screaming in pain and I had visions of having to deliver the baby by the side of the road. That wasn't going to happen. I yelled for assistance as I went to help her out. Though the front of the hospital was shrouded by darkness, there were numerous windows that had light, which meant the backup generators had kicked in. How long they would last was anyone's guess.

Most hospitals ran two types of generators, natural gas and diesel. It was critical that they had some form of backup with so many folks on life support and relying upon equipment to survive. Unfortunately, not all of those backups worked when a disaster hit. When Katrina struck New Orleans, I'd seen reports on the news that 215 patients died in hospitals and nursing homes because the generators had stopped working or had failed completely. It soon came to light that some of the generators were more than 50 years old, housed in basements that didn't even have flood protection and the government couldn't afford to move them to safer locations. If that wasn't alarming enough, the fact that there wasn't a national standard that had to be followed on how and where generators needed to be installed only demonstrated that survival was at the bottom of the list for the government. Unless individual Americans took it upon themselves to act, they were shit out of luck.

Outside a small crowd trying to operate cell phones stared at us. I flagged down a nurse who was smoking a cigarette and having a discussion. Another orderly shot back inside and returned with a wheelchair. It was a chaotic scene as the pregnant woman wasn't the only one needing assistance. Several locals were outside complaining and the second they saw the woman getting attention there was uproar. It obviously didn't factor in that she was about to burst forth life, oh no, that all took a back seat to their needs.

"You want to tell me how this is working?" Some guy was standing at the passenger side window conversing with Chase about why our vehicle was operating when his top-of-the-line motor was as dead as a doornail.

One woman held up her phone and kept shifting position as though that was the cure for a phone that wouldn't power on. She had a better chance of being struck by lightning than having that operate anytime soon.

But the fact was that's how everyone was thinking.

If they couldn't get their vehicles to start they would try to call home, or roadside assistance. Society had become so dependent upon government and local services that the idea of actually preparing themselves for the worst-case scenario had become nothing but a joke shared over lunch.

But how absurd was it?

Most folks were already paying an arm and a leg for auto, medical and home insurance, so was putting aside a small amount of money to pay for a bug-out bag or freeze-dried food really that crazy? If the prepper shows on TV were anything to go by, most of society would have screamed yes. The fact was, the media portrayed survivalists as nutjobs, paranoid crazies who had nothing better to do than overspend on food and water and waste all their time running through end-of-the-world scenarios. No wonder society laughed.

"Sir, just back up, I don't know," Chase replied.

We all did but no one would say a word. Kai made a gesture for me to hurry up. I made sure the woman was taken care of before I dashed back to the Jeep and hopped in. Marlin didn't waste a second hitting the gas and swerving out of there. He nearly ran over the foot of the guy who was now shaking his fist and yelling expletives.

"What now?" Marlin asked.

"I need to get home and make sure that Tiffany and the kids are okay."

"Yeah, I should check in on my mother," Todd muttered.

"How much gas we got left?" Kai asked Marlin.

"Quarter tank."

"Before we check in on our families, let's fill up with gas."

"And how do you expect to do that if the gas pumps aren't working?" I said.

"Well maybe some of them are running on generators."

"Are you kidding me?" I said. "Didn't anything of what Mack taught you sink in?"

"Yeah, yeah, Slater, well not everyone is like you. Some of us actually had better things to do with our time," Kai replied.

What he meant by that was he didn't get around to going through the tapes Mack handed out because by the time he was fifteen, Kai's father had him working in the martial arts school teaching classes. The kid never got a break. He would go off to school and then come home and help his father and then still have to squeeze in time for doing homework. I'd forgotten that until he brought it up.

"Look, with all these vehicles abandoned on the side of the road, we could at least siphon out some. No one is going to see us," Todd said.

Marlin cracked up laughing. "A few hours without power and you are already resorting to theft. Now I know how you support yourself."

"Screw you, Marlin." Todd pulled a cigarette and wedged it between his lips before lighting. That was another thing that was going to be in short supply. Probably for the best. It had taken me three years to kick the habit but with the stress of the present moment weighing down on us and the aroma from Todd's cigarette filling the Jeep, I was beginning to feel the urge to reach for one.

"No, he's right. Let's do it," I said.

"What?" Chase said spinning in his seat as if the idea was that outlandish. "You don't know if this is anything more than a citywide, or statewide outage. For all we know the power could be up in an hour, and what then?"

"No one is going to know but if it's not an accident,

we have gas."

"What, are you planning a road trip somewhere? Because if it was anything like the one we just went on, I'm not going." Kai said.

I sighed and ran a hand over my tired face. I was sweaty, still soaked to the bone from hiking back in the pouring rain, and the weather outside didn't look as if it was going to get any better.

"Well unless you guys have some fuel at home, then tell me where we are going to get some?"

"Brody, right now we just need to make sure family is okay."

"And we will but you can be damn sure if Mack was here, he'd want us to be thinking survival first," Todd muttered.

"No he wouldn't. Family is all that mattered to him in the end. All that shit about surviving and defying the odds and challenging yourself was just bullshit. You know it was. It was just the spillover from an old man who was reminiscing his days in the military," Marlin said as he headed towards Chase's home on the east side.

"Is that why you didn't enlist, Marlin? Cause if anyone could have, you sure as hell could," I said.

"I'm not even having that conversation with you. We are going to Chase's home, and that's it. I'm dropping him off, then Todd, then you and Kai, then I'll drop this Jeep off and walk back home."

I laughed. "You really think this is going to fix itself, don't you?"

"You don't know, Brody. So stop acting like you do. All we know right now is the power is down," Chase said.

"So explain to me then why every fucking vehicle isn't operating except ours?"

"Maybe cause theirs all hooked up to the same damn computer and when that went down, so did the computer chips on their vehicles."

"Oh please, you can't honestly be that naïve?"

"Well I haven't seen a plane come down yet. I would imagine they would be dropping out of the sky right now."

"Look, if you want keep taking the dumb pills, that's fine by me but I'm asking you to stop and let me siphon a few vehicles. If it turns out that the power comes back on, I'll take the gas back to where I got it. How's that sound?"

This wasn't an argument about whether or not an EMP had fried the grid. Chase knew better than that. He wasn't stupid. It was a case of morals. His mother had forced him to go to church when he was a kid until he rebelled in his teen years. It wasn't like he was much of a churchgoer now, but he did have one hell of a guilt complex. He didn't want to be an accessory to theft. And who could blame him? I didn't exactly like the idea but what other choice did we have? I could have given him a lecture about how quickly morals would vanish once society was thrown back into a lifestyle reminiscent of the 1800s but would that have helped? Probably not.

Marlin slammed the brakes on, and we all jerked forward. "Go on then, make it quick."

Eight – Neighborhood Watch

Ten minutes later we arrived on Panorama Drive. Chase's home was a far cry from my own shack. His wife, Tiffany, had her own jewelry line and was making more than enough that he didn't have to work his usual real estate job. He'd quit it two years ago thinking that he'd hit the jackpot only to find himself taking over the position of mommy dearest. That's right, he'd got a promotion to head diaper changer and spent his afternoon ironing, vacuuming and doing anything else Tiffany could put on her man bitch list.

There was no vehicle parked outside as the Jeep turned into their driveway. He lived in a prestigious neighborhood and a home that most of us could have only dreamed about; four bedrooms, four bathrooms, with breathtaking views of Mammoth Mountain.

"You think you can stick around? I'm not sure if she's going to turf me out for the night."

"Why, has she done that before?"

He pointed to the two-door garage. "I've spent many a night inside there."

We shook our heads as he wandered up to the darkened house. I hopped out, stretched my legs and followed him in. In all the years we'd been friends, Chase was probably the one who I'd spent the majority of my time with as the other three were usually busy. However, that was years ago, a lot had changed since he'd got married to Tiffany. Or perhaps, she'd changed him. Until he put a ring on her finger, she was as nice as pie. Back then Chase had his own apartment. Nothing fancy but almost immediately I could pick up vibes that she was expecting him to sell it once they got hitched. We'd go out once a week for beer and wings and shoot the breeze, have a few games of pool and laugh about old times but the moment he got back from his honeymoon that all changed. It was like she didn't want him spending time with me, or any of the others for that matter. It was controlling but he couldn't see that. The last night out had been many years ago, and it didn't exactly go well as I told him that she was trying to run his life and he was going to regret it if he gave up his job to stay at home. But there was no telling him. In his eyes Tiffany could do no wrong.

"Tiff! Kids?" Chase shouted as he entered the dark corridor. I tripped over some shoes that were haphazardly scattered on the floor alongside a coat.

"Perhaps they stepped out to a neighbor's home."

"No, she wouldn't do that. Hell, she doesn't even say hello to them."

"Are you serious?"

He didn't reply, but I knew it was true. That was just like her. Her home was her castle and beyond family she wasn't in the habit of making new friends or even spending time with people she'd met before. I'd tried to get Theresa to bridge the gap. You know, take her out or invite her over so I could hang out with Chase but it was a lost cause. I often wondered if Tiffany hadn't been to blame for my marriage breaking down. The few times

Theresa had swung by her place she would always return and be critical of me as if Tiffany had filled her head with some foolish idea that she could do better. It wasn't long after that, word got around that she was sleeping with Carl Stimms.

Chase reappeared in the hallway holding a note in his hand.

"She's gone to her mother's!" He sighed. "I knew this trip was a bad idea." He shook his head. "I bet you a dime to a dollar she had the kids packed and in the SUV within two hours of us leaving this morning. Shit! And I can't even phone her."

"Well where does her mother live?"

"Bridgeport."

"So it's an hour away. We'll run you over there tomorrow morning."

"Tomorrow? I need to go now. This isn't just about the outage, my marriage is on the line."

"Well best of luck trying to convince Marlin to hand over the wheel. Buddy, it isn't going to happen. Besides, you really think Tiffany would walk out on you just for going on a trip with the boys?"

"Hell yeah," he replied without missing a beat. "That's why I didn't want to go." He leaned back against the wall and let out a heavy sigh.

"What the hell has happened to you?"

He shot a sideways glance. The only light came from the moon that shone through large living room windows. "What do you mean?"

"You act like she's the only woman on the planet and yet she treats you like shit."

"No she doesn't."

I laughed. "You're in denial."

"No, she's just…"

"Controlling."

He raised a finger to me. "That's enough."

"Seriously, Chase, when was the last time your entire clan visited your family?"

"A couple of years ago."

I scoffed. "And you live in the same town. Have they

ever been over to see you?"

"No, but Tiffany has social phobia. She doesn't like to be around crowds."

"You sure people don't like being around her?"

"Careful, Brody."

I shrugged. "Okay then, have *you* been over to see them?"

"I've been too busy with the kids, house and…"

I shook my head and walked out. The guy was blind to it. He was so enamored with her, or worried that he'd never find another woman who would actually treat him right that he was willing to let her use him like a doormat.

He followed me out. "No hey, wait up. Listen, just because Theresa didn't give two shits about what you did, you think Tiffany is controlling."

"You happy, Chase?" I asked.

He snorted. "Oh you are a fine one to lecture me about happiness. You ever asked yourself why you spend nearly all your waking hours listening to those self-help audios?"

"Because I want to improve myself."

"Is that so? So what's the next level for a Von's Superstore manager?" he said in his most mocking tone.

"District manager."

"Oooohh, exciting stuff. Is that when they let you decide what brand of tomatoes to stock the stores with?"

I flipped him the bird as I walked back to the Jeep and he locked up. The truth was neither of us were happy. I didn't really know at which point I made the shift over from enjoying life to enduring it, only that it had happened. It was subtle. I didn't just wake up and think, okay, my life sucks. A shrink might have questioned my marriage, but it wasn't the fourteen years that it had been on the rocks or the divorce that changed the way I looked at life. It started long before that. In reality the last time I could recall truly feeling alive was between the age of fifteen and eighteen. Three years. That was it.

I was just about to get inside the Jeep when someone called out.

"Chase, is that you?"

I turned to see a group of four people holding flashlights. They were walking at a fast pace and shining the light in our direction. I squinted and put up a forearm to block the glare.

"Yeah it's me."

"Oh good, I thought someone was trying to break into your place. We've already had one incident so far this evening."

Chase wandered over, shook the hand of a man in his late fifties, give or take, stocky and going a little soft. I stood by the door while the other three remained inside.

"Who are they?"

"Friends of mine."

"Doug, did you see Tiffany leave this morning?"

"No, when I picked up the mail from the box the SUV was gone. I thought you guys had gone up to the lake."

He shook his head. "No, she's gone to her mother's, I just wanted to check when she left."

He looked back at me and then his neighbor continued his line of questioning.

"This is crazy, right? You heard anything?"

"No."

"I've been trying to get hold of the emergency utilities line but the damn phones aren't working, no Internet and none of our vehicles will start." Then his eyes drifted over to the Jeep. "But you seem to be in luck. You want to give me a ride into town? Maybe a power line is down or something."

"Actually, Doug, we're a little busy right now. Friends of mine are worried about their families and…"

He nodded casting his light down at the ground. "Oh yeah, sure, no worries."

"What else isn't working?" Chase asked. I knew he wanted to verify what I had said it could be.

Doug leaned back on his haunches and scratched the back of his neck. "Better question, what is working? Right now no computers, phones, towers, routers, bank machines, televisions, radios, refrigerators or thermostats are operating. Whoever screwed up down at the utilities company is going to be standing in the unemployment line on Monday."

The other neighbors beside Doug nodded like puppets, mirroring him.

"Bank?"

"Yeah, Shelly over there was getting funds out when the system went down."

Chase pointed to his neighbor's roof. "Solar panels?"

He shrugged.

"What about your generator?"

He shook his head. "Hell, I haven't checked that to be honest. But my portable generator didn't kick in."

"Are you serious?"

"Oh it's not the first time. You remember that storm we had a few years back? Well, my generator was plugged into the local utility line at the time when the storm knocked out the power. Anyway, when the power was restored, the darn thing wouldn't generate electricity. It's like the AC current, which fed into the alternator, fried it. I replaced the circuit breaker, the rectifier and still the darn thing isn't working."

"And the wiring?"

"Clean as a whistle, not a single burn mark."

Marlin shouted over to Chase. "Chase, let's go."

He thumbed over his shoulder. "I should get moving. Thanks for keeping an eye on the house."

"Well, not much else we can do for now until it's light. Hopefully by then they will have the power up."

Keep on dreaming, I muttered under my breath. Chase gripped his shoulder, told him to stay safe and then returned to the Jeep. On one hand I wanted to warn them and say it was only a matter of time before things got worse but would they have even believed? Hell, even Chase was having a hard time wrapping his head around it and he'd grown up around a man that preached nothing but worst-case scenarios. It wouldn't take long for the harsh reality to sink in as people discovered that the electricity wasn't going to be switched back on and all the services they had relied on were gone. In between now and then we could make preparations, figure out where to stay and…

"Guys, you think Mack would have had some kind of bunker in place?"

Chase was still convinced that I was reading too much into this, and he chuckled. "Slater, you need to calm your ass down. Just like Doug said, it's probably just some asshole who has hit a wrong button or pulled the wrong plug in town."

"You better hope it is," I shot back. Our eyes locked as Marlin gunned it out of there and headed towards Todd's mom's home.

Nine – Enemies and Allies

Todd lived in a sketchy part of town. In fact, it was often referred to as "The Ghetto." The ghetto was made up of four streets that ran from Main to Meridian Boulevard. It was located in the center of town and was one of the oldest areas. The street was mainly made up of cabins and residential homes as well as apartments and condos and government-sponsored housing which was what Todd's mother was in because she was on disability.

"Just pull up over there and I'll meet you back here in ten minutes," Todd said hopping out.

"You wouldn't be ashamed of where you live, would you, Fontane?" Marlin said with a grin on his face.

"No. Just my mother is a bit funny about strangers."

"Does everyone else want to see his mom's basement?"

We let out a chuckle. "Hell yeah."

And that was it. Marlin killed the engine, and we all pushed out. "Come on, guys. Shouldn't you keep an eye on the Jeep?"

"Oh, you ain't slipping out of this one, Fontane," Marlin said coming around and putting him in a headlock and rubbing the top of his head like he used to when we were kids.

"God, I wish you wouldn't do that."

"Yeah, it's not the same now you don't have any hair."

That was what annoyed Todd the most in the '80s. Back then he had a rock-star hairdo and used to wear makeup like a lot of the soft metal bands. Marlin teased him to no end. That's why it was a shocker to see him rocking the Kojak style. He said he was going for the Jason Statham look but that would have relied on muscle and his arms were a little too flabby. When we arrived at the run-down digs, I spotted a weathered U.S. flag covering up the basement window. Todd let himself in and called out to his mother, Edith. I'd always liked her. Back in the '80s she'd been one of those women that would think every kid didn't have enough meat on their bones and so she'd offer to make us a Spam sandwich even though I knew she didn't have much money. She was kindhearted, and long before she retired from disability she worked at the local 7-Eleven before they closed it sometime in the nineties.

"Mom," Todd shouted out. I felt like I had been transported back in time. That was exactly what he'd say every time we returned from long bike rides. The outside of his home was still the same. No flowers, just tons of weeds and the stench of dog shit.

Inside a few candles flickered and cast eerie shadows on the walls.

"Todd?" a croaky voice replied from somewhere inside. Todd rushed into the living room and found his mother rising from a deteriorating armchair. It had been years since I'd seen her. In the darkness it was hard to tell how much she had aged but she had to have been in her late sixties, early seventies. Fortunately his father Chuck wasn't alive. He'd died from liver failure due to drinking too much. In many ways it seemed like a fitting end after all the suffering he'd put Todd and his mother through. I never quite understood why she didn't leave him. Police had been called out to their home on numerous occasions and for a while I thought Todd was going to be placed in foster care and his father locked up, but it never happened. Chuck must have been wise to how the system worked as he got counseling and entered rehab. Not that it helped him as he just fell off the wagon again but for a short while it kept the police and child protective services out of the picture.

My eyes drifted around the cramped room. It smelled musty and reminded me of an old person's clothes closet. Everything was exactly as I remembered. School portraits of Todd, and a few from some vacation they'd taken to the Grand Canyon and Mexico lined the walls and rested on side tables. On the table beside her, a newspaper, a cup and a dirty ashtray overflowing with butts and an apple core stuck in the middle. In all the times I had been over to his house as a kid, I'd always wanted to have a shower after I left. It felt like grime lingered in the air. I don't think it was because his mother was unclean, just busy with life and trying to cope with an alcoholic husband while attempting to raise a child.

When she caught sight of us, she gave a warm smile.

"Brody, Marlin, Chase and oh wow, Kai, you really have grown up," she said noticing us standing in the hallway. She came over and hugged each of us like we were her own, and pinched Kai's cheeks.

"So we good here?" Marlin asked eager to get back out on the road.

"Actually, I'm wondering if it's safe to stay here?" Todd interjected. "I mean if that was a high-altitude nuclear weapon from North Korea that detonated in the atmosphere, won't there be fallout? Radiation and whatnot?"

"Korea?" Chase screwed up his face.

Todd nodded, turned and picked up the newspaper off the table. It was a copy of *USA Today*. Plastered across the front in huge bold lettering was the headline:

Presidential Administration Pressures North Korea to

Give Up Nukes

I took it from his hand and cast a glance over it. My eyes scanned fast.

Below were several articles about the U.S. getting backlash for bombing Syria, and another from experts warning that a single North Korean nuke could black out the national grid and kill 90 percent of Americans.

I turned to the others and held it up while using a candle to show them the headlines. "He's right. The first few weeks after a fallout are the most dangerous, at least for those who are closest to the blast region."

"Fallout decays rapidly though," Chase added. "And again, we don't know if that's what it was."

I shook my head. "You really think that eruption we heard up in the foothills was thunder?" I threw my hand up in the air, tossed the paper down on the chair. I was unable to grasp that Chase was acting so gullible. "Please!"

"Is it so naïve to think that our government could actually prevent what you think has happened?"

"Well, their track record is a bit shaky," Kai muttered. He coughed and muttered, "9/11, Pearl Harbor."

"Oh give me a break!" Chase said.

"Better to be safe than sorry, right?" Todd said with his arm around his mother. He looked as if he was trying to figure out what to do.

"Look, we don't have time for this. This was not the plan. I was going to drop you all off and go home, Amanda is probably going out of her mind with worry," Marlin said.

I directed my attention to him. "Well, I hate to piss on your parade, Marlin, but I think until we find out exactly what has happened, we have to assume the worst."

"Why?" Chase asked.

"Why what?"

"Why do we have to assume the worst? Because Mack would have?" He eyed me through narrow slits, his features barely visible in the dark. Before I could respond, he leaned forward and took a hold of my left wrist and pushed up my shirtsleeve, then did the same with the right.

I scowled. "What are you doing?"

"Seeing if you're wearing a 'What Would Mack Do?' wristband. Because you keep bringing him up as though we are expected to live and die by his word."

I leaned forward and poked a finger into his chest. "You want to take risks, be my guest, but the signs are pretty damn clear to me. Hundreds of vehicles just don't stall all at the same time."

"Have you even considered the thought that this could be Chinese hackers?"

"Oh great, let's blame the Chinese," Kai said shaking his head. "It's not like we don't have better things to do."

Chase let out a chuckle. "Buddy, maybe you have had your head under a rock for the last few years but your people are not exactly innocent. Haven't you read the news?"

"My people?" Kai said straightening up. "I'm an American!"

"You know what I mean. China has repeatedly hacked

the U.S. and stolen data on nukes, FBI and war plans. Hell, they even hacked into the Pentagon a couple of years back."

"Bullshit," Kai replied.

"You want to act ignorant, that's up to you but only a few days ago the Chinese tried to hack the THAAD missile system set up in South Korea."

"THAAD? What the hell is that?" Todd asked.

Chase leaned forward. "The anti-missile defense system, dipshit. If North Korea decided to unleash one of its intercontinental ballistic missiles at California or even South Korea, that's what would attempt to stop it. So it makes you wonder why are they trying to hack our technology that could save us?"

Kai laughed. "Well, that wouldn't even happen. A missile that could travel 5,500 miles? Good luck, the last I heard they failed to launch a missile that could go half of that," Kai added. "And anyway everyone knows they don't even have the engineering in place to threaten the American mainland. They would need a working ICBM system and a warhead for one of those missiles. Then they would need to make a rocket that could survive the vibrations of launch, the G-force of flight and temperature changes of takeoff and re-entry," Kai said in one breath before exhaling hard. We all stared at Kai who began picking some food out of his teeth as though what he'd just reeled off was common knowledge.

Chase directed his attention back to me. "There you go, satisfied? North Korea doesn't have the means to reach the U.S. You're just buying into media fear tactics."

"Oh and you're not guilty of doing the same? What were you just saying about the Chinese?"

Marlin groaned. "Can we just get going?"

This was driving me insane. "Okay, you have me really confused now, what the hell has that got to do with vehicles stalling?" I said throwing a hand up. "Todd, look, just go grab a few things and we'll take you and your mother over to Mack's place, I'm sure Bridget would know if he had something in place for this kind of event. And anyway it's probably best we stick together."

"This kind of event? Brody, you don't even known what this event is. All we are dealing with right now is what-ifs and unknowns. You talk about people panicking but the only one that seems to be panicking is you!" Chase barked.

As Todd went to head out with his mother, Marlin stepped forward and placed a hand on his chest. "Hold on a second. This is not the plan."

Todd ignored Marlin and pushed past him. His mother looked worried. She had good reason. Sure, I didn't have official information straight from the horse's mouth on what we were dealing with. It could have been a solar flare.

"Look, perhaps the Chinese hacked into our power grid. Who knows, maybe this is some backlash over some trade agreement. Maybe the USA forgot to make a payment on the trillions that they owe them. Who the hell knows? Who the hell cares?"

"I care."

Kai had been sitting quietly observing but the whole

pointing the finger at the Chinese sent him over the edge. "The Chinese are our allies. If anyone is going to want to help the USA, it would be them."

"Not exactly," I said. "While I don't agree the Chinese are behind this…" My eyes darted to Chase. He was clearly barking up the wrong tree. "I'm not convinced that they are friends of the U.S. Trade allies maybe, but with the recent change in power, here in the States, and the U.S. dropping that bomb on Syria. Right now I think our country is on shaky ground."

I grabbed up the paper and used a candle to read out one of the articles.

Tensions are high between North Korea and global powers after the missile strike on Syria. Though many world leaders were in agreement, the United States has received backlash from Russia, China, North Korea and Japan, who say the U.S. has broken international law.

They are calling for the U.S. to withdraw its military presence from foreign countries. It's believed that there are currently 800 U.S. bases dotted around the planet in 80 countries, while there are no freestanding foreign bases in the United States.

"It's a threat, plain and simple," the Chinese foreign minister said.

China and Russia have dispatched ships to shadow the armada sent by the U.S. after the continual testing of ballistic missiles by North Korea.

I looked up briefly and could see Chase listening closely. All of them were. I continued.

Russia has warned the U.S. after the vice president said the era of strategic patience with Pyongyang was over. The Russian foreign minister said in Moscow that while they do not accept or condone the nuclear testing that breaches United Nations resolutions, that does not mean the U.S. can break international law. He warned that there had better not be any actions like the one in Syria.

"So Russia has a bee in its bonnet over what our boys are doing. What's new? They have had a beef with us since the cold war. But let's face it, why did they drop the bomb on the Syrian airfield? Because no one else was taking action against President Bashar al-Assad's use of chemical weapons against his own people," Chase said defending the decision that was made by our government.

"I still don't see how China has anything to do with this?" Kai said. "They are just worried because North Korea is their neighbor. If the USA fires on North Korea they'll be in the blast radius."

"That's not all," I said.

"Okay, North Korea's largest trade partner is China. They would lose out."

"Not just that. Why do you think the USA has bases in eighty countries? They have 28,500 troops in South Korea, 34,000 in Germany, and 39,000 in Japan. And that doesn't include Singapore or Guam. China is concerned because North Korea is a physical buffer against U.S. forces. If the U.S. bombs North Korea and plants a base there, they'd be right on China's border and in a good position to contain China as they continue to rise in world power."

"Dude, why would they worry now? We've been out there since World War II. It's precautionary."

Chase went and slumped down on a chair. "Hurry up, Todd, I'm getting tired of listening to Brody's fear-mongering drivel."

"Fear-mongering?" I shoved the paper in his face and pointed to the article about how experts were warning the USA that a single North Korean nuke could black out the national grid and kill 90 percent of Americans.

He slapped it out of his face. "Ninety percent dead, really? Oh I've got to hear this crap."

"Chase, it's not from the blast, it's from the aftereffects of an EMP. They're talking about starvation, disease and society collapsing. Come on, man, tell me you didn't bypass that tape?"

He didn't reply but just continued to stare at the wall as if he was ignoring me. Chase might not have been willing to admit that this was serious, but he wasn't an idiot. I knew he'd listened to Mack's tapes as any time Mack grilled us on them, he was one of the first to reply with an answer. Being as he was going to be difficult about it I decided to read the article.

"Okay, Chase, you want hard facts from our government? This article cites their source as the former director of the CIA and the executive director of the EMP Task Force on National and Homeland Security."

My eyes drifted across the text. It was hard to see anything in the dark. "Marlin, you got that flashlight?"

"It's out in the Jeep. You want me to get it?"

"Ugh, don't bother."

I continued to hold the candle close to the paper as I scanned it looking for snippets that might provide any insights into how North Korea might have been able to pull this off.

Chase snorted. "You're not going to find it, Brody. Like Kai said, they don't have the capability to pull off a strike on the U.S. with nuclear weapons." Chase huffed and shook his head as if I was wasting his time. This was less about proving a point and more about finding out if it was even possible.

"Here it is. Russia paraded an intercontinental ballistic missile that could carry four miniaturized nuclear warheads through Red Square in Moscow last month."

"Oh great, so now you think it's the Russians?"

I ignored his jab and continued.

"They have stated that North Korea also has the sophistication to miniaturize warheads and deliver them by satellite, so that they are specifically designed to make a high-altitude electromagnetic pulse attack against the United States. And listen to this... A former commander of NORAD gave a warning a year ago at a press conference that North Korea already had the means and capability to do this after a photo was released of Kim Jong-Un beside what appeared to be a genuine miniaturized nuclear warhead. Detailed information has been released that North Korea does have two ICBMs — the KN08 and KN14. But that's not all. It goes on to say that a congressional EMP commission said that if the North Korean satellite delivered a single warhead, it could black out the nation's grid for over a year and kill nine out of ten Americans purely through starvation and collapse. There are currently two North Korean satellites, the KMS-3 and KMS-4, orbiting over the U.S. as we speak. There you go!" I dropped the paper on his lap like a microphone. "And that's if they launch one. Imagine if they unleashed two or more?" I paused for a few seconds. "And you know what? It doesn't matter if it's North Korea. If Russia has the means, does China? Makes you wonder, doesn't it, Chase? Who really is our enemy or ally?"

Chase stared at the paper as Todd came back into the room.

"Brody, can I speak to you a minute?"

I walked out casting a glance at Chase who was letting that sink in.

Ten - Desperation

"What's up?" I asked as he led me into the kitchen. Edith was sitting at the table smoking a cigarette. Her hands were trembling. She was wearing her coat and shoes but they still hadn't packed a bag of clothes.

"She won't go and I don't think it's safe to stay here."

I shrugged. "So explain it to her."

"I tried but she won't listen, and well, you're good with old folks, right?"

I screwed up my face and cleared my throat, then chuckled a little. "What, because I work in a supermarket?"

"Yeah, I mean you have to deal with confrontational old geezers all the time. Folks who don't understand why that 50 percent off deal isn't available on the weekend, or are confused over why you're sold out of their favorite brand of peanut butter."

I rubbed the bridge of my nose feeling a tension

headache coming on. "It's your mother, Todd."

He spoke out the corner of his mouth. "I know but she doesn't listen to me."

"I can hear you," Edith said. "I might be old but I'm not deaf."

Todd leaned in and spoke quietly in my ear. "Look, she still thinks my father is here."

"Chuck?" I blurted out his name and Edith started looking around.

"Where is he?"

Todd gritted his teeth together and waved his hand. "Keep it down. Like I said, she still thinks he's here. Anyway..." He trailed off, and I glanced over to her. Getting old was tough on many levels. I didn't look forward to losing my mind. I felt I could handle anything but that. How many of the elderly were out there sitting in the dark, wondering what was going on? Thankfully it was the summer months, as had it been the winter, many might have succumbed to the drop in temperature. I took a seat beside her and placed my hand on top of hers. They were cold and clammy.

"Hey, Mrs. Fontane. Do you remember when I used to show up here in the winter with no jacket and you used to insist I wear one of Todd's?"

I was keen to jerk her memory. The fact that she had remembered us made me wonder if her memory was fine and she was just coming up with an excuse because she was afraid. It wouldn't have been the first time I'd had to deal with old folks who acted all out of character.

She nodded.

"It used to annoy the heck out of me but I did it because it made you happy. Well, Todd here wants to take you over to see an old friend of ours. You remember Mack Sheldon and his daughter Bridget?"

She frowned for a second then shook her head. "No. Where is Chuck? I should really get his supper ready. He doesn't like to wait."

I shot Todd a sideways glance. She wasn't making an excuse; there was definitely some mild dementia at work. I rose from my seat and crossed the room.

"Maybe you should stay here."

"What and succumb to the fallout? Like hell, I'll drag that old bat out of here if I have to."

"Todd."

He shook his head. "I know, I'm sorry. This is just stressing me out." He took a hard pull on his cigarette and ran his hand across his bald head.

"Look, go pack a bag for her and I'll grab some of yours."

"No, I'll do it. Or you can get my mother's things."

I frowned. "I'm not rooting through your mother's underwear. Shit."

"Okay. Um, just wait here," Todd said.

Todd looked over to his mother with a concerned expression. I had no idea how we were going to convince her to get out. After Todd went out I began looking around inside the cupboards to see if there were any sleeping pills or something that might sedate her. The last thing I wanted was for her to start screaming. That had happened on two occasions in the supermarket. It was painful to watch and sad.

I thumbed to Kai and asked him to keep an eye on her while I went down to the basement. I hadn't been down there since we were nineteen. It was around that time that we each got busy with work. Of course I'd seen him several times over the next twenty-odd years but most of the time he met me outside of his home, or at a bar. It was like he was embarrassed to be still living with his mother.

As I rounded the corner that led into an open space that doubled as a downstairs living room and bedroom, I could see why. The place hadn't changed one bit. It literally looked exactly the same as it did back in the '80s. Plastered all over the walls were posters of Metallica, Iron Maiden, Depeche Mode, Poison, some were of pinup girls in various states of undress and others were from classic movies like *Back to the Future, Ferris Bueller's Day Off, Top Gun* and *Gremlins*. On the counter was his old record player and collection of vinyls. Hell, the only thing that was new was the bedspread. Gone was the NBA duvet and in its place was some tacky leopard-skin eyesore.

Right then Todd came barreling down the stairs. "Brody, I told you to wait."

"You haven't changed anything in here."

His cheeks flushed red as he hurried over to his closet and started filling up a duffel bag with a few items.

"Why didn't you move out?" I asked. He didn't immediately reply. "Or join the military? I mean out of all of us you actually told me you had enlisted. How did you get out?"

He cast a glance over his shoulder as he continued haphazardly tossing clothes into his bag. "Delayed enlistment process. I signed up and was meant to ship out for basic training but I couldn't do it."

"Why?"

He stopped packing and his chin dropped for a second. "Who was going to look after my mother? My father? All he cared about was himself. No. Anyway I had an attorney help me get out. Seems that once you sign on the dotted line, you can get out but the recruiter kept hassling me. The attorney told me that the Department of Defense's policy is that anyone can request to be released from DEP, even though they did try to threaten to court-martial me but that never happened. It was just a scare tactic. According to my lawyer, the military is a volunteer force and well, they don't need or want to have anyone who doesn't volunteer. Even my recruiter knew that, but he worked on a quota and so they tried a bunch of unethical tactics to keep me from dropping out."

"Is that why you resent your mother?"

"Resent?"

"The way you spoke about her upstairs, like she was a burden on you."

He cast his eyes away. "You know how many times my father beat on me?" He didn't give a number but I knew it was high. "I wished my mother could have stopped it but he was already wailing on her."

"So you blame her?"

"No," he said shaking his head. "She's the only good

person in my life." There was a long pause as he seemed to reflect on the past.

"Did you quit to piss him off?"

Todd looked at me and he got this smirk on his face as though I had hit on the real reason he bailed on the military.

"Maybe."

Nothing would have pissed off Chuck more than having his son enlist and then quit before he got shipped out. He acted like it was his civic duty to tell anyone that would listen to his shit that they should enlist. Perhaps that's why he sent Todd over to Mack's place. He wanted some form of guarantee that he wasn't just going to make it into the military but that he would pass the training required to become one of the elite. It was as if he was trying to live his life through Todd. You see, Chuck had never managed to go beyond being a soldier in the army. Not that it made him less of a man but he was always heavy on Todd for not aspiring to be something more. For someone that expected his kid to join the military he sure had a strange way of encouraging him.

It made sense that Todd would go against his wishes.

I went over to his bed and reached underneath his mattress, hoping to cheer him up.

"Todd Fontane, you still have the July 1985 issue of *Playboy* magazine. You dirty bastard." I burst out laughing as he rushed over and snatched it out of my hand.

"Hey, that's a classic."

I wagged my finger. "Wasn't that the one with Grace Jones and Dolph Lundgren?"

He sucked air in. "Oh yeah. Hot! Gotta love me some Grace Jones."

I frowned. "Each to their own."

"What does that mean?"

Before I could reply I heard Marlin yell "Hey!" It sounded as if chaos was breaking out upstairs. I sprinted up the stairs taking two steps a time to find them gone. By the time I made it outside, Marlin was straddling the side of the Jeep as it pulled away while Kai had dived into the back. I broke into a sprint just as the Jeep came to a standstill. Marlin was on the driver quicker than I could identify who it was. He yanked him out of the seat and dropped the guy with a hook to the side of the jaw. He was about to continue laying down a beating when I caught up and hauled him off.

On the ground was a kid in his early twenties with spiked blond hair and wearing black camo gear. He had multiple tattoos and was sporting some motorcycle patch on his back. A look of fear spread across his face as he held up his hands and cowered back.

"Look, I didn't know anyone was using it, and besides you left the keys inside. I thought it was abandoned."

"You left the keys inside?" Chase was the first one to ask Marlin.

He shrugged. "What? It slipped my mind. I didn't think we were going to be in Todd's house for as long as we were."

He turned his attention back to the kid. "Get up!" Marlin said giving him a kick in the leg.

"Marlin," I said before shaking my head. The kid got up and brushed off dirt from the back of his pant legs. His shirt was torn and blood trickled from the corner of his lip.

"What's your name, kid?" I asked.

"Markus."

"Well, Markus, where are you from, and how did you end up here?"

"I'm staying with friends of mine on the east side of town at the Best Western." He looked nervously at Marlin who was twice the size of him. "Look, I'm real sorry. I wouldn't have taken it if I'd known—"

"That we were going to beat your ass?" Marlin interjected.

"It's just crazy out there right now. I'm not even from the area. I'm from Carson City, Nevada. We were down here on a biking trip when this all kicked off. Our group was trying to find a working vehicle to get back."

"Well look, kid, you are going to have to find another vehicle," I said. "And if you're smart, you'll find a grocery store and stock up with as much food as you can before all the supplies are gone. And if you're looking for a vehicle, keep your eyes out for anything that was manufactured before 1980. All the computer chips in the modern vehicles have been fried."

Marlin stared at me with a frown as the kid nodded. He turned to leave and then said something that was a little odd. "Does this town have a gun store?"

"Why, you thinking of returning?" Marlin flashed him the Glock 17 he'd stashed in the front of his waistband. Markus' hands shot up.

"Hey, I've got no problem with you."

"No you don't. Now get the fuck outta here before I bust a cap in your ass."

The kid turned and bolted into the darkness.

"Marlin, was that really necessary?" Chase asked.

"You're damn right it is. My friend, we are in a different world now! Like it or not, people are going to come knocking and I for one am not going to be caught with my pants down."

"Like the way you left the keys in the vehicle?"

It was mistake any of us could have made. Outside of a stressful situation anyone could say what they would do but saying and doing were two different things. But regardless we were going to have to start thinking about every action we took and the consequences.

"Whatever. I'm not the one who's been taking all this time. Look, let's just leave Todd with his mother and get out of here before any others show up."

I turned and headed back towards the house. "She's coming with us."

"Oh great, how many other strays are we going to pick up tonight?"

He grumbled as he got back into the Jeep and started the engine. I watched him drive by. Marlin had only managed to drive a short distance away from the house but it raised an important issue. How long would it take before we'd start turning on each other in order to protect what we had? Marlin could have easily shot the kid and driven off and no one would have been the wiser.

Emergency services weren't operating, at least not in the same capacity they were before. Law and order would soon spiral out of control as confusion turned into desperation.

Chase strolled beside me.

"So I've been thinking. If this is a nuke, we need to get our hands on some battery-operated Geiger counters as soon as possible."

"So you did listen to the tape," I muttered.

"Of course. I'm not stupid, I guess I just don't want to admit the worst."

"Hell, I don't want to believe it's happened, man. I wish the power could come back on and this was all just some screw-up by the local utilities company but until then, we need to take precautions, find out what Mack might have had in place and go from there."

Eleven – Hideaway

Crestwood Hills was located on the west side of Mammoth Lakes. It would take ten minutes to get there on a good day, except this wasn't a good day. We didn't have time to mess around, so we coaxed Todd's mother out under the premise that we were going to take her to meet her dead husband.

We drove east along Meridian Boulevard and had just turned north on Minaret when I slammed the brakes on. Farther up I saw a large group of people filling up the road, many were families clinging to their children, there had to have been at least a hundred.

"Where the hell are they heading?"

"Main Street probably, city hall, police station… who knows?"

The headlights washed over a cluster, and several of them turned and pointed.

"Move. Move," Marlin muttered slapping me on the

arm.

I jammed the gear into reverse and spun around taking the Jeep up onto the curb. We bounced around in our seats as I gave it some gas and peeled away before things got out of hand. We'd only seen two other vehicles in operation around the town, and it wasn't that I expected people to resort to violence immediately, but I figured some would hassle us for a ride and right now we were already jam-packed.

"Go southwest on Meridian, hang a right on Majestic Pines Drive and that will take us onto Lake Mary Road," Marlin said.

"I am familiar with the route, you know."

"Sure you are but—"

Before he managed to finish, I eased off the gas as we came around a bend and saw the glow of fire in the distance. A vehicle must have stalled and drifted into a propane supply store. The entire place was engulfed in flames. One big fireball had ignited nearby vehicles. There were several people watching in the distance as smoke covered the road making it feel even darker than it was. No emergency services were on scene as their vehicles would have been stranded at the station and even if they could have dragged hose pipes and hooked them up to a fire hydrant, the pressure would have only lasted so long.

Had anyone died in the crash? Death would become the norm, as locals struggled to survive and seek safety. The crowd we'd seen was probably seeking out emergency services, some kind of main base that might have been set up by the town.

I pressed down on the gas and got closer; vehicles that had come to a standstill blocked the road itself.

"Okay, turn back, we'll take a different route," Chase suggested.

"What, and drive into a crowd of people looking for a ride? No, I can squeeze by using the walkway."

Chase leaned forward and grabbed a hold of my shoulder. "There's not enough room and if anything explodes…"

"There's plenty of room."

I gunned it and headed up onto the curb, Kai grabbed the passenger side handle and held on for dear life as I was about to plow through two vehicles that had come to a halt on the walkway itself.

"Mack is going to kill you."

"Hold on!" I yelled.

A sudden crunch of metal and we all jerked forward as the Jeep slammed into the corner of the vehicles. A split second of headlight glass breaking and metal scraping, along with a few golden sparks and we were through. Along the way, people filled up the sidewalks and streets. Several times I had to honk the horn to get people to move. I cast a glance back in the mirror and saw some toss up their hands as if they expected us to stop and help them out. It was too overwhelming and too many people in need. I hung a right and followed the twists and turns of the road until we finally reached Crestwood Hills.

It seemed strange flocking to his home, but I figured if anyone would have Geiger counters, gear and a plan of action in place for SHTF events, it would have been

Mack. It's all he taught, and he was never a man to do things by half. Though he never told us what he'd prepared, I had to hope there would be something, anything we could use.

I killed the engine and shoved out the door. This time we weren't taking chances; I grabbed the keys and pocketed them. Kai and Marlin watched over the vehicle while the rest of us headed in to find Bridget. I headed around the rear of the truck and stuffed a Glock 17 into the back of my waistband and jogged up to the front door.

"You think she's even here?" Todd muttered after I gave the door a hard knock and waited for an answer.

"Bridget! It's Brody."

Todd stood with his arm around his mother. He looked like a giant beside a small child. There was no answer. No movement could be heard.

"I'll go around back. Stay here."

I jogged to the corner and down the side until I reached a gate. Once inside the yard, I shuffled up to a wide double sliding door and peered in. It was completely dark. I banged on the glass and had my face up real close when a dark mass slammed hard into the window causing me to jump back. My pulse raced as I took in the sight of the huge beast. It was Bridget's dog, a Tibetan mastiff. It snarled and clawed at the windowpane. If the dog was there, she had to be nearby. There was no way in hell she would have left that dog alone. She loved it. I took a few steps back and was considering climbing the drainpipe and entering through an upper window that was slightly ajar when the silhouette of a figure appeared.

"Brody?"

"Bridget, thank god. I thought for a second I was going to have to break in."

"I'll be right down."

I stood for a minute or so on the back porch gazing out at the yard. There was a large fountain, and a shed at the far end. A BBQ was off to one side, the same one that Mack had used each summer when he invited us out to his house. Bridget came to the double doors and pulled the beast back before letting me in.

She frowned. "What are you doing here? I thought you'd still be camping."

"Yeah. It didn't exactly go the way we expected." I looked around inside. "Didn't you hear me knocking?"

"I was in the basement."

I arched a brow. "But I saw you upstairs."

"I wanted to see who it was without being seen."

"Listen, did Mack have a cabin or something in place for events like this?"

She sucked in her gums and then turned her head at the sound of voices outside.

"It's the other guys and Todd's mother."

She gave a confused look. "What?"

"I thought Mack might have something in place. Look, I'm sorry to have bothered you."

I turned to leave feeling as though I'd overstepped a line by showing up.

"You didn't make it to Iron Mountain, did you?"

I swiveled and met her gaze. "No, how did you know?"

She smirked. "Because if you had, you would have arrived at his cabin. The coordinates he gave you were for a property. A bug-out location he'd built back in the '80s when the whole cold war was going on." She chuckled. "He was convinced the Russians were going to nuke us. Anyway, part of that package he put together was to give you guys a place to reconnect. He thought you could use the cabin. Of course it will stay in the family but he looked at you five like family."

I frowned. "He did?"

She smiled warmly and moved across the room and peered out the curtains. "Oh yeah, you guys were like the sons he never had. I mean he made time for me but I always felt that he wished he'd had a son or several."

Right then a figure emerged holding a rifle. I put a hand up. "Whoa!"

"Jason, put that down," she said to her husband. "It's just Brody."

"Oh hey Brody," he said before crossing the room and gazing out. "Why are they outside?"

"You know what's going on?" Brody asked.

"I think I have a good idea," he replied. I'd only met Jason a couple times over the years. Once at Bridget's wedding, and once when I was visiting Mack. He always struck me as a guy that was slightly timid. The kind of man that would have probably shoved his wife out first to see who it was rather than risk his own neck. So it didn't surprise me that she had appeared at the window, and only now he'd shown up.

"Bridget, beyond the cabin, did your father have anything else in place?"

"For this?" she asked before looking over at Jason. I caught him shaking his head.

"He'd want us to help them, Jason."

Jason stepped toward her. "But you said…"

"I know what I said, but they meant a lot to my father."

She turned back to me. "He built a bunker below the basement of this home."

My eyebrows arched even though I kind of figured he

would have had something in place, but why hadn't he told us? I imagined he would have been eager to show it but he hadn't. Nope, not even the cabin was mentioned. Then again, it made sense; a real prepper would have kept his cards close to his chest. The fewer people who knew, the better. As much as he considered us family, there was no way of knowing if one of us would let it slip. That was the worst thing that could happen. He'd spoken at great length about being prepared, like having a 72-hour bug-out bag, keeping a storeroom of freeze-dried food and several gallons of water on the ready. He'd even discussed the process of building a bunker and what were some of the essentials that would need to be stocked. Yeah, when Mack took us under his wing, he wasn't just preparing us for the military but for surviving life.

Bridget went out of the room and I heard her open the front door. Jason stood there holding his rifle and looking pissed. They didn't have kids, so it wasn't like we were going to be taking their supplies. We just needed a place for the first seventy-two hours until we could figure out what exactly had occurred, the danger level and then we'd take steps from there. Some of us could head up to the cabin at Iron Mountain while the rest could stay in the bunker if Bridget was okay with it.

The rest of the guys filed in along with Todd's mother who looked completely lost.

"Chuck, you here?"

While Todd tried to keep his mother calm, Bridget showed me the bunker Mack had built in the early eighties back before they constructed the house on top.

"Chase, you want to bring the Jeep into the garage? At least it will be out of sight for now."

"I still need to get to Tiffany's mom's place."

"And you will."

"I'm not waiting until morning."

I sighed. "That's fine, but it's best you don't go alone, and we need to go on a food run before then." I tossed him the keys, and he strolled off looking annoyed. Bridget led the way down into the basement.

"He wanted something that was close just in case he

couldn't make it to the cabin, something that would protect us from nuclear, biological and chemical attacks."

"But I've been down here before and never seen it."

"He kept the entrance well hidden behind a false wall. There are two entrances, one through here and the other out in the yard. It comes up under the shed so no one would know."

At one time the basement had become a sanctuary, a safe zone away from home where we could play pool, watch TV and shoot the breeze. He never harped on at us about drink or smoking, in many ways he saw it as a rite of passage. I remember the first time he gave me a shot of whiskey.

"You sure you want to do this?"

"I've had it before," I'd said to him. I hadn't, in fact I'd stayed away from my mother's liquor cabinet and only occasionally swiped a beer and that was on special occasions.

At the far end of the basement behind the tacky wood-paneled bar that was still stocked with various liquors was a large cabinet that housed all the glasses. Bridget gave it a shift, and it seemed to slide to one side with ease. Behind it was a section of drywall. She pulled at it and it opened to reveal an arched entranceway carved into stone. On the ground was a steel hatch.

"It's blast-proof. Something else, huh?" she said. I didn't say anything as she tapped in a code on a keypad and opened it wide. A light illuminated a series of steps. I felt like I was privy to something Mack had built only for the eyes of his closest family members. Our boots clattered as we descended into the steel coffin.

"It's buried twenty-five feet underground, the actual shelter itself is made from corrugated steel and then encased in concrete and then there is another twelve feet of earth above us. It has two 2,500 gallon tanks for gravity-fed water, and two generators."

"What about waste?"

"It runs on a marine system which means it can be hand pumped out or gravity fed into a drainage system. My father thought of everything when he built this. I still remember him hiring the company who installed it. He was so excited, showing us the blueprint. My mother thought he was out of his mind but he believed that one day it would come in handy. I guess he was right," she said.

"What about storage?"

"Beneath it, it runs the full length which is forty-eight feet."

"And what about ham radio, hand-cranked radios? Some kind of communication that doesn't rely on digital?"

"I'm sure he had it. There wasn't much he didn't have in place. I'll dig around for it. If not you probably can find it down at um…" She scratched at her dark hair. "Atomic Jim's Military Surplus. When I was a kid, it was his favorite place to take me on a Saturday morning after we got a milkshake."

I chuckled. "Oh that dive."

The place was owned by a real nutjob who folks nicknamed "Atomic Jim" after his store because he collected all manner of discarded and weird military items, some of which were from the era when they built the atomic bomb. Though he did have a great collection of army fatigues, survival gear and whatnot.

When we made it to the bottom, I took in the sight of the space and smiled. It was absolutely perfect. Well, not better than living in a house but being as it was partially built off to the side of the basement, it gave us options. If there was no danger from fallout, we could still use the house and the bunker.

Bridget turned around in the close quarters. "Okay, this is the mud room slash decontamination room. This room and the next are divided by a gastight marine door."

It looked like a submarine hatch made from super-thick steel. On the front was a yellow sticker with a gun on it and the words:

PROTECTED BY HOMEOWNER. I WILL BLOW YOUR ASS AWAY!

I chuckled thinking of the way Mack would strut around when he gave his lectures on survival. He didn't mince words, and he said there would come a time when we'd have to make hard decisions. Whether that was in some dusty shit hole in Afghanistan or right in our own backyards, it didn't matter, the line between what was right and wrong would soon blur.

I pulled back a curtain to reveal a shower mounted off to the side to allow people to decontaminate before entering the main area.

"Hey, anyone down there?" a voice called out from above. Chase had returned.

"Yeah, come on down."

Bridget led me through into the next area, which housed a marine-grade toilet where waste could be hand pumped out or gravity fed through the bottom. Chase came down and his eyes widened as he stepped inside. Immediately off to our right was a weapon rack, which was jam-packed with several AR-15's, a Springfield M1A and two Remington 870 12 Gauge Pump-Action shotguns.

"If you guys want to step to one side, let me show you

something."

Bridget crouched down to the floor and opened a hatch that was several feet in length. Inside were bags of grain, salt, oil and MRE's.

"There are several of these storage areas that go all the way down to the far end."

Either side of that were the living quarters. Bunk beds with striped covers and American flag pillows. There were four. But she said there also was a double bed at the far end and if needed they could drag down single mattresses which could be placed into some of the open areas.

She continued giving the tour and brought us into the living room, which had a leather couch, TV, kitchen counter, sink and stove along with regular cupboards for storage. A fridge and microwave were off to one side, along with a place to store coats and even books.

"Just a bit farther down is the power center."

I could tell she was proud of what her father had created. She lifted another hatch and showed us what looked to be at least a hundred batteries hooked up, along with an inverter.

"These are charged using a solar system that is above ground on the shed but just in case he also added a large thirty-kilowatt diesel generator with block heaters and battery chargers on board. It also has two hundred gallons of fuel powering it. It runs in conjunction with the battery backup and solar power, which means you only have to run this beauty for around one or two hours. Most of the time the solar panels will charge the batteries so we have more than enough power to keep this place ticking over."

"Nice," Chase said. "What's that?"

Chase pointed to a machine at the far end.

"That's the climate control and air filtration system."

"How much food do you have?" Chase asked.

"Enough to last six months, give or take, but that's feeding four people."

"Which means we need to get more. You up for doing a run?" I asked Chase.

Twelve – Von's

Starvation. It would be the first thing that people would die from if not violence. The average household in America probably stocked four to five days' worth of food, maybe a little more if they had a large family and shopped at Costco. But it wouldn't be food that people would be lacking initially. It would be water. The human body could exist without food for several weeks but water? People would start dropping in a matter of three to five days. Sure there had been cases of folks surviving eight, even ten days without water but those weren't typical. With the grid down, water would soon run in short supply and it would be the first thing that folks would try to buy or steal. Of course pipes, wells and water heaters in basements could be drained before the pressure ceased but most wouldn't think about that. Their worried minds would be preoccupied with rushing down to their local supermarket.

The Jeep careened into the parking lot at Von's Supermarket. Usually it was open twenty-four hours but Gregory the assistant manager had locked it up after the blackout. The lot was empty but it wouldn't be that way for long. At what point would folks begin to start looting? Had they already begun?

"I still don't think this is a good idea, I need to get back and see Amanda."

I parked near the front entrance and hopped out. Marlin, Chase and Kai had come along while Todd stayed at Mack's place to keep his mother calm.

"Marlin, by the time we check on everyone, that window over there is going to be smashed and all the shelves will be bare. You want that?"

"But there is more than enough food back at the bunker."

I thumbed through keys looking for the one for the main entrance. "Yes, to keep four people alive for six months. And anyway we aren't going to be staying there. There's not enough room for all of us. Besides, Mack wanted us to use the cabin."

"How do you know that?" Kai said.

I couldn't be bothered to explain it to him. I stuck the key in the lock and then heard the alarm system kick in. It beeped getting steadily faster. It gave up to thirty seconds to disarm it. I dashed inside nearly slipping over in the process before punching the code into the system. After, we used flashlights to illuminate our way and locked the doors to prevent anyone from getting in.

"Grab a cart each and only fill it with the essentials. Jugs of water, canned goods like fruit, beans, vegetables and so on. And don't forget protein or fruit bars, dry cereal, peanut butter, nuts, ramen noodles, crackers, soup, salt, oil and sugar."

"What about medical supplies?" Chase asked.

"Grab some pain medication, gauze, hydrogen peroxide, sterile pads, compresses, and anything else that you think will come in handy."

We flew into action soaring up the aisles. Marlin was shouting out what he had as we went. It was only when I made it over to aisle one that I began to slow down. As I was loading two-gallon water jugs into the cart I spotted a wash of headlights outside. I squinted trying to make out who it was.

"Chase, you see that?"

He was one aisle over and farther down, certainly more likely to spot who had disappeared out of my line of sight.

"Yep. Looks like a truck with a bunch of people inside."

"Turn your flashlights off," Marlin hollered.

The place was engulfed in darkness as soon as the flashlights went out. Each of us made our way around to one aisle and crouched down.

"They'll probably leave in a minute once they see the place is closed."

"And the Jeep?"

"Don't worry, I have the keys," I said dangling them.

"What about the rifles?"

"They're locked inside," Chase said.

We watched in silence as three individuals came

rushing up to the door and began shaking the handles. One of them kicked the window out of frustration while the other two looked to be having a discussion. They shouted back to the rest of their group who were now taking an interest in the Jeep.

"Great, they're probably going to jack it."

I shuffled forward and made my way down between a checkout counter so I could get a better look. Several guys tugged on the doors of the Jeep and peered inside. One of them commented to another, and he rushed back to their pickup truck. It was what he grabbed next that caught my attention, but before I could yell to the others that he was about to break in using a tire iron, the front entrance window shattered. I turned to see the three that had initially approached the door kicking the glass out. They had slammed a metal cart into the door.

I shuffled back to where the other three were and pulled the Glock.

"You carrying?" I asked the others. Marlin showed his but the other two didn't have one.

"Great, maybe I can toss ramen noodles at them," Chase said.

I sighed. "We need to get out there and prevent them from getting those rifles in the back. Marlin, take Kai with you and head out the side exit." I pointed in the direction of where it was.

"As soon as you get out there, fire off a round in their direction otherwise we are going to lose those rifles."

They shuffled away fast.

"No seriously. What do you expect me to do?"

"Stay close." I handed him a can of tomatoes. "It's better than nothing, or you can slip down to aisle three. We have a deal on kitchen knives at the moment."

"Oh wonderful, can I cash in a coupon?" He rolled his eyes and followed me as we made our way down. We could hear them yelling at the top of their voices.

"What supermarket doesn't have an alarm system? Dumb fucks!"

Another one was making whistling noises and yelling like a six-year-old in a jungle gym. He snatched up a shopping cart and jumped inside it. "Davey, give me a push."

The third was serious and told them both to shut the hell up and get busy collecting as much food as they could. I cast a glance outside to the four individuals who had now smashed the front passenger window on the Jeep and were rooting through it. Where was Marlin?

There was no easy way to do this and I couldn't see if they were armed. If they were, this situation was about to get ugly real fast. "Listen up, I want you to slip down to aisle two and around to the far end, as soon as they enter the first aisle, be ready for my signal."

I turned and started to move.

"Which will be what?"

"You'll know," I muttered and flashed a grin.

"And how am I meant to protect myself?"

I didn't reply but scooted into a better position. I was trying to see if they were packing but it was just so damn dark it was hard to see anything but their silhouettes.

No assholes were breaking into my store. Sure we were

about to rob the place blind but that was different. I worked here. I ran this damn store and I sure as hell had gone far and above duty. I wasn't going to have some pissants smashing my window and ransacking the joint.

Chase dashed out of view up aisle two. I checked the magazine for ammo and then slapped it back in and moved out.

"Stay right there," I yelled in the most authoritative voice I could. As I was wearing army fatigues, and it was dark inside, I figured they would think I was SWAT or a security guard for the building. They were shoveling cans of food into a cart by the armload and cackling when they turned.

Would they leave nicely?

A sudden gunshot and I dived out of view. Well, that answered that. I slid down to the far end of the aisle and peered around the corner. Where the hell was Chase? I soon got my answer.

"Shit!"

He came rushing back down under a hail of gunfire.

Bags of sugar exploded and went everywhere. The noise was only intensified by the sound of rounds from outside. Glancing around checkout number five, I could see Marlin coming into view firing multiple rounds at them while moving in on the Jeep. The group started backing up and then one of them returned fire.

"I don't know who you are but you are making a big mistake," a guy's voice shouted out.

I was about to say, "I'm the manager of this store, asshole." But instead I blurted out, "Who gives a fuck? Get the hell out of here now or you'll leave in a body bag."

"You sell those here?" Chase asked with a grin, keeping low and trying to stay out of view. I could hear the thump of feet getting closer. I moved around Chase just in time to see a guy racing down the aisle. I fired off a round, and he slid across the floor. I wasn't trying to kill them; I was hoping they would have the good sense to run but not these fools. Oh no, they weren't about to run away from a shitload of food and water. Whoever they were, they knew the value of getting to it before anyone else and…

"Markus, head down."

Markus?

I heard a voice reply and recognized it as the kid that had tried to break into the Jeep. Chase tossed me a frown and mouthed the words, "Is that him?"

I cleared my throat and called out. "Hey Markus."

There was no reply.

"Markus. This is Brody. The guy whose Jeep you tried to steal."

There was whispering between them. No doubt they were asking him if he knew us. A few seconds passed before he replied.

"Oh hey there, seems we keep crossing paths."

"Seems so," I yelled back. "But I'm gonna go out on a limb here and take a wild guess that you didn't just happen to be in the area, did you?"

"Desperate times call for desperate measures."

"Listen up, you're not meant to be in here."

"And you are?"

"I'm the manager of this place."

Laughter echoed back.

"Do they issue handguns to all Von's Supermarket managers nowadays?"

"It's a rough neighborhood," I yelled back. We'd been in there at least ten minutes and in that time my eyes had become adjusted to the dark. While Markus was speaking, in the reflection of the window I could see someone making their way down. They were armed and within twenty feet of us.

"You might want to tell your buddy to back up before I turn him into Swiss cheese."

The guy stopped walking and started backing up quickly. Outside Marlin had managed to get over to the Jeep and now he was exchanging bullets with four individuals who were also taking cover behind their vehicle. I shook my head. "Shit." I had visions of coming out to find the vehicle riddled with bullets. But worse than that, if it pierced the engine we were screwed.

"Listen, grab what you've got in your cart and get out

of here. I'll let you take that but you need to go now."

"Is that so?" another guy yelled.

"Or you can check out another way," I replied.

Thirteen – Fortify

The sound of boots pounding the ground and a cart being wheeled away made it clear they'd opted to escape. It was a gamble but at this stage; they didn't know what had caused the blackout, and it certainly wasn't worth dying or going to jail over. The second I saw them leave, I sprinted towards the side exit with Chase in tow and went to assist Marlin and Kai. By now Kai had managed to get inside the Jeep and grab a rifle. Both of them had dropped to the ground and were squeezing off shots as we rushed over.

"Stop shooting for a minute."

"Are you kidding, those mother—"

"Wait," I said watching intently as the silhouettes of the three individuals joined their group and loaded what they had from the cart into the truck. A minute or two passed before their engine roared and they tore out of the parking lot at high speed.

It was an intense moment and all four of us stayed on alert just in case they had second thoughts and doubled back.

"Listen, let's grab what we have and get the hell out of here. I don't know how many more of them there are but I doubt it will be long before others show up looking to loot. It's only going to get worse."

I hopped into the Jeep and brought it up to the side door. Marlin and Kai remained with the vehicle while Chase and I dashed inside and gathered together the carts we'd filled up. Once the goods were loaded in the back, I cast a nervous glance over my shoulder and then hopped into the driver's side.

Within a matter of days the place would be ransacked. This was only the beginning. People would arm themselves and next time the outcome might not end well.

The only positive to come out of the evening was that no one had got hurt. The thought of taking someone's life remained at the forefront of my mind as we drove back. What if I had killed someone, could I have lived with that? It was one thing to be trained on how to kill, another to actually do it.

"So that guy Markus. He was with them," Chase said.

"Are you serious?" Marlin barked. He was riding in the passenger seat and glanced over at me. I knew I was going to get an earful from him. "I knew we shouldn't have let him go. That bastard has probably been following us since Todd's place. Which means…"

"The house." My mind swirled. "They might know about Mack's place."

I put my foot down and gave it some gas.

Out the corner of my eye I could see Marlin's knee bouncing up and down, his other hand was holding a Glock and he was acting all twitchy. It was the adrenaline pumping through his system. All of us were wired.

"You know, if this is what we think it is, there is going to come a time when we'll have to make that decision. You know, to kill someone."

He glanced over his shoulder to the two guys in the

back who were staying quiet.

"And?" I asked.

"I'm just saying. We could have been killed tonight."

"But we weren't."

"Not this time, but…"

"What are you trying to say, Marlin? Spit it out."

"I'm saying we should have…." He trailed off unable to say it.

"Killed the guy back at Todd's place? Are you serious?"

"I don't know. I just…" He cast a glance out the window and his bobbing knee began to slow.

Marlin was never one for having anyone tell him what to do, that's why he went into business for himself. It seemed appropriate that he ended up being a fitness boot camp instructor. Had he made it into the military, there was no doubt in my mind he would have become a drill instructor. He loved to yell and get up in people's faces. He was never one to back down. There was a fight in him that I admired but many times it had got him into trouble. The first time was when we were fourteen. A math teacher by the name of William Gras had taken a disliking to Marlin or any kid that talked back. I'd heard stories from my brother back when they had corporal punishment in schools that he would heat up a sneaker and use it to hit kids. Of course that was all abolished in 1982 so by the time we made it into his classroom, all he could do was yell and shout at kids and threaten to send them to the principal.

Now I don't exactly recall what it was that pissed him off that day, but Marlin was the focus of his wrath and by God did he rain down on him that morning. All I remember was Mr. Gras poking his finger into Marlin's chest and telling him that he wouldn't put up with his attitude and if he continued to be a pain, he would move his desk outside the classroom. Of course Marlin didn't take it well and warned him to stop touching him. Mr. Gras continued, so Marlin unloaded one hell of a right hook and knocked the teacher on his ass. You could have heard a pin drop that day. I don't know who was more surprised, the rest of the kids in the classroom or Mr.

Gras. No one had ever stood up to him and here was a fourteen-year-old kid half his size looming over him telling him to get up and try it again.

Well, that nearly got Marlin expelled. Thankfully his father knew the principal well and managed to get the punishment reduced to a ten-day suspension. When Marlin returned to school, he was hailed as a hero. No one in the history of Mammoth High School had done anything remotely that bad, or in the eyes of the kids, that cool.

After that day, anytime Mr. Gras walked by a crowd of kids, they would mock him by singing a line from the Pink Floyd song "Teacher Leave Those Kids Alone."

But that was Marlin, a rebel, and a nuisance and yet a guy that was as loyal as could be. There were times I wanted to slap him around the head but I knew his heart was in the right place. And he had a point; perhaps this was what Mack was referring to in his tape on the Battle of the Mind. I mean every soldier that went into battle faced it. A split second, a moment when they had to decide who lived or died. Certainly for those who didn't give a shit about human life, or the psychotic, it didn't matter. Hell, some guys got off on it but for the average Joe, it wasn't as easy as that. That kind of act of aggression or self-defense would weigh on a man's mind long after. For some they could live with it, for others not so much.

"Listen, we'll drop off what we have and head over to your place," I said to Marlin. He nodded but didn't reply. He was lost in thought, all of us were. Tonight's incident had cleared away any doubt in our mind about where this was all heading regardless of what had caused the blackout. Whether it was a solar flare or an electromagnetic pulse, this was going to send the country back to the mid-1800s. The use of electricity was woven intricately into every facet of life from transportation to communication to the services that were provided to keep society in a place of order. Now it had all gone out the window, and that was downright terrifying.

"If the EMP was the first wave, do you think North

Korea will send troops to invade?" Chase asked biting at his nails.

"Their army is not big enough."

"That's not what I heard. In fact I'm pretty sure it said they had 1.2 million active soldiers and over 7 million in reserves. We have roughly 1.4 million active and 802,000 reserves, and a large chunk of the military is stationed overseas. Besides, if they are behind it, who's saying they haven't fired upon some of the warships? Multiple attacks and whatnot," Kai replied.

"Shit, dude, is stats like porn to you?" Marlin laughed as he turned in his seat to look at him.

"What? I like to stay abreast of financial, political and nationwide issues."

"You are such a nerd. If I had a memory like yours, I would use it for something useful like playing poker and memorizing a deck of cards. I've always wanted to visit Vegas and clean up."

"Well, I'm sure they still have jobs for street sweepers," Chase said before chuckling.

I remained quiet weaving the jeep around stranded vehicles, occasionally braking to avoid pedestrians but never stopping. In the distance the fiery glow of another fire flickered in the night. Had it been caused by an accident or were roving gangs like the one we'd encountered taking matters into their own hands?

"You got a cigarette?" I asked Chase.

"No, I gave up. Tiffany was riding my ass for years over it. I shifted over to those vapes but she said it was embarrassing to be out in public with me blowing big clouds. So I had to toss those as well. Besides, didn't you give up years ago?"

"Yeah."

I knew Kai and Marlin didn't smoke. Both of them were health nuts and had always been big on eating green and devouring lots of roughage. It was strange to have a craving for something that I hadn't desired in years.

"Perhaps the troops are already here?"

"What, disguised as Japanese tourists?" Marlin said putting his feet up on the dashboard and snorting into a sigh. "Yeah, I can see that."

"Japanese?" Kai said.

"Japanese, Chinese, Koreans, you all look the same. Throw a large camera over your neck and no one could tell the difference."

I looked in my rearview mirror at Kai and he rolled his eyes.

Not all the streets were filled with people but there were large groups out watching as the Jeep rumbled by. Some of them called out but their words were lost in the growl of the engine. It was like watching a natural disaster on TV; the expressions were a mix of fear, confusion and desperation. Some would choose to remain inside hoping to ride out what they probably assumed was a momentary glitch, but as the hours and days passed, they would soon figure out that power wasn't going to be restored and then the real show would begin.

* * *

Upon arrival at Mack's place, I backed into the garage and hopped out and we began unloading the food and water. Marlin wanted to take the Jeep by himself but after what we'd been through, I wasn't going to risk losing the only vehicle that worked.

Todd emerged from the basement. "Thank god you're back, I'm going out of my mind. I'm telling you, if she doesn't get a grip, I'll put a bullet in her."

"Who?"

"Who do you think? Amnesia Annie."

That's what he'd started to call his mother.

"Did you bring any beer back? As I'm thinking of getting shitfaced tonight."

"Nope, just the essentials," I said lugging bags of potatoes and sugar past him with cans on top.

"Liquor is essential. What the hell are we meant to do, make moonshine with that shit?"

"Maybe you can stop flapping your lips and actually give us a hand," Chase said following close behind. Todd grunted and headed off. Bridget smiled as we came in carrying more supplies.

"Hopefully this will help."

"Thanks."

I didn't want her to feel the burden of trying to feed more mouths. At least this way we'd have enough for a couple of weeks more until we could decide who was going to head up to the cabin on Iron Mountain. After that we could ransack stores or hunt if push came to shove.

"By the way did you find that hand-cranked radio?"

"Still looking. My father had so much crap stored in the basement. It could take me days to get through it."

"Maybe you can grab one of the guys to help."

I dumped the bags down into one of the gutter-style containers below the bunker and guided Marlin and Kai to place their load farther down.

"What's that banging?" I asked Bridget.

"Oh it's just Jason. He's nailing in some boards on the windows to prevent anyone from getting in."

I shook my head. "No, he doesn't want to do that." I double-timed it up the stairs and made my way to the front of the house. He had managed to talk Todd into giving him a hand. Some of the supplies that Todd had been carrying were lying on the floor.

"Take it down," I said.

"What?" Jason said turning his head.

"You want people to think that we have something to steal in here? Take it down."

"But we need to protect the house."

"And we will but there are better ways to create a deterrent than making it obvious that people are inside. We want to blend in not stand out."

"Like army fatigues," Todd muttered.

He stood there on a short stepladder and stared back looking confused. "And what if someone breaks in through the window?"

"Then they are going to have some trouble prying their soles from the six-inch nails that will be embedded in their feet. We're going to build some nail boards."

"Are you serious?"

"Damn right I am," I said beginning to pick up some of the food that Todd had left on the floor. "If you want to board up windows, only do the sides and back. Do it in areas that people can't see from the main road. But for the rest, we are going to create some nail boards and place them under the windows. We'll secure the doors and enter and exit through the garage or the secondary escape hatch in the shed."

"That's some serious A-Team shit," Todd said with a smirk. I could see his eyes light up. "Oh yeah, I've got some killer ideas to add to that but I'll get started on that first. Where's the wood and nails?" I glanced over to Jason as he told him to head out to the garage and the yard. Todd disappeared and Jason gave me a hand gathering up some of the food.

"Have you filled up the bathtubs with water?" I asked him.

"Why would I do that?"

I shook my head in disbelief. I figured that if Mack had let him marry his daughter, he would have at least grilled him on some of the basics.

"Because the pressure in the pipes will give out, if they

haven't already. You are going to need to empty as much as you can and save it. We'll boil to purify."

"We have enough jugs in the bunker."

I stared back at him.

"Forget it. I'll do it myself."

"Just for the record, I want it to be clear that I don't like having you here. None of you. You are a danger to my family. I don't give a shit about whether or not Mack liked you or what survival tactics you learned when you were young. If you endanger Bridget, I will end you. Do you understand?"

I snorted. "Oh I understand," I said in a sarcastic tone as I purposely brushed past him. He wasn't going to do shit. It was all words. Nothing but hot air.

He grabbed a hold of my arm as I walked away and pulled me around. He scowled and straightened up as if he was about to throw a punch.

"I don't think you do."

"Let go… of my arm," I said to him in a cool and calm manner. Years of working with the public had taught me that butting heads with customers rarely ended well unless there was some form of threat to one's life. Communication was always the first line of defense. Right now the last thing we needed was conflict. At the end of the day we were in Mack's home, and whether or not we liked it, we were guests and Bridget would take her husband's side first and ask questions after.

He held it for a second or two and then released it.

"We have enough trouble on our plate, whatever problem you have with us being here — put a pin in it, as we might be the only reason you get through the next seventy-two hours," I said before walking away.

Fourteen – Boot Camp

It was eleven in the evening when we pulled up the Jeep outside Soldiers of Fitness Boot Camp on the west side of town, just across from Old Mammoth Road. He'd purchased a property that was close to Mammoth Creek Park because he'd received permission to use it in conjunction with his own property so he could provide indoor and outdoor options for fitness. I had to admit, he'd outdone himself. Marlin's facility was unique in that it offered military-oriented fitness training. Essentially, he'd taken all the physical aspects of what Mack had used to train us, hill runs, an obstacle course, stair climbing, push-ups, pull-ups, calisthenics, long-distance running, swimming, weight training, marches and basic self-defense, and had combined it all together to create an intense workout that focused on teamwork.

Though I hadn't signed up myself, I'd heard nothing but good things from folks who came into my store.

According to Marlin he had a good mix of guys and women using his facility. It was mostly single mothers looking to get back into shape after giving birth, middle-aged guys wanting to lose that potato sack around their gut and young whippersnappers eager for a challenge.

Countless times I would drive past the park on my way to Von's and see him out there shouting at them through a megaphone as a group would jog along with what looked like a log on their shoulders. I always got a kick out of that as it would bring back flashbacks of being wet, muddy and cold and having Mack harp on about how pain was just weakness leaving the body.

We all bundled out of the Jeep and waited as Marlin hurried into his home leaving the door wide open. His business wasn't far from the Mammoth Police Department, which was located north. Two police officers shot by at blistering speed on bicycles, and that's when I knew that maybe the world hadn't gone to shits completely. Even though vehicles weren't working, some of the boys in blue were still out trying to maintain order.

It wasn't going to be easy or a fast job. I squinted into the darkness. Then it dawned on me as they turned around. They weren't cycling to get to an incident; they were heading our way. Shit! Someone must have seen or heard the gunfire in the supermarket lot.

It was too late to hide our weapons. We were all carrying, and the Jeep had several rifles inside. They were all legal, so it wasn't having them find the firearms that bothered me. It was what they assumed we'd done. I was about to race inside to alert Marlin but it was too late.

"Police. Stop where you are!" a voice cried out as one of the bike patrol came barreling towards me. The two bicycles were Cannondale full-suspension mountain bikes fully equipped with strobing lights and sirens. Their bike headlamps focused in on us and for a brief second one of them put on the siren and then switched it off.

"Can we help you, officers?" I asked.

One of them launched off his bike, letting it fall to the ground before pulling out a pair of handcuffs. "Get over there with your hands behind your back."

"What?" Kai said stepping forward. The officer's partner dismounted from his bike and placed a hand on his gun.

"Are any of you carrying?"

It was pointless lying. "Yeah, we are."

"Get up against the Jeep."

"Are you serious?"

The officer pulled his firearm but kept it low. "Now!"

All four of us complied, except Todd who tried to protest and was thrown down against the wet asphalt. It wasn't raining as hard as it was before, just drizzle was coming down but the parking lot was still soaked.

"What the hell is this about?" Chase asked.

"Any vehicles that are currently operating will be held by the police department."

I felt a pair of cuffs cut into my skin as he slapped them on. The officer had me pushed up against the front of the Jeep with my legs spread.

"You can't do that!" Todd said.

"So you're arresting us so you can use the vehicle?"

Chase asked.

They didn't reply until they had all of us in cuffs. "No, you're under arrest because you match the description of the individuals fleeing the scene at the local Von's Supermarket where a B&E has occurred and multiple gunshots were heard."

"Um, officer, I'm actually the manager of Von's."

The officer shined his flashlight beam into my face. "Well, then you won't have a problem explaining what happened."

They began searching us for weapons and placed my Glock on the hood of the vehicle. After that they began reading our Miranda rights.

"Look, it wasn't us. There were seven individuals."

Right then, Marlin came out with Amanda and he began yelling. "What the hell is going on?"

One of the officers approached Marlin.

"Sir, are you with them?"

He nodded. "Yeah, I just came by to pick up my girlfriend."

"Turn around."

"Why?"

"Turn around, I'm placing you under arrest."

That was the worst thing he could have said to Marlin. He pushed the officer back. "Get off. I have rights."

"I'm warning you right now. Turn around or I'm going to taze you."

"Taze?" Amanda yelled. "This isn't right. Look, you don't…"

Marlin continued to struggle, so the officer pulled his tazer and sure enough, lit him up like a Christmas tree. His body jerked around like a fish out of water before hitting the ground. The other officer stepped in to keep Amanda back while his partner cuffed Marlin. Then we were assisted back into the Jeep with myself, Chase, and Kai in the back seat and Marlin and Todd in the rear. They left their bicycles behind, along with Amanda, and used the Jeep to take us to the station. How on earth they were going to manage with no electricity remained to be seen. It was obvious that just because the power had gone out, emergency services were still going to continue operating even if they were running at a disadvantage.

The Jeep rumbled along as each of us tried to explain but they weren't listening. There was too much distracting their attention. Vehicles littered the road, and we noticed that the liquor store had been broken into. Glass was everywhere and multiple people were streaming out with armfuls of wine and spirits. The cops just looked over and kept on driving. Things were already starting to spiral out of control and they had probably been given instructions to deal with one thing at a time and make confiscating any vehicles that were in operation, top priority.

They pulled into a plaza-style lot and killed the engine outside the small police department that was located between a Mexican diner and some design studio. The red brick building had several black-and-whites out front.

"Wait here," said the officer in the driver's seat before he hopped out. His partner remained in the vehicle to keep a watchful eye on us.

"Look, we can explain. This is just a big misunderstanding."

"I'd like to see where it says in the bill of rights that you can confiscate a civilian's vehicle?" Todd muttered.

"Shut up, Todd," Kai said.

Meanwhile in the rear Marlin was going apeshit, shouting about police abuse, Rodney King in L.A. and how he was going to sue the entire department. That was followed by him yelling, "Black lives matter." To the curious locals who had shown up to find out what was going on, it must have looked like quite the spectacle. A large crowd had gathered, some had even pitched tents along the sidewalk. They must have figured that it was better to be close to the police than to take their chances staying in their homes. No two people would handle this event the same. Some would remain calm and collected, others would panic, and the rest would lose their minds, like the group of six people who were camped out and wearing silver foil on their heads. I couldn't believe what I was seeing. They had a board in front of them welcoming their alien brothers and sisters. I chuckled. Did people honestly think this was some kind of alien attack? Farther down a religious group was going from person to person handing out blankets and bottles of water.

The door opened on my side and the grizzled officer returned with two more to assist in strong-arming us into the station. I squinted as they flashed a light in my face.

"You mind not blinding me."

"Just hop out."

I struggled to squeeze out with my wrists locked behind my back. One by one we were brought into the station and made to take a seat while they began the paperwork.

"Look, isn't there someone I can speak to? Um, what's your staff sergeant's name?"

"Just settle, you'll get a chance to explain."

As he walked away, we chatted among ourselves. I made it clear that we weren't to mention taking supplies from the store. We were there because I had to pick up some belongings.

Uncomfortable, annoyed and frustrated, I was glad to hear a friendly voice.

"Mr. Slater?" A female voice came from the left side; I jerked my head to see Nancy Dolman, one of the girls who worked at my store. She was holding a cup, steam swirling out of it. My brow knit together.

"What are you doing here?"

"My father is an officer. Brett Dolman," she said as if I should know his name. I wasn't exactly familiar with all the officers in town. We'd had to call them in a few times when someone shoplifted but it was always quick. They were in and out the door and generally didn't stick around to shoot the breeze.

I shrugged but was pleased to at least have someone recognize me.

Her eyes swept across the others before smirking. "What did you do now?"

"Why would you assume I've done anything?"

"Because..." She looked as if she was going to say something but then closed her mouth as an officer came over.

"Okay, come with me," he said. We all rose from our seats and he shook his head. "Not all of you. Just you," he pointed to Todd. "I'll get to the rest of you in a minute."

"You mind doing me a favor," I directed the question to Nancy. "Can you let your father know who I am and that we are not responsible for the recent break-in at Von's. There were seven guys out there that shattered the window at the store and fired at us."

Her face was a mask of concern. "Are you okay?"

Nancy was like the other eighteen-year-old girls that worked at Von's. She was a good kid but a little slow on hearing.

"Nancy, can you do that?"

She nodded, cupping her hands.

Chase sniffed the air. "Is that hot coffee?"

"Hot chocolate."

He groaned. "I would kill for a coffee right now."

"I'll see what I can do," she said walking away. I leaned my head back against the wall and took a moment to go over what we had done so far and all that had happened. I still had to check in on my daughter Ava, and Chase needed to get to his family. I glanced down the line as an officer adjusted the cuffs on Kai's wrists because he was complaining that they were too tight. That's when I noticed something that hadn't been there earlier — a wedding band. I waited until the officer walked away.

"Kai," I muttered. He glanced sideways.

"Yeah?"

"You married?"

He pursed his lips together and ignored me as if avoiding the conversation was going to get him off the hook. But Chase had overhead and so had Marlin.

"Of course he's not married, he's dating Kristy and Misty, ain't that right, Kai?" Marlin said proudly as if his friend had scored a home run with those two hotties.

"So what's the band on your finger then, huh?" I asked.

"What band?" Marlin said screwing up his face.

"Kai," I repeated.

"It's just…"

He seemed a little lost for words. Chase was now leaning back and trying to get a better look at his hand behind his back. Kai leaned back to block his view.

"C'mon. Are you married?" I asked again.

He hesitated and then spat it out. "Yes, I am," he hissed out in frustration. "You mind not speaking so loud."

I chuckled with a confused expression on my face. "But you came to the funeral with two women. You want to help us out here?"

"Oh I know what's going on here. Kai is a player, aren't you?" Marlin said before bursting into laughter. "Oh my god, now that is what I call doing it Don Juan style."

I shook my head in disbelief. "But you told us you were dating tons of women and avoiding marriage."

"It's complicated."

"I bet it is," I said.

"That is unbelievable. You're cheating on your wife?"

Chase asked.

"It's not like that."

"How else can it be, if you're married? Unless of course you just got married twenty-four hours ago."

"Yeah that's got to be it," Marlin said snickering to himself.

"You wouldn't understand."

"Try us," I said.

There was a long pause as we waited to see if he could clarify. While he was thinking about it, I glanced over to Todd who looked like he'd been pulled into the principal's office. He had had his head down and occasionally would direct it our way as if referring to us. Kai took a deep breath and looked as if he was about to explain when Nancy returned with her father.

"Mr. Slater. Come with me."

Fifteen – Emergency

Tonight was going from bad to worse. The last thing we needed was to end up spending the night in the can. I followed Officer Dolman down a corridor and into a small office. On the table was a wind-up lantern illuminating the room. He closed the door behind us and unlocked the restraints.

"Please, take a seat, my daughter was telling me that you manage the local Von's Supermarket."

"That's right," I said glancing around the room.

"So you want to tell me what happened this evening?"

"Look, I'm sure you guys have better things to do with your time, don't you?"

He smiled and rocked back in his seat. "We have fifteen active officers in this department and most of them are not on shift at the same time but right now every single one of them is out there, barring a few that are here right now. We are doing our job and part of that involves making sure folks don't break and enter until the power comes back on."

"It's not coming back on."

"I know it might seem that way but…"

"Seriously, officer, how many times in the past has the power gone out and all the electronics have stopped working? Vehicles, cell phones and computers? This wasn't a freak accident."

He ignored the issue at hand and seemed more interested in the break-in.

"So why were you at Von's?"

I sighed. "Do you honestly think I broke into my own building? I have keys."

"No one is stating you did break in but what about the gunfire that was heard?"

I knew they would want a reason and I couldn't exactly say that we were robbing the store blind and stocking up in preparation to hunker down and avoid the fallout of a nuclear weapon, as one, he didn't seem to think that this was anything more than a local power outage and two, that would have been confessing to a crime. So I opted to lie.

"I left a set of keys there. I was dropping by to pick them up."

"Keys to what?"

Police loved to get specific; it was how they caught you in a lie.

"To my apartment."

"Don't you carry your key on the same set as your vehicle?"

"Usually but I had taken it off that day. Anyway," I said quickly shifting the topic away from the lie, "while we were there a group decided to break in. I approached them and instructed them to leave and they fired upon us."

"Lucky you didn't get shot."

"They left of their own accord."

He nodded, tapping a pen against the table in front of him and not looking convinced. "Armed individuals broke in, then left after you appealed to their good nature? Did you fire any rounds back to motivate them out that door?"

"Yes I did. But it was self-defense, and no one got hurt."

"And why were you carrying?"

"Does it matter? I'm legally allowed to carry a concealed weapon in the state of California."

"I'm just asking?"

"We were returning from a camping trip."

"And you usually take firearms with you?"

"A man has a right to protect himself, officer. Besides, staring down a bear or cougar without a weapon isn't smart."

He nodded. "Well, you are fortunate this evening. While California doesn't have a stand-your-ground law so to speak, the castle doctrine is similar and the penal code does say you are allowed to use deadly force within your residence if you have a 'reasonable fear of imminent peril or great bodily injury to self, family, or a member of the household when that force is used against another person.' Though technically your workplace is not your residence, it could constitute as your dwelling being as you manage the place, so to speak." He breathed in deeply. "And since no one was harmed, and you have legal permits, I gather, for the firearms?" I nodded. "Of course we will have to see those and in light of this evening's unusual event which has placed this department at a bit of a disadvantage, we should be able to have you out of here shortly once we have the paperwork squared away. Okay?"

I sighed heavily. "Thank you. But what about the Jeep?"

"Well, as you are aware, our vehicles are not operating so we are requiring locals whose vehicles are working to allow us to use them."

"Are you even allowed to do that?"

He smiled. "If you want to know if it's legal, Section 150 of the California Penal Code outlines what we can or can't do. Again it mainly covers that you are required by law to oblige or face a fine if you neglect to aid and assist in preventing any breach of the peace or criminal offense. In this case we need to prevent crime and that requires a vehicle as bicycles aren't exactly the fastest means of covering this town."

"Right but that's only assisting *you*. Does it refer to *property?*"

"Well that's where exercising posse comitatus gets a little gray, but then again so is this event that's happening."

"We really need that vehicle."

"Going somewhere?" he asked.

I cast my eyes down and gritted my teeth. Arguing with him right now wasn't going to do us any favors. The fact that he'd been willing to listen and seemed like a reasonable man with some common sense was a bonus.

"Anyway, how's my daughter doing working at your place?"

"She's good. No complaints."

He nodded and started scribbling down on the paper in front of him. I looked at the name tag above his badge.

"Listen, Brett, is it?" He glanced up. "What is being done in the town about this event?"

"I just told you. We are handling it the best we can right now."

"But surely they have issued a state of local emergency? Before the power went down, were the police alerted to any potential threat?"

He shook his head and cleared his throat and stared while twisting his pen around in his hand. "Steps have been taken to maintain order. I'm not at liberty to discuss that with you."

"As a citizen, I have a right to know what is being done. You know as well as I do that little incident down at Von's is just the start of what is going to happen on a larger scale. They might not be out-of-control right now but people will begin looting supermarkets, pharmacies and hardware stores."

"And like I said, we have officers patrolling the town."

"Fifteen cops? You really think that is going to stop hundreds of panic-driven people? It's not going to be long before people learn what has happened. We need to get our hands on a ham radio, and several Geiger counters."

Officer Dolman screwed his face up. "Geiger counters?"

"Yeah, to check on radiation poisoning from the fallout. Now I know there could be a very natural explanation for all of this and it's very possible it could be a solar flare but we need to take precautions now. If there is fallout, people in this town should know the truth so they can seek out shelter or rapidly travel away from the known areas of the blast. Those indoors will need to shut ventilation systems, windows, fireplace dampers, exhaust fans and clothes dryer vents, and make use of battery-powered radios."

He raised a hand and rocked in his seat. "The fallout? Hold on a minute. I think you're heading down the wrong road with this. You want me to believe that a nuclear weapon is responsible for this blackout?"

"Brett, how many other towns have this power outage? Better still, how many states? Do any of you know what has caused this?"

The fact was, it was not like all the police in every state would have got a heads-up warning. If our own government hadn't seen this coming, there was no way local police would have. Beyond the newspaper headlines of unrest in Korea, which had become a daily occurrence, there had been no warning of an imminent threat.

"Mr. Slater, calm down. I understand this is very unusual but let's not jump the gun here. The last thing we want is to evoke panic."

"Officer, take a look outside this department. People are waiting for answers. You might not have the entire town on your doorstep right now but how long is it going to be before you do? How long are you going to wait? At the bare minimum you need to get your hands on a battery-operated radio or hand-cranked one, or even better, a ham radio to find out if the Federal Emergency Management Agency has issued an alert."

He arched his eyebrows. "You some survival nut?"

I shrugged. "A little."

"Like I said, we are doing what we can right now. What I can tell you is that the existence of a local emergency has already been declared by the town manager. Just like he did in January with the snowstorm. Okay? An update will go out to the public as things progress and steps are being taken to assist anyone in need, to protect life and property as well as public infrastructure."

It was a nice sound bite, like the kind that may have been given over the local TV channel to reassure the public, but it didn't sit well with me. Without TV or Internet that kind of information would trickle out by word of mouth. "Oh I would be interested to hear how he managed to accomplish that feat. Did the town manager go door-to-door?"

Brett squinted and inhaled deeply. There was no denying the situation that was before us. Whether it was a nuke or a solar flare, not being proactive was going to lead to a loss of life. He tapped his pen for a few seconds against the table as if contemplating what to do.

He got up from his seat and though I could see he was troubled by what I had dropped on him, he remained composed.

"Just hang tight here, I'll be back in a minute."

"Brett. I don't have to tell you that an interruption in supplies of water, gasoline, diesel fuel and fresh food as well as communication is just the first wave. But once civil unrest erupts, the police are going to have a major problem on their hands."

He nodded and closed the door behind him. Through the slats of the blinds I saw him heading down the corridor and then out of view. I leaned back in my chair and tried to relax. I rubbed my wrists and glanced at a framed photo on the table in front of me. It was a snapshot of Brett with his wife, daughter Nancy and a young boy. Regardless of what his duty was to the town as an officer, he was a father and a husband first and that meant he knew the importance of being responsible and prepared. I was fully aware that he probably thought I had lost my marbles but in that moment I didn't care. All that mattered was making sure that others were aware of the gravity of the situation. That was no thunder shaking the earth when we were making our way back to the lot. Trouble had been brewing for months, unrest in the east, and if the American people were honest, many had lost their faith in government to protect them. When it came down to it, everyone was responsible for his or her survival. No matter how stupid or ridiculous it would appear to others, as Todd said, it was better to be safe than sorry.

The door cracked open and Officer Dolman made a gesture with his head for me to follow him. I got up, and he led the way down to a large conference room that was being used as a central hub for emergency management. There was a large town map on the wall with colorful pins pushed into it, and several whiteboards off to one side with details of what they were currently focusing on. Already there against the wall were the other four guys and near the front talking with who I came to know as Administrator Sandy Tanner was Chief of Police Bernie

Raymond.

"Sir," Dolman muttered.

The chief's eyes bounced from him to me. "Ah, Mr. Slater, nice to meet you." He extended his hand. "Dolman and I were just discussing the conversation you had with him." He breathed in deeply, his expression a mask of seriousness. "Ordinarily, and under any other conditions we aren't in the business of involving the public in emergency situations, however, this doesn't appear to be any ordinary situation. As you can appreciate we have limited resources and officers, and are unable to call in for assistance that might be found from the Red Cross, National Guard or so forth. And… the one officer who we have managed to get down to the closest town, which has another police department, has said they are in exactly the same situation as us. So we are pretty much up shit creek without a paddle. With that in mind, it's important that we establish some communication with the outside world. Dolman mentioned you had suggested a ham radio, which of course would be ideal. Do you have access to one?"

I snorted, and yet it was to be expected. At the end of the day emergency services were run by regular folk. There was only so much they could do in a disaster before they would require assistance from the public.

"I don't have one but I think I know someone who might."

"Good, then I'll have Dolman go with you."

"Actually we should be fine," I said motioning to the other four. "But um… I'm going to need my Jeep back."

Sixteen – Atomic Jim's

"I still think they should have made it official and given us badges," Todd said puffing away on his cigarette. I cast a glance at him and shook my head. It was a miracle that they had had even released us, let alone allowed us to continue to use the Jeep while assisting them. And that's exactly how they saw it. We were assisting them so they could dedicate their limited resources to other critical needs including watching over key areas in the town such as grocery, pharmacy and hardware stores, most of which were located off Old Mammoth Road, Main Street and Minaret Road.

"Just be thankful they didn't push the issue with Dolman," Marlin said. Under any other conditions, I was pretty sure they would have sent Dolman with us but they needed every officer they had available for critical situations. "Can you imagine that, having a cop looming over our shoulder? Anyway, let's pick up Amanda and get back to Mack's."

I turned slightly in my seat, taking my eyes off the road. "We're not going back there yet."

"What?" he protested leaning forward.

"I said we'd locate a ham radio, and that's what we're going to do."

"But I need to get Amanda to safety, and Chase still has to check in with his family."

"And I still need to find out about my daughter," I said. "But right now establishing communication with the outside is critical. We need to know for sure what's going on."

"You seemed pretty sure earlier," Chase piped up.

I sighed. It was to be expected everyone would have their own opinion about what they should or shouldn't do. Of course every person would think they were right, and they were to some extent if viewed through a limited perspective and right now that was exactly what we had. A limited view of the event that was unfolding. How could we take specific preventative measures without knowing the state of the country? Would help arrive? Had the nation's grid gone down or was it just isolated to California?

"You know Jim isn't going to just let us waltz in there, right?" Kai muttered glancing out the window lost in thought. He was fiddling with his wedding band on his finger and looked concerned.

"He has a point. That guy is a few sandwiches short of a picnic," Marlin said.

"What, because he sells a lot of weird shit?"

"That and the fact that he roams around town in the back of a convertible with a bunch of peace activists while holding up a banner that reads 'Sorry for Dropping the Bombs.'" And then who in their right mind mails a can of plutonium to the White House?"

I had to admit he was a little quirky. That one stunt with the plutonium had caused an uproar and a visit from the Secret Service to see if he had any history of mental illness. That was the first and only time I had seen them show up and the media had a field day with that one.

"I mean I wouldn't mind if his store sold anti-war goods but everything in there is a warmonger's heaven. You would think he was advocating for it with all the shit he sells. The guy is a bloody hypocrite."

"He's confused," I said. "Or perhaps he has mixed feelings on war."

"Well then pick a side but don't bark 'end the war' out of a megaphone on Sunday, only to sell a gun to me on Monday."

"Man's got a right to earn a living," Kai muttered.

"And I have a right to protest."

Marlin had been one of several folks including war vets who gathered on Main Street twice a year to protest against the peace activists who came out in droves to voice their disgust about so many troops being overseas. He'd called me up a few times and asked me to go with him but I would always come up with some excuse related to my work. It wasn't that I didn't think he had a point, but I preferred to keep out of any political, financial or religious arguments, they only ended up being bootstrapping discussions that pissed people off. And being as I dealt with enough pissed-off people on a daily basis, the last thing I needed was some loon seeing me out there and then coming into the store and giving me a tongue-lashing.

When we pulled up outside his store just off Alpine Crescent, the sign on the door was flipped over to "Closed" and the steel shutter was down on the window. Interestingly enough he had pulled in all his usual crap that was stuck outside. Normally it was like pulling up to a yard sale. Jim Brewster was a guy in his mid-seventies who had a cloud of white hair and rarely was seen out of his camouflage pants and multicolored sweaters. It was like an ugly Christmas sweater party every time I rolled up there. I'm surprised the town didn't get complaints about him being an eyesore.

On the days I visited, he was usually found in a rocker, smoking a pipe with his Doberman pinscher beside him and some light blues music playing in the background. Behind him an American flag would flap in the breeze and multiple cameras would be angled at different spots in the event someone fancied snatching an item. Not that they would have got far, rumor had it that dog was as fast as a racetrack whippet. It was on its last legs, had a face full of gray whiskers and the damn thing barely lifted its head off the ground in all the times I'd visited.

That evening the place was locked up like Fort Knox. Like Mack he would have been on the ball the second the power went out. I imagined him hauling all his stock back inside and then making an escape to his bug-out location.

"Great, looks like he's not in, let's go home," Marlin said before I killed the ignition and hopped out. "Or we can take a look," he muttered after.

You see, even though he paraded around town as a peace activist, I thought it was just a front to draw attention to his store. Like the way someone might pretend to be gay just so they could hang out with a bunch of hot females.

"I don't like this," Marlin said pulling out his handgun.

"Put that away! You want to spook the old guy?" Kai muttered.

He was known for being a little trigger-happy. A rumor circulated that he'd run anyone out of his store with a double-barrel shotgun if he thought for a second they were trying to shoplift. Of course, his peace activist buddies flatly denied that rumor and said he wouldn't harm a fly. I wasn't too sure about that.

"Can't we just search Mack's place for his ham radio?" Marlin said. "It would be so much quicker."

"Yeah, best of luck," Todd said. "It took me two hours to find an extra hammer."

He probably wasn't the only guy in town that had a ham radio, and there was a good chance, scratch that, a very high chance that Mack had his own but months before he passed away, he had boxed up most of what he had to make it easier for his daughter. Unfortunately he hadn't marked any of the boxes, so it was like searching for a needle in a haystack. Mack was a lot like Jim in that regard, he collected a bunch of crap and wasn't exactly the most organized individual, at least when it came to storage. Perhaps that's why they got on so well. Other vets in the town called Jim a traitor and yet the same people who cursed him on a Sunday would thank him on a Monday. It really was an odd relationship he had with the town but somehow he made it work.

We made our way over to the door and I banged on it a few times with a closed fist. The steel slapped back and forth. There was no answer. I took a few steps back and squinted up at the apartment directly above. The curtains were drawn.

"Well, that's that. Let's go," Marlin said turning and heading back to the Jeep.

I placed my ear up to the metal and listened intently. "Shhhh," I said waving with my hand. I was sure I heard movement inside. I gave it another bang. "Jim!" I yelled. "It's Brody Slater. From Von's. Mack's old friend. You remember me?"

The silence was unsettling.

"Perhaps we should go," Chase said. I knew he was

eager to find out what had happened to his family and I certainly didn't want to get in the way of him leaving but right now there was more at stake. This wasn't just about us, or our own families, there were more lives that hung in the balance.

"I'm going around the back."

"Are you outta your mind?" Chase said grabbing the sleeve of my jacket. "He's liable to blow our damn heads off if he catches us snooping around. And that's if that beast of a dog doesn't get you."

"Just stay here and watch the front. I'll be back in a second."

I circled around the back and hopped over a tall fence into a yard that had a dog kennel that appeared to be empty. A single chain lay on the floor unattached. Okay, that was a good sign. It wasn't like I was scared of the thing. I hadn't once seen it bare teeth and Jim would let small kids come up and pet it but that wasn't to say that I didn't think it was capable of tearing me a new one

Around the back of the house, I saw an extra-large dog

flap. As I got closer, I paused for a second, checking for movement. There was nothing. I went over to the windows and tapped on them and called out to Jim. I wanted to make it clear that I knew him and I wasn't there to rob the place.

"Jim. Can you hear me? The police department sent us over to speak to you about getting use of your ham radio. If you can hear me, can you open up the back door?"

I waited for a response and again I heard the same movement. I glanced down at the flap on the door, hesitant to do what I was thinking. It wasn't just the dog that concerned me, it was Jim. His eyesight wasn't what it used to be, and in this darkness it would have been easy to mistake me for an intruder.

I glanced back at the fence wondering if we shouldn't just follow what Marlin said and go back to Mack's and spend the next few hours digging through his belongings. But the lazy side of me refused. I dropped to a knee and pushed up the flap ever so slowly. I figured that if the dog were on the other side, it would give me a chance to bolt.

I felt like I was disarming a bomb pushing that flap in. I fully expected at any moment to find myself coming face-to-face with Jim's shotgun, or the beast of Mammoth Lakes, as I liked to call the dog.

It was like looking into a dark void and being as that Doberman was black, the chances were it would see me long before I caught sight of its teeth. Once the flap was up, I breathed a sigh of relief. Thank fuck for that! I thought, as I leaned in and tried to reach up and unlock the door.

I was about to break the law but I figured I had the cops' permission and if Jim was anything like Mack, he was probably squirreled away inside a bunker or miles away in some cabin.

Just as I got my hand on the door lock and gave it a twist I heard a sound that made my blood run cold. Paws padded across the hardwood floor, a dog panted, and then a growl. I turned my head ever so slowly. Ten feet away was his snarling, drooling dog. It barked once, and I felt my heart slam against my chest. That was the moment I knew I was fucked. Instantly, I yanked my arm and shoulder out from the flap and scrambled across the ground just as the dog burst out of the flap. I lunged at the fence from several feet away and my fingers raked into the chain link as I made my escape.

But I wasn't getting off that easy. That dog leapt into the air and latched onto my pant leg. Here I was hanging from the top of a fence with one pissed-off dog trying to have me for supper. I was making such a commotion trying to free my leg that the other guys had made their way over. However, instead of assisting me, they simply burst out laughing.

"A little help?" I yelled.

That's when I heard a gun cock.

"Don't struggle, he'll tear your leg off."

I turned to find a double-barrel aimed at my head. The gun was bigger than the man himself, and he looked as if he was struggling just to hold it up.

"Well, hey there Jim."

He made a whistling sound with his teeth and the dog

released me and he instructed me to get down slowly. He cast a glance over to the others.

"Assholes, you want to join your friend?"

They didn't exactly look eager. Within minutes we were all standing in his backyard with a heavy flashlight being scanned over us as we were questioned. It felt like an interrogation by Elmer Fudd.

He shouldered his shotgun and drifted it back and forth in front of our faces.

"You have ten seconds to tell me why you are snooping around my place."

"I already told you. Didn't you hear me?"

"What?" he stammered. "Hold on a second, this damn hearing aid keeps playing up." He whacked himself in the ear a few times and then fiddled with the back of it and then I repeated myself.

"Oh, right. Well why didn't you say?"

I looked over to the others, and they threw back the same confused look.

"Come on in but mind the land mines that I've

planted."

"Land mines?" Todd asked.

He burst out laughing. "Man, you should have seen the look on your face."

Jim chuckled to himself as he walked back inside with his dog leading the way.

"Excuse the mess. I haven't had a chance to put everything away with this blackout and all."

We tried to navigate our way around all manner of crap that was filling up the narrow hallway. Metal shelves lined the walls and on either side were degraded brown boxes full of useless junk and aged military surplus. The whole residence smelled of electronic oil, mold and surface rust. Our flashlights lit up dusty old computers from the '90s and card punches, ohmmeters and floppy disk drives. Then he led us into the main store itself. I cast my flashlight around the walls. There was a rack full of modern firearms, clothes racks full of military apparel and tactical gear behind glass counters along with knives and swords. At the far end of the store it catered to camping equipment and all manner of military accessories such as tents, parachutes, helmets, vests, flags, tape and paint.

"Now why do you need to use the ham radio?"

"Well I think it's pretty obvious, isn't it?" Marlin snapped back and Jim turned around and glared at him. I elbowed Marlin.

"What he means to say is we need to hear if the federal government has issued a warning. More specifically, one related to a high-altitude nuclear weapon being detonated in the atmosphere."

Without missing a beat, and said in a tone as if he wasn't the slightest bit concerned, he replied, "Well I can answer that right now. That's exactly what's happened."

Seventeen – Under Attack

"Holy shit, we need to get to a shelter ASAP," Todd said becoming all jittery and nervous. The rest of us stood there slack-jawed. It wasn't that he'd dumped on us something that we weren't expecting to hear, it was his nonchalant response to Todd and his overall laid-back demeanor that seemed peculiar.

He continued leading us down into his basement to where his ham radio was stored.

"Settle down. Everyone hears nuclear weapon and they freak. You have a good chance of surviving this unless you are a complete asshole." He stopped and turned to Todd. "Are you a complete asshole?"

That was debatable but Todd shook his head.

He puffed away on a pipe and continued shuffling along like the elderly in a retirement home. All the while his dog kept a close eye on us. It would let out a growl every couple of minutes and Jim would make a clicking sound with his tongue and the dog would become silent again. "There are number of variables to take into consideration, the weather, more specifically wind speed and direction, the time of day it was detonated, where it hit, how many hit and whether it exploded in the air or on the ground."

He guided us over to a bunch of radio equipment he'd set up alongside his computers which of course were no longer in use.

"Did you store all this in a Faraday cage?" Chase asked.

"What do you think?" he shot back before taking a seat and switching it on. "Now I've already got it tuned into a public safety frequency. I hope you boys are ready for this."

The unit began clicking, and it let out some white noise. As he began fiddling with the knob and adjusting the volume, a voice came over the speakers that sounded almost robotic. It started by beeping several times. We looked at each other while Jim tapped his fingers against the table looking as if he was about to doze off. I had to wonder if he had been expecting this. There was a different attitude among preppers compared to ordinary folk. Preppers always had their ear to the ground, they were ready for the worst and so when an event hit, they just handled it like it was a walk in the park. For the average Joe, shock would overwhelm them.

"This is a national emergency. Important instructions will follow… This message is transmitted at the request of the United States government. This is not a test. A nuclear attack has been commenced. Several high-altitude nuclear bombs released by North Korea have detonated in the atmosphere over several geographical areas of the country. They include Washington, California, Texas, North Carolina, Kentucky, Colorado and Oklahoma. At this time the entire electrical grid is down across the nation. All residents within a four-hundred-mile radius of the locations mentioned should seek a fallout shelter. Fallout is the product of a nuclear attack. Prolonged exposure to fallout will result in certain death. It is advised that if there is a nearby location that is being used as a fallout shelter, go there now. Otherwise seek shelter in the interior part of a strong building on the lowest floor. Take with you food, water and a battery-powered radio if available. Do not leave the fallout shelter until you have received notification that everything is clear."

The radio began making more beeping sounds.

Jim glanced up at us and the reality sank in hard and fast. Our country had come under attack and we were now at war.

"This is an emergency action notification. All broadcasting networks will continue to transmit this emergency action message."

And just like that it began to repeat. Jim switched it off and for a few seconds there was silence. It was one thing to assume what had happened, another to get specific details and official confirmation. Could all the nukes have come from North Korea or was it possible that Russia or China was involved? Maybe North Korea fired the first but who was to say that they were the only ones involved? That all those nukes were theirs? There was no denying that Russia had been against the USA since the cold war. What better way to engage than by piggybacking on the actions of North Korea? I shook my head unable to believe it. No. It couldn't be. And yet in the back of my mind I couldn't shake the feeling that there were more figures lurking around the war table, just waiting for the moment to bring the USA to its knees. According to the news prior to the event, tensions were high between the USA and other global powers. Who really were the USA's allies or enemies?

Right now it didn't matter. All that mattered was dealing with the situation at hand.

"We need to get this unit over to the police station."

Jim leaned back in his chair and removed his pipe. "You're not taking this. It's my property."

"But they're not going to believe us unless they hear this for themselves."

"Then maybe they should have sent an officer with you."

I looked at the others and ran a hand through my hair

before blowing out a lungful of air. I began pacing back and forth. The dog growled again.

"You're making the dog antsy."

"You're making me antsy," Marlin said.

"Why those locations?" Todd asked.

"Pretty obvious," Jim replied. "Some of the largest military bases in the United States are located there. Fort Bragg, Fort Campbell, Fort Hood, Joint Base Lewis-McChord and Fort Benning, Peterson Air Force Base."

"It's not just that," Kai interjected. "The U.S. electrical systems are interconnected but made up of three main interconnections. The western encompasses the area from the Rockies west. The eastern covers the east of the Rocky Mountains and some of the Texas Panhandle and the Electric Reliability Council covers most of Texas. My guess is they were looking to kill two birds with one stone."

"Well at least one of you isn't a complete asshole," Jim said rising to his feet. "Now it's time for you fellas to be on your way. I was in the middle of saving my own ass when you imbeciles showed up."

"Jim, we need to take the ham radio."

As quick as a flash, Jim brought up his shotgun. "I keep my gun well oiled. I've never once had a glitch. Can you smell that, boy?" He shoved the barrel against the tip of my nose. "You ever smelled death? Sniff real hard. Now you have." His eyes darted across to the others. "Now there's the stairs, head out now before Ruby takes a fancy to your balls." His dog growled, and we all began backing up slowly with our hands up. Could I have knocked the shotgun out of his hand? Probably but we didn't have a beef with him and right now as long as we knew what was happening, the police could tackle him if they really wanted it that bad.

"You think we could grab a few things from your store before we go?" Without my head moving, my eyes drifted to Marlin who was pushing his luck. "I mean I'll pay. I have money."

"You have money?" He let out a huge belly laugh. "Ruby, they have money. Oh that is rich. Boy, that money is no better than toilet paper right now. In fact you might want to hang on to it and save it for when you have a bad case of the shits." He continued laughing while motioning with his gun. "Now get the hell out of here."

We double-timed it up the stairs, Todd tripped and let out a yell as his knee cracked into the stairwell. You'd think anyone with a heart might have given him a chance to recover — not Jim, nope.

"You better move it now."

As we rushed outside, and made it back around to the Jeep, Marlin was holding several tactical vests in his hands. "Where did you get those from?"

"Grabbed them on the way out. Don't worry, I left money behind. And you'll thank me for it later."

He tossed them in the back and hopped into the passenger seat while I slipped in. I wasn't going to stick around to argue. If Jim found out, we'd be picking shotgun pellets out of our asses for the next few days. The engine roared to life and Chase was having some argument with Kai in the back as we pulled away.

"Would you guys shut the hell up?" I said gripping the steering wheel tight and chewing over the emergency message. Would foreign troops be next? How many people had been wiped out from the initial blast? It was estimated that when Hiroshima exploded the temperatures near the site were 540,000 degrees Fahrenheit, which was three hundred times hotter than the temperature of what bodies were cremated at. Those closest would be incinerated, others burned, and falling buildings from the pressure released in the explosion would likely crush others, and if that didn't kill people the radiation could. Of course the amount of radiation encountered would be greatly affected by whether someone was outside or inside, behind wood or cement. My mind drifted back to what Mack had taught us. He'd become almost repetitive in the way he drilled us in the rules of survival, as if he could foresee the future.

They were still arguing in the back and raising their voices. Kai was taking offense to the fact that Chase was pointing his finger at the Chinese even though the message had clearly stated that the nukes were from the North Koreans.

"Guys. Enough!"

"He still thinks China is involved," Kai said.

"How the hell do you know they aren't? The fact that they hacked the U.S.-built THAAD system in South Korea only a few days ago seems a little suspicious to me. For all we know the Chinese might have launched a cyberattack on the U.S. to bring down the power. I mean think about it. What other countries have trade deals with North Korea? Huh? We don't. But China does. Russia does. Hell, China is their biggest trade partner. Are you telling me these global powers are not in cahoots? Please. Keep on drinking the Kool-Aid. Who the hell has been shadowing the USA armada since it was sent out to North Korean waters?"

"China and Russia," Marlin said.

"Exactly! Point made."

"They are there to assist!"

"Assist who? North Korea?"

The back-and-forth was starting to drive me nuts, and yet it was expected. Everyone would chime in with his or her two cents on what would or wouldn't happen and how it would happen if it would happen at all. But none of that mattered.

I slammed my brakes on and everyone jerked forward.

"Would you two shut the fuck up?" I slammed my fist against the steering wheel. "Who cares who initiated it? Who gives a fuck who's behind it or whether or not it fits in with your world viewpoint? Opinions matter very little now. The fact is the grid is down. Nukes have been detonated and there is a threat of fallout. We need to alert the police and then seek out shelter."

"Alert the police?" Marlin said letting out a chuckle. "Are you out of your mind? You want to go back there and allow them to confiscate this vehicle?"

"I didn't say we were going to drive in there. But I'm going to alert them."

"You already have!" Marlin hollered.

"They have a right to know and prepare as much as we do. This is not every fucking man for himself. If we are to survive, we are to work together. If there was anything Mack tried to drill into us, it was teamwork. The military succeeds because they work as one unit. As a team." There was silence. I put my foot back on the gas and eased out.

"We should be thinking about thermal radiation and black rain right now. All it takes is exposure to 600 rem radiation and it could lead to fatal illness and at 450 rem it's estimated to be deadly to half of those affected. And even if we managed to recover from that, it's seriously going to mess up our molecular structure and DNA and you know that means?" Kai rattled off stats like a damn computer.

"Mutations," Todd chimed in. "This shit is going to end up like something out of *The Hills Have Eyes*."

"Actually you kind of resemble the bald guy," Chase muttered. "Yeah, he was one ugly mother—"

Todd flipped him the bird. "Screw you."

"No, guys, this is serious. Fallout can travel for

hundreds of miles when carried by the wind. The first two weeks are the most dangerous."

"But doesn't it decline? I remember Mack saying something about it dropping?"

Kai nodded. "Yeah, I mean, within seven hours the intensity of the initial radiation level drops to 10 percent, after two days to around 1 percent, then to around 0.1 percent after two weeks. However intensity is dependent upon the size and power of the nukes. Hiroshima was 15 kilotons, Ivy King was 500, Castle Bravo 15,000 but are we dealing with something that strong? If they were mini nukes, the yield may only be .005 KT. Either way we should still get inside and underground soon."

Marlin slammed his fist against the door. "Two weeks in a shelter?"

"Forty-nine hours to be exact but I would advise to stay inside for the first two weeks or longer just to be on the safe side," Kai replied.

"We could already be exposed! We need to know what the radiation levels are." He clicked his fingers. "You can bet your ass Jim had Geiger counters. Damn it! I should have thought about that." He threw a hand up. "Doesn't matter. Brody, turn the Jeep around, let's go back."

I frowned and shook my head "We're not going back. We're heading to the station."

"Really. And who put you in charge?"

"Jim's not the only person who will have one, I'm sure Mack owned one."

"Yeah and I bet he purchased a dozen CBRN suits?" Marlin said before rolling his eyes.

"Actually CBRN suits aren't going to be of much use. It doesn't exactly protect you from gamma radiation, which is the short-term threat that we're facing. It mainly shields from particle and compound contamination that would harm you, such as alpha and beta radiation. Gamma is photons, and it's practically impossible to uh… 100 percent stop that," Kai said, pushing his glasses back up to the bridge of his nose. "But it would be handy to have some available."

"Well, thanks for weighing in on that, brainiac,"

Marlin replied. "Now can we turn around?"

"Look, Marlin, we'll find one as soon as we get back."

"Oh, sure we will. Maybe you can spend the weekend searching for it while I swallow a healthy dose of radiation." His voice got louder. "Turn. The vehicle. Around!"

"No," I said strongly while glancing at him and taking my eyes off the road for a second. "Emergency services need to know about this now. We deal with Geiger counters after."

"I said, turn around."

Right then Marlin leaned across and grabbed the steering wheel. He yanked it towards him and the Jeep jerked hard to the right. Tires screeched across the wet ground. "What the hell do you think you're doing?" I yelled as I tried to maintain control.

"Watch out!" Chase yelled pointing ahead as the Jeep veered towards several stalled vehicles. I yanked at the wheel just in time to prevent a near collision but as the roads were shrouded in darkness, I didn't see the black sedan that was off to the left until it was too late. I slammed my foot on the brake hoping to avoid it but it was impossible at the speed we were traveling. The Jeep slammed into the back of the vehicle. Metal crunched and golden sparks flew, sending it shooting forward. I lost consciousness in that moment and when my eyes blinked open, my head was leaning against the steering wheel, I could hear Chase shouting and the horn blaring out one single deafening note.

Eighteen – Fallout

Even after I pushed off the steering wheel, and the horn stopped blaring, I still had ringing in my ears. I reached for my chin, feeling something warm trickle down it. Blood? Then a sharp pain came from my chest where I'd hit the steering wheel. I turned to find Marlin arguing with Chase. I wanted to lash out but instead; I pushed out of the vehicle to assess the damage, and check that I hadn't hit a pedestrian. I staggered a little as my body caught up to my brain. The vehicle we hit had flames coming out of it. I stumbled over and checked inside. Thankfully, there was no one there. Farther down I saw a crowd of people heading our way, some of them were running.

Not wasting a second, I hopped back in and turned over the ignition. It spluttered.

"Come on," I yelled giving it another go. Second time it started up, and I jammed it into reverse and backed out without saying a word to Marlin. There was no point arguing and right now all that mattered was putting some distance between us and those heading our way. I took an alternative route back to the station. Along the way we saw a few more fires, mostly coming from vehicles that had crashed, others from what looked to be acts of vandalism. Not everyone would act civilized. Some would try to take advantage of the situation and draw the police away to different areas so they could raid stores.

"Listen up, I'm going to park a few streets away on Chateau Road and Azimuth Drive. Wait here with the vehicle. I'll give them the heads-up and then we'll head over and grab Amanda and return to Mack's. You can use the vehicle after that, Chase."

Marlin looked as if he was about to say something, a look of guilt flashed across his face but I didn't stick around to find out what he was about to say. I slammed the gear into park and hopped out taking the keys with me. It wasn't that I didn't trust him but after what had just happened, I wasn't taking any chances. He was unpredictable, and all I needed right now was to find myself stranded because he'd decided he wasn't going to stay put. I took my Glock with me, tucked it into the back of my shirt and high-tailed it along Chateau Road. I wasn't thinking about what the cops would say. My mind was churning over what I was going to do about Ava. In all this time I hadn't stopped to think about collecting her. You see, the whole relationship had become so strained, and depending on the month, Theresa could either be a bitch or as nice as pie. For a short time I was allowed to see Ava on weekends. I would drop by and take her out to the YMCA for a swim, snowboard in the winter or we'd go hiking in the summer, and for a time that worked, that was until Theresa wanted more money. We'd come to an agreement whereby I would pay her a fixed amount each month instead of going through the courts. But that changed along with her taste for expensive clothing. So, she resorted to threats.

"*My brother is a lawyer, he'll make your life a living hell. I will end up with full custody so either we do this my way or*

I'll see you in court," she'd said. The agreement worked for a while until she moved in with Carl Stimms, and then everything changed. It was as if he warped her mind and purposely brought out the worst in her.

"I want more money. My income alone isn't going to pay for those school trips, and new clothes she needs."

"You mean those designer labels?"

She scowled.

"Look, I just gave you money and a little extra."

"Brody, if you're going to give me hassle, I'll have my brother handle this."

After I agreed and said that was probably best, she absolutely flipped her lid and stopped Ava from seeing me and came up with these bullshit excuses that I was too busy, or I didn't want to see her because she was a burden. Anything and everything was used to twist the truth and turn my own daughter against me. But I don't think it stopped there, there was more to it. Ava had removed me from her social media and the few times I had waited to speak to her outside her school, she would just head in the opposite direction. It literally killed me inside. So, I ended up taking it through the courts and her brother got involved and somehow managed to get her full custody. She came up with some bull crap reason that I was living in an area of town that was unsafe, and that I was a heavy drinker, which was a lie. Not a drop of alcohol had touched my lips in over six years. It wasn't that I had a problem with it, but my body had changed, it just couldn't handle it the way it used to. Nope, Theresa was bad news. There was no hope for us. I didn't want her in my life, and she had made it damn clear that I wasn't in her future the moment she cheated on me. It wasn't like I was a bad guy. I treated her right, never forgot an anniversary or birthday and I went out of my way to make sure she had everything she wanted but it was never enough. Mack had said that some relationships were doomed from the moment they started. He joked that I must have had mud in my eye from all those hours of training. I had to find the humor in it all otherwise I would have lost my mind.

Upon arriving at the station, I wandered in to find the place was practically empty. Besides the administrator, the chief and two staff sergeants, all the rest of the officers including Dolman were out on patrol.

That suited me fine; I didn't want to end up in some big discussion with Dolman over why I hadn't returned with the Jeep. I was going to tell him that a group had overrun us, but he probably wouldn't have bought it.

Instead, I approached Staff Sergeant Moloney and relayed the information that was being broadcast. I also told him that Jim refused to hand over the ham radio and it was probably best a couple of officers visited him if they needed it.

He thanked me and I was just about to step out when the chief came into view.

"Mr. Slater."

I squeezed my eyes closed with my hand on the door. I could pretend not to hear and hurry out and race off but with an officer arriving on a bicycle outside, I figured I wouldn't get far.

Grimacing, I turned and then smiled. "Chief."

"Any luck?"

"I just uh… explained to your sergeant, he should be able to fill you in."

I turned to leave and then he asked.

"Did you bring back the Jeep?"

I winced with my hand on the door for a second time. "Actually no. Um…" I turned to face him, and couldn't believe I was going to lie to the chief of police but the way I saw it — the country was under attack. In a matter of twenty-four to forty-eight hours very little law and order was going to be in place. Bike patrol would cease; any vehicles on the road would be stored away. The United States was not going to bounce back from this a week from today, or even a month. It didn't matter what he heard. So I unloaded the lie. His response caught me off guard.

His cheeks blew out. "Yeah, I'm not surprised."

Shit, he actually bought it.

"There have been a number of fires started around

town on purpose. Your store is one of them. The entire place is up in flames. That's where Dolman is right now. I hope Von's has good insurance."

"What? How?"

"No idea, all I know is this is going to be a long night," he said turning to leave.

I'd seen smoke rising over the tops of buildings but I assumed it was just another car fire. "Chief," I hollered back just as he was leaving the room. "The country is at war. It's suffered a nuclear attack over multiple regions. The entire nation's grid is out." I felt obliged to be the one to tell him, even though I knew his sergeant would have conveyed it. He twisted around and stared at me as if I was a ghost. "The Federal Emergency Management Agency is transmitting an emergency message across all networks. It's official, the United States is under attack."

"You're certain?"

I don't think he thought I was making this shit up, but it was a natural response to want to be sure about a life-threatening disaster.

I nodded. "Heard it with my own ears. Alert the town. People need to find shelter inside, preferably in a fallout shelter, and prepare to hunker down on the lowest floor for at least two weeks. Gather what food and water you can, and battery-operated radios and wait it out. Tell them to block off air vents, seal windows and avoid going out until further notice."

His head shook as the grim reality weighed heavily on him. Officers, town folk and officials would be looking to him for answers and protection but there was only so much they'd be able to offer. The fact was, what town was prepared for something of this magnitude? Some were capable of dealing with quakes, floods, ice storms and hurricanes but even then people died. How many would die this time? How many had already died? I hated being the bearer of bad news but it was important that as many people as possible in the town knew the truth.

I figured some would be ready, Mammoth was full of families that were outdoor enthusiasts, there had to be preppers among them like Mack and Jim, but many wouldn't be. I cast a glance outside to the long line of people that had gathered in droves waiting for news updates and direction. There were more there than when we left.

He continued to look at me with eyes of disbelief or perhaps it was shock.

"I couldn't get him to give his radio over. You'll need to send officers over if you want further confirmation."

He nodded, and I turned to leave.

"Mr. Slater. How come you know so much about this?"

"I had a good teacher."

"Perhaps you can stick around. We could use someone like you. Give it some thought."

I shrugged and exited. I breathed in the warm evening air. That was all I could find to be grateful for right then. Had this occurred in the dead of winter, a loss of electricity would have caused the death toll to rise faster due to a drop in temperature. I sprinted back to the waiting truck, pleased to see it was still there and Marlin hadn't taken off. I hopped in and sat there for a second trying to catch my breath.

"So?" Chase asked.

"We've done what we can. Let's go collect Amanda," I said, turning to Marlin who nodded. I started up the engine and pulled out. Regardless of my relationship with her mother or what she'd told Ava, I had to check in with Ava. First, we'd collect Amanda and then we'd swing by Theresa's place.

"What about my wife?" Kai asked.

I frowned as my eyes flicked to the rearview mirror. We all had questions but they would have to wait. We were pushed for time and Chase still needed to make sure his family was okay, and that meant another hour's ride north. A journey that I didn't think was a good idea but had I been in the same position I would have driven it. All of us were anxious, regardless of what we knew about how to survive. It didn't matter. I felt like a fish out of water, like someone getting back in the saddle and becoming comfortable in the uncomfortable. That had always been repeated to us when we were cold, caked in mud and had hours of hiking ahead of us. The words of Mack echoed at the back of my mind.

"You will learn to perform at your best under the worst conditions, because that is what the military will demand of you, that's what America expects of you. Get comfortable with discomfort."

* * *

The home of Carl Stimms was located on Starwood Drive. A beautiful wood and brick home that had four bedrooms and four bathrooms, it was another reason why Theresa had jumped ship. She was never content with what we had, even though I worked all the hours under the sun to provide her with a home that we really couldn't afford. As the Jeep swung into the driveway, it was close to midnight and there were no vehicles outside. The headlights washed over the property and I saw movement.

The second I hopped out, the door to the home opened up and my daughter came rushing out, teary eyed and her face swollen from crying. When she caught sight of me, she bolted back towards the house but I caught up with her and grabbed hold of her arm.

"Get off."

"Ava. Where is your mother?"

"Please, just go away."

"What is going on? Where is Carl?"

By now the guys had got out and were glancing up and down the road and looking as if they wanted to help.

"They said they were going away for a couple of days and would be back this evening but they haven't returned."

"What? They left you by yourself?" She was thirteen years of age. It was one thing to nip out to the store or go out for the day but to leave a thirteen-year-old alone overnight? Two nights?

She shrugged. "They do it all the time."

"Holy crap." And here she was saying I was a bad father. I swallowed hard and kept a firm grip on her as she tried to wriggle free. I didn't know what lies Theresa had filled her head with but I sure as hell wasn't going to leave here there by herself.

"You're coming with me, go grab a bag and a few clothes."

"I'm not going with you."

"Yes you are."

"You don't get to tell me what to do."

"I'm still your father. And without your mother around and until you're of age, you are going to do what I tell you. You hear me?" I shook her a little and then realized that I was losing my temper. It wasn't with her that I was angry, it was Theresa. How could she have done this? "Now go and get your stuff."

She shot inside and I rose from a crouched position and cast a glance back at the guys. None of them said anything, hell, they hadn't even met my kid. For the short amount of time I had been allowed to spend with her, I felt more like a stranger than a father. But I knew what a father was meant to do, and I would protect her at all cost.

Nineteen – Neighborhood Watch

Tensions were high as we made our way back to Mack's. Kai wanted to collect his wife that none of us even knew existed. Chase wanted to drive an hour away to check in on his family and Marlin was still harping on about revisiting Jim Brewster's store and gathering the Geiger counters and CBRN suits. It didn't matter what Kai tried to tell him, he wouldn't be deterred.

Stress was the fuel in our tank, and with smoke rising above the town it was clear it was only going to get worse. At the same time I knew the chief had his work cut out for him if he was going to alert the town. It would take more than fifteen officers to do it that was for sure. Of course, some might have known by now, those who had been prepared and had working radios available to them, but the largest majority wouldn't. I couldn't help feel some burden of responsibility, even though there was no way of helping everyone in Mammoth Lakes. But now I had Ava to think about. I glanced at her beside me. She'd brought along a backpack full of clothes and hadn't said a word to me since getting in.

When we pulled up in front of Mack's place, many of the neighbors were out on the street, including Bridget who was talking to one of them. I reversed into the garage and everyone hopped out. Amanda took Ava inside and Jason stood at the door with a scowl on his face. He clearly was against us being there and in some ways I couldn't blame him. It couldn't have been easy to have a bunch of strangers showing up out of the blue, wanting to use the same shelter and yet we had no other option. Heading out to the cabin on Iron Mountain would have taken too long.

"What's going on, Bridget?"

The neighbor beside her walked away, and she remarked that they would chat later.

"Not long after you left, I heard the sound of gunfire on the street. I went up to the top floor and looked out to see a truck, and several armed men going house to house."

"What color was the truck?"

"Hard to tell. It was too dark but if I had to guess, maybe red?"

"How many men?"

"Seven, maybe eight. Anyway, they were beating on doors and dragging people out. No clue what they wanted. It didn't last long as thankfully two officers were in the vicinity at the time. They escaped by driving their truck through Ms. Thompson's backyard."

"Probably ended up on Juniper Springs Drive," I muttered. There was a neighborhood directly behind Crestwood Hills that led to Juniper Springs Resort.

"Anyone hurt?"

"Tracey Harper and her husband, Matt, suffered a few cuts and bruises but they got off lucky. If those cops hadn't shown up, I'm pretty sure it would have been much worse."

My thoughts went wild as a crowd gathered farther down the street. Had the group from the supermarket followed us? Were they searching for us? Perhaps they had seen us enter the neighborhood but didn't know which home we had pulled into. I turned and Jason still had his arms folded and was scowling. His words echoed in my mind. *If you endanger Bridget…* I wasn't scared of the guy but he had a right to be protective of her. If we ventured out again, we would need to make sure several of us stayed behind to watch over them and the house. If it were learned that there was a shelter below the place, those guys from the supermarket wouldn't be the only ones banging on doors.

"You think you can introduce me to a few of your neighbors?"

Her brow knit together. "Why?"

"I think they need to know the truth."

"Which is?"

"We are at war."

We made our way down to the crowd that had gathered at the home of the Harpers. No medics had shown up as the injuries weren't life-threatening and from what I could tell most of them would be stranded at the hospital on the other side of town. They had already tended to the wounds and someone had brought out a kerosene camping stove to make each of them a hot drink. They were both draped in gray blankets and hunched over sipping their drinks. I immediately noticed that two neighbors were bearing hunting rifles and were still scanning the area for potential threats. That was a good thing. Perhaps if we all worked together, we could protect the homes on the street.

"Tracey, this is Brody Slater."

She looked up, her face a mask of anguish. A flashlight shone in our eyes. "I know you. The manager of the supermarket."

"The people who did this to you. Did they say what they wanted?"

"No, they were barking all manner of orders. I barely understood what they were saying. Masks covered their faces. At first I thought it was the army or police as their lights blinded us."

"Anyone else injured?"

"Martin Walton a few doors down. He fought back and threw one of them to the ground. Someone struck his leg."

"I heard what they were looking for," a familiar voice called out from the darkness. I turned to see none other than Kurt Donahue.

"Kurt? You live down here?"

"Yeah. We bought number eight, around the bend there, a few months back."

He came over wearing a tight-fitting green T-shirt and he was holding a Sig P320 off to his side. A flood of memories came back, most of which were not pleasant. Had the years changed him? Had his time in the military knocked some sense into him?

"What did they want?" another neighbor asked.

"I heard one of them say they were searching for a Jeep." His eyes darted over to me and I knew what he was about to blurt out. I cast a glance at the ground for a second to contemplate what I was going to tell those who'd been injured when Kurt spoke again. "I figure they got their bearings wrong, unless of course they were looking for yours?" Kurt said.

The others turned, and I now regretted wanting to speak to them.

"Yeah, we have a Jeep that's operating. They must have seen us around town."

"You brought them down here?" Matt muttered. "You need to get rid of it."

Bridget stepped in seeing that this was about to escalate. "Now listen up, that's my father's Jeep. No one is getting rid of it. Besides, it's the only one right now that is working barring a few others in the town. Now Brody has something important to tell you all. It would be advisable that you pay attention."

I gave Bridget a short nod of thanks and stepped forward into the light coming from all the flashlights and lanterns. There was no easy way to tell them and I wasn't going to cherry coat it.

"Today our country came under attack by North Korea. This blackout is the result of a nuclear attack."

Several gasped and one woman grabbed a hold of her husband for support.

"Are you joking? Because if you are, this is not the right time," Donahue said.

"This is not a joke. We've received official confirmation. Which means right now you all need to get inside, block off all your vents, seal up the windows and get to the lowest part of the house. There's no way of knowing when the fallout is going to be carried this way by the weather or how strong it will be. We've already had a good dose of rain, and more is on the way. Unless you want to get radiation poisoning, I recommend you stay inside."

"Come on, are we supposed to believe this?" a neighbor piped up, while others looked stunned. Donahue looked over but didn't say anything. He must have known what I was telling them held some merit.

If anyone should have understood, it would have been him.

"If any of you have a ham radio, you can tune in and

hear the FEMA message for yourself. I don't have any reason to lie to you. The police have been notified but without vehicles, and with the amount of need in town, we aren't going to be able to rely on them to show up every time."

"Why don't you give the police your Jeep?"

"It was actually being used for that purpose this evening."

I was going to mention what I'd told the chief but the thought of heading down into the shelter and leaving the responsibility of alerting everyone was weighing heavily on my mind. The chief needed as many people to help as possible and we were familiar with how to survive an event like this, even if our expertise was only in theory.

Donahue snorted, but he didn't say anything. He didn't need to, his pompous stance and attitude spoke volumes. The idea that he'd changed was a little too much to wrap my head around, military or not.

A larger crowd began to gather and talk among themselves.

"Listen up," I said. "For those of you who didn't hear. Several high-altitude nuclear bombs from North Korea have been detonated in the atmosphere and that's what's knocked out the power. Now whether you want to believe it or not, California is one of the areas that was hit, which means sooner or later we are going to experience fallout if we haven't already."

Kai stepped into view and cut me off.

"Actually, sorry to interrupt, Brody. It's not good news but… the fallout will be less because the nuclear weapons were detonated in the air. It's called an airburst. It tends to produce less fallout compared to a ground explosion. However, that doesn't mean it can't travel fast." He looked back at me. "Sorry, continue."

I nodded, I was used to Kai jumping in, and he'd been that way since we were kids. "Right, either way we all need to be prepared. Now look, what happened tonight is just the beginning. It's getting worse. Von's Supermarket in town is ablaze, so any chances of you guys stocking up on food and water are next to none, unless you want to break into the few other grocery stores in the area tonight. Money isn't going to be much use. No Internet. No ATMs, no cell phones, we are on our own right now until further notice. It won't be long before law and order will be out of control, which means, with what happened here tonight, we need to work together to survive this. So regarding water. The pressure is gone but there should be some water left in your pipes and water heaters so I would suggest filling up your bathtubs and sinks with what remains. Make sure you boil it before using and the rest, well, we'll figure that out. Now it's late right now and there isn't a lot that can be done tonight. But we can meet in the morning and work together to secure the neighborhood."

As I continued to speak, more people on the street began to gather. There were twenty-seven homes in Crestwood Hills. The street itself looped around like the eye of a needle. It was still unclear if the area could be secured. It would require the assistance of everyone and being as for the next two weeks it was going to be unsafe to venture out, the first order of business was to find the Geiger counters and determine the threat level from radiation. I yawned and ran a hand over my face. It was closing in on one in the morning and we weren't even close to getting everything done. Chase would still be eager to leave, Kai wanted to pick up his wife, and I was going to have to convince them to hold off until the morning. A task I didn't imagine would be easy being as I already had my daughter there. I cast a glance back to the house for just a second when Donahue grabbed my arm and pulled me off to one side.

"You using his shelter?"

"What?"

"Mack's. That's the only reason you would be here."

"Get your hand off me, Donahue."

Donahue released his grip without me having to ask again.

"Don't you think these people should know about that?"

"There is barely enough room for all of us."

"So you're just going to batten down the hatches and enjoy the protection of a fallout shelter while the rest of this street has to resort to hoping they don't get radiation poisoning?"

"No, maybe they can use your shelter."

"I don't have one."

I snorted. "And yet you made it into the military?"

"Don't get snarky with me, Slater. Some of us weren't expecting this."

I would have argued with him but the fact was, neither was I. If it weren't for the kindness of Bridget we'd be in the exact same position.

"It's not my call. Bridget is letting us stay there."

Donahue took a few steps back. "Well then I'll ask her."

"Donahue," I went to tell him that wasn't a good idea when he strode over to her. A few seconds later he took a step back and pointed his finger at her then stormed off in the opposite direction. I wandered over to find out what happened.

"Look, I'm sorry about that. I tried to explain but…"

"He's not getting in. After what he did to my father, I don't trust him."

"I don't blame you." I turned and looked back at Donahue who was marching away. His presence on the street was going to be a problem. However, the problem had started a long time ago, back when Mack was still training him. Some would say his need to be in control and rebellious attitude caused Mack to kick him out of the training group but that wasn't entirely the case. He was the only guy who had ever been kicked out which was saying something because Mack had the patience of a saint. At first I thought it was just a conflict of character but I soon came to discover that he'd actually stolen personal items from Mack's home. He never told me what was taken, but it meant a lot to him and one thing he didn't put up with was thieves. Loyalty meant everything to Mack, and perhaps that's why he handed us the keys to the Jeep, and had offered to let us use the cabin on Iron Mountain.

I turned back to the group of neighbors that were still discussing what could be done. Food and water appeared to be an issue. On one hand I wanted to tell them that we had some that could be shared but in a SHTF event, the last thing you wanted to do was flap your lips. It would have been like constructing a sign outside the house that read, Come and Rob Us!

"Look, tomorrow morning I will go and see what is left of Von's. Hopefully the entire place wasn't burned down but according to the chief it's not looking good. Once we know some more details, perhaps the town emergency operations will have something in place to distribute food out. I can't guarantee anything but I'm sure we can figure out something. In the meantime, go back inside, shut your vents, seal off your windows and stay safe."

The crowd dispersed, and I walked back with Bridget.

"What now?"

I was about to say sleep as my mind wanted to switch off when I noticed Chase pulling out of the garage with the Jeep.

"Chase!" I called out, and he flashed me a glance before driving off.

Twenty – Morning After

Day two since the attack and I don't think any of us slept well that first night. Chase returned in the early hours of the morning and woke me up sometime around five when he opened the hatch. I knew where he'd been but was surprised to see that Tiffany and his kids weren't with him. He refused to speak about it and settled in to get a few hours of sleep.

I'd spent the better part of an hour searching boxes for a Geiger counter and eventually found one stashed away beneath a collection of survival magazines. Marlin was boiling some water for coffee and giving Todd a hand making some breakfast when I stepped outside and switched the unit on. I flipped on the audio switch and turned the fast and slow knob to slow to get a more accurate reading. From there, I checked the battery by turning the dial. The needle shot over to the BAT TEST area. Good, it was still working. There were four scales on the front; X1, X10, X100 and X1000, each one determined the sensitivity of the unit. After setting the knob to the smallest scale X1 so that it would measure even the smallest amount of radiation, I raised the Geiger-Muller tube probe to the sky and began to check for radiation. It had been a long time since Mack had shown us how to use one. When I found this, I thought for a second it wouldn't work but the battery was still running strong and it appeared to be in fair condition.

The unit started making some noise as I began walking the distance of the yard. I monitored the needle and it let out a few small clicks. This was normal if it was picking up background radiation. Not all radiation was harmful and background radiation was present in the environment and originated from both natural and artificial sources. Normal background radiation was safe from 5 to 60 CPM. As I raised the probe up and began moving it back and forth, there was an increase in clicks and the needle shifted giving me a reading of 112 CPM. As I had the setting on X1 that meant that was accurate. Had it been set to X10, I would have had to multiply 112 by 10 and that would have given me 1120 CPM. I recalled Mack saying something along the lines of if the reading was over 100 CPM the danger varied based on exposure and number of days exposed at the same rate. Also there was the fact that the CPM might increase or drop being as the bomb was detonated in the air and the wind might not have brought it this way yet. It could be hours or days we were looking at before it registered differently.

"Kai! Are you there?" I hollered over my shoulder. I remembered some of what he'd taught but not everything. Kai was like a walking computer, I swore he had a photographic memory but he denied it. The fact that he hadn't gone on to get a job as a scientist or become some kind of whiz kid was baffling. Then again, his upbringing wasn't exactly what someone might call ordinary. When he wasn't helping his father at the martial arts school, his family would make him do all manner of extra homework. I couldn't get my head around it. He said it was something to do with Chinese families expecting more from their kids.

He poked his head out with a cup in his hand. "What do you need?"

"I'm getting a reading of 112 CPM, any ideas on measuring the risk?"

"It's actually a mixed bag of opinions depending on who you ask. Some say that up to 200 CPM is considered normal background noise while the Radiation Network uses 100 CPM as the warning threshold. Then of course you have to take into account what the average annual human exposure to radiation is, you know... from having dental X-rays, mammograms and other sources..."

"In English, Kai!" I hollered, my arm was growing tired of holding it up.

"So 112 CPM is kind of high but then again Hawaii back in 2011 picked up a reading of 141 CPM and then it bounced back to 37 CPM within two hours and then picked up to 100 for close to five minutes. Spikes in radiation can come from a surge in background radiation. It's not uncommon."

"Okay, that's not helping, brother," I said letting out a chuckle, looking off to the side to see Marlin hanging from the doorframe doing ab crunches. The guy was obsessed with staying in shape. Even in an apocalypse he was doing sets.

Kai sighed. "It's not as easy as that, man. There is the amount of dosage and how long you are exposed to it. Annual radiation for Americans is around 600 milliRem, increase of cancer is 1,250, radiation sickness is about 75,000, poisoning you are looking at 300,000 and death around 400,000 mRem. Then you have to base that on how long it would take to experience those kinds of numbers based on a CPM number. So if 100 CPM is the threshold, you are looking at around 207 days for the average human exposure, 432 days for increased cancer and around…" He squeezed his eyes shut as if he was trying to figure out some super-hard equation. "Around 25,000 days for radiation sickness based on 100 CPM. So the higher the CPM, the quicker it would take to experience poisoning."

"In a nutshell, Kai?"

"The lower the CPM number, the better, and the less exposure we have, the better. We should really be limiting the amount of time we are outside, staying clear of the blast site and using water, concrete or lead to block gamma radiation. Though having said that, I wouldn't rely on what I've just said as my memory is a bit foggy."

I snorted. "When did you learn all that? Last week?"

"Fifteen years ago."

My eyes widened as he walked back inside. I switched the unit back off and headed in. I had to hope that Kai was right about airbursts and that perhaps the CPM number would drop. We'd have to keep monitoring it throughout the day and if it increased we'd have to stay inside. Hopefully if there was less fallout because of it being an airburst we wouldn't have to stay inside for longer than a few days, two weeks tops. Then again, was that the only risk we were looking at? The threat of foreign troops was ever present and at the forefront of my mind.

"Did you hear Chase come in?" Marlin asked handing me a cup of coffee. The rest of them were farther down inside the bunker. I'd placed my mattress close to the front alongside Chase, so he'd managed to get in without waking the others.

"Yeah, you might not want to crack any jokes about Tiffany today."

I walked over to the front window and peered out the curtain. The street was quiet, neighbors were probably still sleeping, trying to catch up after the previous night's incident. A lot would change today. Now that it was light we'd be able to see the aftermath of the EMP. I was eager to know how we could be of use to the chief. I didn't like the idea of staying inside when there were folks out there trying to help the community. Though I had my issues with people in the town, I wasn't one for sitting on the sidelines and doing nothing.

"I'm going to head out in five to pick up Zhang Ling."

"Ah, so we finally get a name?" Marlin said scooping out some of the slop from an MRE packet. "So come on,

Takumi, how did you meet her? Was she a foreign exchange student? Oh no, let me guess, she was a mail-order bride. That's it!" He burst out laughing. Kai continued eating an apple and thumbing his way through a day-old paper paying no attention to him. I grabbed up a banana and a muffin and sat down beside him and I could tell he was uncomfortable.

"I was thinking I might go by myself," Kai muttered.

"Oh no you don't. You are not wiggling your way out of this one, Takumi. Give up the goods. Tell us why you didn't tell us you were married. Better still, who are Misty and Kristy and what do they think about it?" Right then Marlin stuck his finger out as if he had just been enlightened. "Oh I've got it. They are involved, aren't they? This is some kind of polygamy deal you have going. Let me guess, the Chinese one stays at home cleaning while the other two tend to your every whim and pleasure. Oh that is beautiful. You old dog!"

I elbowed Marlin. "Man, you have a really warped view of women."

"Oh give me a break, Slater. Are you telling me you wouldn't jump in the sack with three beauties?"

I swallowed hard and glanced down at the paper but didn't answer.

"Just what I thought." He slurped another mouthful of food down. "Anyway, I'm not saying it's a bad thing. Hell, there was some guy on TV who had four on the go. Can you imagine how many headache pills he must swallow, or contraceptives he gets through in a given month? Shit! Well, we know what he'll be stocking up on."

Kai got up and tossed his apple core into the garbage and went off to get ready.

"Do you have an off switch?" I asked getting up and following him out.

With his mouth full, he hollered back. "What? What did I say?"

As I was heading down to grab a jacket, and my firearm, Ava emerged rubbing her eyes and still clinging to the backpack.

"Hey hon, you sleep okay?"

"Can you take me back this morning?"

"We'll check today but you won't be able to stay there. It's not safe."

"Why?"

I realized I hadn't explained to her what had taken place; I breathed in deeply and took her to one side. "Look, I know things between your mom and I have been strained, and I don't know what she told you about me but it's—"

"You said you didn't want to see me," she blurted out cutting me off.

My eyebrows arched. "That's not true."

"Then why didn't you come around? Why haven't I received one birthday or Christmas card from you in over six years?"

My heart stung. "She wouldn't let me see you, Ava. Well, that's not exactly true, the lawyers..." I trailed off sighing. A flood of memories came back. It was tough. It didn't matter that I was holding down a full-time job at the time. Theresa had a way of twisting the truth and making it seem as if I'd wanted nothing to do with Ava. No wonder she'd acted so cold all those times I'd shown up at her school.

Ava studied my face as if trying to find a crack in my expression. "That's because you drink too much."

I snorted. "Ava." I reached for her hand but she just pulled away. "I don't drink. I mean, I may have a beer once a month but that's it."

"Because you can't afford to drink?"

I shook my head, my face screwed up. "No, that's not the case."

What had her mother filled her head with? I looked off to the side as Kai came out. "I'm going to head out, be back in half an hour."

"No, I'm going with you," I said. Before I could explain what would happen for the day, Ava walked away. "Ava."

She didn't look back, and I didn't blame her. The kid was messed up. She had her mother telling her one thing, and me giving her another story. I snatched up my jacket and stuffed a Glock into the back of my waistband before heading after Kai. He was already in the garage with the keys in his hands. I went around to the passenger side and hopped in.

"Where are you going?" Kai asked.

"I told you. With you."

"I don't need a babysitter."

"Look, Kai, I don't know what the issue is with you and your 'wife,'" I said using my two fingers to create quote marks in the air. "But we've nearly lost this vehicle twice now and after last night, I'm making damn sure it doesn't happen. Whoever those goons are that were looking for the Jeep, I expect them to be back this way today and this time we're going to be ready."

He slammed the door shut. I could tell he didn't like it but Kai wasn't one for arguing unless of course it was some jab against his home country. The whole idea that the Chinese might be involved in the attack upon America was absurd. The Russians, I could see but China?

The Jeep eased out into the humid morning air. The after smell of rain stung my nostrils as I wound the window up and we drove out of the neighborhood. In the light of day, it was easier to see the effects of the EMP. Vehicles littered the roads, their metal bones clogging up the road like a morgue of bodies.

Kai was silent for the first ten minutes of the trip. A band of sunlight came in and warmed my face as I leaned it against the window still feeling tired from a lack of sleep.

"She was an arranged marriage," he blurted out. I blinked. My eyes opened, and I looked over to him. "When I was twenty we got married."

I just let him continue. I was floored. Sure, we hadn't been in contact for a while but I had seen him around town and never once saw him with a Chinese woman. It was always some bronzed beauty. I just assumed he was having a difficult time finding the one.

"I thought the whole arranged marriage was some Indian thing?"

"It's not as common in China as it used to be, and it's considered old-fashioned now, but my father and mother believed in it."

"And you didn't want to go against their wishes?"

He shook his head.

"But you were an adult. You could do whatever you wanted."

"I know."

"It's 2017, Kai. An arranged marriage?"

He nodded without taking his eyes off the road.

"And what about the other women?"

He looked embarrassed now. His cool bravado had disappeared and in its place was a look of shame. "Just escorts."

I couldn't believe I was hearing this. This was a guy who never had a problem landing a date with a girl back in high school. Out of all of us I assumed he would end up with some beautiful woman and be the first one married. And now I was seeing another side to him that I wasn't sure I liked, I certainly didn't agree with it.

Especially after being cheated on. I knew what it was like to be on the other end of the stick. At least Theresa had the decency to try to cover up her infidelity but Kai had been brazen with it.

"Does she know?" I asked and then shook my head. "Of course she knows. How could she not in a town like this?"

"She does." He tightened his grip on the wheel, his knuckles turned white.

"How come she hasn't divorced you?"

"Because she sees other men too. We made it an open marriage."

My eyes really widened. "Are you serious? C'mon, you're pulling my leg."

He turned his head and his expression was flat.

"And yet you still live in the same house?"

He nodded. That just opened a whole can of worms. Questions spilled over in my mind about the logistics of how that worked and did the guys she was dating know about him and what about the escorts? Well they wouldn't care as they were just getting paid but... I exhaled hard. We had changed a lot over the years but this one caught me off guard. I didn't know what to make of it.

We traveled in silence for the rest of the journey

Between the disturbing Geiger counter readings, Theresa's lies and Kai's unusual marriage, this day was just full of surprises. I didn't even want to know what lay ahead.

Twenty One – Death's Door

The Jeep idled as I waited for Kai to emerge from his home. The vehicle was positioned on a rise at the end of a cul-de-sac providing a sweeping view of the town. Gone was the rain that had fallen almost non-stop the day before, in its place a hard sun bore down on us, browning the tips of the grass in the yards. While I waited for him, I continued to monitor radiation with the Geiger counter. It clicked, and the needle continued to hover between 110 and 115 CPM.

As my eyes drifted over the town, I could see several areas that had been affected by fire. Faint remnants of smoke twisted up into a cloudless sky while in other areas it was dark and full. I brought a pair of binoculars up to my eyes and leaned back in my seat searching for any signs of life. I saw a police officer on his bike shooting by in the distance, a cluster of people walking down Main Street and two people working under the hood of their vehicles. They must have thought they could get them working.

I lowered them as Kai emerged with a Chinese woman yelling at him and tossing his clothes all over the ground. He cast an embarrassed glance my way and continued engaging with her. She wasn't exactly eye candy. Neither attractive nor ugly, certainly unlike the kind of women I'd seen him out with. Was that why they'd agreed on an open marriage? Why not just divorce and be done with it? At least they wouldn't have to pretend they were married. It wasn't like he had to keep up appearances for anyone. This wasn't China. These weren't ancient times. No one was going to turn up their nose if they separated. People split up every day in the United States. It was worse than a pandemic. Very few seemed to want to tough it out through the hard times and every marriage had them. Once the honeymoon period was over, the things that once were adorable became pet peeves.

Kai charged back inside the house and she followed, slapping him on the back. I continued gazing out figuring he wasn't even close to being done. Perhaps the whole attack on the USA was the final straw, maybe now they would have a reason to part ways. *Crazy.* Mammoth Lakes had become a town ghost. Where had everyone gone? I didn't imagine people would up and leave just because of a power outage unless of course the cops had managed to somehow spread the word. We couldn't have been the only ones to know, so I figured people were taking precautions.

I was just about to bring the binoculars down when the glimmer of something caught my eye. I focused in on the west side of town and could see someone holding a shard of mirror in one hand. It was a white guy with long dreadlocks, and his clothes weren't anything out of the ordinary, though they did appear to be a little tatty. *Okay, what are you up to?* I traced a line from the direction he was pointing down the street to... then my eyes fell upon the truck. It was then I realized where they were. Jim's place. I zoomed in and could see them loading up a bunch of boxes into the back. One of them was acting as a lookout and notifying another who was farther down.

"Kai!" I yelled out. I dropped the binoculars and checked how much ammo I had in my magazine. I slammed it back in and hit the horn. Whoever these guys were, there was no way in hell that Jim would have allowed them to take anything from his store.

"Kai!" I shouted even louder and let the horn ring out. He emerged looking extremely pissed off.

"We need to go."

"I need longer, she's gone berserk and has cut up most of my clothes."

"Screw your clothes. Jim's place is being robbed."

A look of resignation, he was torn between staying and going.

"Forget it. I'll swing back and pick you up."

I slammed my foot on the gas and shot off over the rise. I sure as hell wasn't going to lose these guys this time. They had to have been following us to know about Jim's unless of course they were local in which case, they as well as many others would have thought about visiting him. The place was a survivalist's gold mine. Right now Jim's place was as enticing as an open vault of money to a thief.

My body bounced as the Jeep tore around the twists and turns that led down to his store. I had no idea what I was going to do when I got there, only that if they had managed to rob the place blind, that meant… well I didn't even want to think about it. I took a shortcut down Forest Trail expecting to slash a few minutes off my time only to come to a screeching halt because several stalled vehicles had blocked the road.

"Shit!" I backed up and spun the vehicle around and had to head back to Sierra Boulevard and take the other exit. Perhaps I might have made it if it wasn't for a group of individuals who had seen me heading back their way and had parked themselves in the middle, determined to stop the only vehicle on the road. I considered for a second going up the curb but there were kids out, I couldn't risk it. I slammed the brakes on and leaned over and locked both doors. I kept my one hand on the gun just out of view and watched as a guy in his forties came around and tapped on the window. He had a gaunt face, sunken eyes, long hair and a beard the texture of wool. There was a rifle slung over his shoulder. I cracked the window just a touch so I could hear him.

A yellowed grin stretched across his face while a cigarette hung from his teeth. He pulled it away and blew smoke through the window. "You want to step out."

"No."

"Listen, so far I have only seen two other vehicles that are operating and the police are using those, so I gotta ask myself, why don't they have yours?"

"I'm actually on my way to give it to them."

"Well that's real generous of you. I'll escort you as I'm a reserve police officer."

"Where's your ID?" I asked. My eyes flicked to the rearview mirror. A group had formed an arc around the Jeep and was peering inside looking for anything of value.

I honked the horn. "You want to keep those folks back."

The guy muttered something to them and they took a few steps back but they were still blocking the way. The pulse in my neck began to throb.

"Listen, I don't have my ID on me right now."

"Then it's best you stay back from the vehicle."

"Can't let you do that," he said swinging his rifle off his shoulder. Before he could raise it, I pulled the Glock and lifted it to the window and he froze.

"Now I figure it's going to take you a good few seconds to bring that up and squeeze the trigger. That's more time than I need to drill a hole in your skull." My eyes drifted around to the passenger side where two guys carrying baseballs bats were standing. There weren't many of them but enough to cause a problem if they wanted to. I'd never felt this threatened before but I figured it wouldn't take long for people to start getting antsy. "Now I'm warning you. Back up from the Jeep."

I slammed my hand against the horn and it blared. There was hesitation in the response of the man. He nodded slowly and took about four steps back. "Now tell your family or friends to get out of my way."

"You're not being neighborly. We're just trying to figure out what's going on. People are scared. They want answers."

"You want answers? The nation is at war. A nuclear bomb has detonated and fallout is coming this way. The police are doing what they can. I would advise you to get inside and batten down."

With that said, and the road ahead clear, I slammed on the accelerator and tore out of there looking back in the rearview mirror for just a second. They weren't doing anything anyone else wouldn't have under these conditions. Would they have harmed me? Who knew? In the world when everything functioned, people lashed out at others when they wanted something they didn't have, was it a far stretch of the imagination to think that they would do it now? People were confused and there was no way in hell the police would manage to spread the news to everyone.

As I got closer to Jim's place, I knew it was too late.

The truck was gone. I slammed my fist against the wheel and pulled into his driveway and killed the engine. Hopping out of the vehicle with my gun held low, I could hear the noise of thunder in the distance. Impossible. There were blue skies. Was it more nukes? I cringed and hurried towards the gate that was open. "Jim!" I yelled. "It's me, Brody."

The second I entered the backyard I deflected my eyes away from the sight of his dog. Lying on its side with two shots to the body, blood pooled.

"Jim!"

From inside I heard a groan; I burst into the house and found him lying in the corridor with his hand clamped over the left side of his abdomen. His face looked as if it had been battered. The second he saw me he looked scared and tried to move away. He must have thought I was one of them.

"Jim. It's me, Brody."

I passed by the store area; I glanced inside to see that half of his supplies had been cleared out. There were still a few weapons on the walls, and survival equipment remaining but not much. They obviously didn't have enough room in their truck for it all, which meant they would be back soon.

Dropping to a knee, I grabbed a hold of him and he let out a scared whimper like a child who thought they were going to be struck.

"It's okay, it's me, Brody."

"Brody."

I pulled back his hand to take a look. He'd already lost a lot of blood, and it didn't look good. I sprinted into the store area and grabbed up from behind the counter a med kit, ripped it open and took several of the bandages. I placed them against his wound and told him to apply pressure. His pulse was weak, and he kept drifting in and out of consciousness. There was a strong chance he wouldn't make it, so I hauled him up and literally carried him out. With one hand I opened the passenger side and laid him in the back.

I kept talking to him as he drifted in and out of

consciousness. "Stay with me, Jim."

He groaned and his eyes closed. I knew we didn't have long. Back in the vehicle I threw the gear stick into drive and gunned the engine. It roared as we shot down the streets, reaching speeds of up to eighty. On any ordinary day, I would have had to stop at traffic lights and stop signs but not today. I didn't even worry about other vehicles. I blew through neighborhoods making what usually would have been a ten-minute drive across town in less than five.

"You still with me, Jim?"

He let out a faint groan. It was less than before but something.

The tires squealed as I veered into the hospital grounds. There were no nurses outside, no patients waiting to be seen. I entered the open doors and shouted to the first nurse that I saw, who was helping someone else.

"Gunshot wound."

She rose from her seat and shouted to someone in the

corridor before following me out to the truck. I was pleased that at least the nurses and doctors hadn't abandoned their posts. The reality was, they would continue just as they did in times of war. That was just their way. Hard-working people who didn't receive a lot of thanks were still working, still trying to help the afflicted. When I opened the doors for them to bring out Jim, a nurse leaned inside and I went around to help bring him out. That's when they noticed he was no longer breathing.

"I'm getting no pulse."

Another orderly came along and helped bring his body out onto the ground. Right there in front of the hospital on the hard asphalt they began performing CPR. One of the orderlies raced inside and returned with a mobile battery-operated defibrillator. The nurse tore his shirt open, and they placed the pads, pressed a button on the unit and a second later his body jolted. The nurse then continued with chest pumping and rescue breathing for another two minutes before she stopped and shook her head.

"There must be something you can do."

She shook her head and offered back a despondent look.

I pressed two fingers against the bridge of my nose.

"Sorry, he's gone."

I nodded slowly and went to get back into my blood-strained Jeep.

"Sir, hold on a minute. Who is he? Who are you?"

I started the engine and spoke to her through the window. "His name is Jim Brewster, the owner of Atomic Jim's. It doesn't matter who I am. Just a friend."

"Sir, you really should stay until we can get a police officer."

"It was an accident. Someone shot him by accident."

I pulled away and could see the woman return to her colleagues. I could have said that someone murdered him but it didn't matter now. Within a matter of twenty-four hours others would die, if they hadn't already. Whether it would be at the hands of another or simply from the fallout that was to be determined. It would get worse from here on out. Police weren't going to begin an investigation. The few who were still on shift and not sleeping from having worked crazy hours last night would be either alerting town folk or preventing chaos from erupting. More than likely both.

As I drove back through the streets on my way to pick up Kai, I wondered how anyone could have reacted so violently, so soon. Some would have said that violence wouldn't have started for three, maybe five days after a disaster but that was just wishful thinking. The truth was, people would take whatever steps they felt were justified in order to survive, even if that meant taking innocent human life.

Nothing could be done now to help Jim but there was something that could be done to prevent them from harming anyone else. The store wasn't completely emptied which meant there was a good possibility they'd be back and when they did, we'd be waiting. It was time to turn the tables.

Twenty Two – Catch a Mouse

Kai was waiting outside with a cigarette in his mouth. An unusual sight being as he didn't smoke. His clothes were still strewn all over the ground though some now stuffed into a suitcase. I put the gear in park, and heard the thud of the case. As he came around to the passenger side, he stepped back and squinted at the handle.

"Is that blood?" he asked and then opened the door to get his answer. When he saw the mess on the back seat, his eyes grew wide. "What the hell?"

"Get in, I'll explain."

He jumped in and I brought him up to speed. While he continued to puff away on his cigarette, I reached over and took it from his hand.

"I know, I shouldn't but…" Before he could say anything I took a hard drag and then tossed the rest out the window. I didn't care to know where he got it from or what other skeletons he had in the closet. My mind was too preoccupied with what had just happened and what we were going to do. It felt as though I was standing on the precipice of a vast gap, deciding if I should jump or walk away. I knew that I had a choice to make, and this one would lead to more bloodshed.

"You want to slow down?" Kai said gripping the handle above the door. The streets were mostly empty, with some of the diners and coffee shops along Main Street nothing more than burnt-out husks. The smell of burning plastic mixed with pine saturated the air.

"We need to get back and tell the others to secure the street because no matter how this goes down today, they are going to come."

"Who? Who is going to come, Brody?"

"Have you not been listening to a word I've said?" I flashed him a sideways glance. "The men who fired at us, the same ones who busted up Tracey's and her husband's faces, the same ones who killed Jim and his dog, and the same ones who are going to show up again looking for this Jeep, and whatever else they think we have."

"We don't have to do this. We can lock ourselves in the fallout shelter and come out in two weeks. Hell, I could use a break from society right now."

I veered around some burnt-out vehicles. They didn't look as though they had collided with anything, which meant someone had set them on fire. For light? For fun? Or had it been used as a distraction? That's when the cogs of my mind started connecting as Kai droned on about how the world didn't need a nuke to explode for it to go to shit, it had already gone to shit. People were killing each other long before they had a good reason.

I interrupted his line of thinking. "We need to create a distraction."

"What?" Kai said

"Today. If we don't, the cops will show up. Society might be on the brink of collapse but it's not there yet. Emergency services are still operating as best as they can and so are the police."

"Are you losing it? You are really thinking of doing

this, aren't you?" Kai asked.

"Jim might have been a paranoid control freak, but he was a good man. He wanted peace. That's all he wanted. That's why he kicked us out. A man has a right to protect his home and business. They showed up and killed his dog and shot him in the stomach and left him to bleed out. For what? Some of his stock? Hell, we could have done the same, but we didn't."

"That's because we're civilized," Kai said glancing out the window.

"You really think so? How civilized are we, Kai? Huh? Because we haven't been pushed into a corner yet? Is that why? Because we haven't killed anyone? Because believe me, before this month is over, we are going to have blood on our hands."

"We don't have to."

I snapped. "Wake up, Kai. What did your father teach you?"

"Self-defense was only to be used in situations where there were no other options. Right now we have other options."

"That sounds like a passive approach to me."

"Whatever, Brody. You are just angry and looking for a reason to lash out."

"Am I? Maybe I am. You didn't look into that man's eyes as the light went out. You don't have his blood on your hands."

"Oh and you want to get more blood on your hands? If you wanted to do that why didn't you join the military?"

"I could ask you the same thing."

I eased off the gas as a group of women crossed the road. They looked nervous but determined and purposeful in wherever they were heading. We continued on our way as the sun pushed high in the sky, and a distant rumble of thunder rang out. The clear blue sky was now almost gone as thick gray clouds rolled in. I reached over and turned on the Geiger counter and stuck the probe out the window again. It clicked and the needle shot up to 106 CPM.

"It's dropped a little."

"I told you it might. We probably picked up a spike of background radiation."

"Or this damn thing doesn't work."

It was old and even though the battery test had worked that didn't mean it was accurately reading. Inside the unit it had a sealed ionization chamber and if any air got inside through rust or a weld breaking, it would no longer work correctly. Ideally we needed two to be sure.

"Anyway, there's a good reason why I didn't join the military," I said.

"Oh, I would love to hear. It seems all of us skipped it."

"Todd didn't. He enlisted but bailed before he was shipped out."

"Yeah, I bet he did. Let me guess, it would cut into his gaming time?" Kai snorted.

"Actually he stayed back to look after his mother."

"Oh." Kai paused for a second feeling like an idiot. Sure, some might have said that wasn't a good excuse, and maybe not, but who was to say what a person should or shouldn't do? Everyone had to live with their own decisions. He wasn't any less a man because of his choice. "So what about you?"

"I was ready to enlist. Fit as a fiddle. I have no excuses except…" I trailed off.

There was a long pause and Kai reached his own conclusion. "You didn't join because of Sam?"

I tapped the steering wheel thinking about my brother again. Memories flooded in. The day we received news of his death. The well-dressed military personnel who showed up at the door and delivered the news. My father breaking down in tears and my mother collapsing into his arms.

"I couldn't do it. I couldn't put them through that again. It nearly killed them last time. I really wanted to but the thought of what it would do to them if I didn't come home…" I shook my head. A spring of emotion welled up in me. Mostly regret. "Anyway, I went back and forth. Spoke to Mack at great lengths and surprisingly he understood. I thought he was going to tell me to stop being a bitch or give me some macho speech about how my parents would be proud of me but he never did."

"At least you have a reason."

I glanced at him and Kai dropped his chin a little. He removed the wedding band from his finger and tossed it out the window.

"So it's over?"

"Yep. I tried to explain to her what was happening but she wouldn't listen. She said she finally found someone that she wanted to settle down with. The guy was even in our house — comforting her and helping her get through this difficult time. Can you believe that?" He shook his head. "I can't blame her. It was to be expected."

"Did you feel anything for her?"

"Not at first. I absolutely resented my parents for making the arrangements. She was the same. She didn't want to come to America, and she certainly didn't look pleased when she saw me at the end of the aisle. But we each dealt with it as best as we could for a few years and then I said if she wanted to get a divorce she could. But she wouldn't do it. I was going to go ahead but… well, I know this is going to sound crazy but we decided to see other people. We figured if it didn't go well, perhaps we would realize that what we had was good and worth working on." He took a deep breath. "I guess we just got lost in it. I would come home and sleep in a different room, she did the same. When our families would visit, we would put the rings back on and act as though nothing was wrong."

I couldn't make sense of it. I couldn't understand anyone getting married without knowing the person or at least wanting to be married to them. Then again, I had to wonder how different it was from regular marriages that ended up in divorce. People came together under the premise they were in love only to find out years later they hated each other, or had nothing in common. Was love blind?

The Jeep bounced into the driveway and I reversed

back into the garage. Marlin was the first one out of the house, and I spotted Todd halfway down the block chatting with several of the neighbors.

"What's going on?" Marlin said in a cheerful voice until I hopped out and he saw blood on me. "You hurt?"

"It's not my blood. I need to talk with everyone, inside."

Kai came around the vehicle and Marlin strained his neck looking to see if Kai's wife was with him.

"Let me guess, she wasn't gangbusters for the idea of a ménage à trois so you killed her?"

Kai passed by him without saying anything.

"You could have at least brought Misty and Kristy with you."

It didn't take long to gather all the guys together. I didn't want to involve Bridget in it but she was adamant that if we were staying there, she wanted to know what we were up to. It probably didn't help that I still had blood on my hands. Jason stood off to one side leaning against the wall waiting to pounce but in the mood I was in, I was liable to knock him out without any reason.

"The men who visited here yesterday, the same ones who shot at us, we know they're coming back so I propose we strike first before they do. Right now we might be able to rally the neighborhood to secure the streets with stalled vehicles but there is no time to teach them how to fire weapons. Maybe if we had a week or two but we don't have that. They hit Jim's place this morning. Jim's dead."

Eyes widened, and I gave a moment for that to sink in. They needed to understand these weren't people who were going to be open to negotiation. It was the very reason why they fired at us in the store. Desperate or not, they were ready to kill. Hell, I had to wonder if they already had before the attack on America.

"Who are they, Brody?" Jason asked with a look of disdain.

"Your guess is as good as mine. Look, there's still a lot at Jim's store that we can use and you can bet they are going to swing back sometime today and get the rest."

"Go to the cops, let them handle it," Jason said.

"Under any other conditions I would agree, Jason, but this is not something they are going to handle. Those men are coming, I'm telling you, they will be back. Now even if the cops have a vehicle to get across town, could they get over here in time if they fired on us? Maybe, but highly unlikely because we have no way of communicating with them."

"Actually that's not true."

Jason disappeared out of the room. While he was gone we continued discussing what I had in mind.

"I say we go over to Jim's and wait for them to show up."

"Fuck yeah, sounds good to me," Todd and Marlin said almost in unison.

"And what then, Brody? Huh? You going to have a shootout?" Chase chuckled. "Please, we are not fifteen anymore. And their weapons don't shoot paintballs. This is serious shit you are suggesting. What are you going to do, huh?"

I didn't say anything. It wasn't that I hadn't chewed it over, but the fact was we were all in new territory. Chase was right. This wasn't some game in the backwoods. Some training routine that Mack had put us through where we would all come out of it laughing and covered in paint. People could die. It wasn't a decision you made at the drop of a hat. Sure, if someone was shooting at you, then it was self-defense. But going in with the intention of killing them just so they wouldn't kill us? Were we ready to step over the edge and do that? How did that make us any better than them?

"Right," Chase said. "So I think this discussion is over. We stay here. We notify the police like Jason said, and we let them handle it. If they show up here, we'll deal with it. But I'm not going in there and killing anyone. I'm sorry about Jim, Brody, but Mack wouldn't have wanted this."

With that said, Chase walked back into the house.

Jason emerged holding walkie-talkies that Mack had stored inside a Faraday cage which was made from a galvanized steel garbage can, a cardboard box and antistatic bags, or otherwise known as EMP bags, to protect the electronics. That was just one of the ways they could be protected.

Perhaps I was responding out of emotion. None of them were there with Jim so of course they were viewing this from a different perspective, one that was out of sight, out of mind. However, all I could see was blood. I looked down at my hands and felt myself getting riled up by the injustice. The police weren't going to do shit about this. That's why I said it was an accident. They were already pushed to the limit and trying to provide service to an entire town with nothing more than bicycles, and perhaps one vehicle.

Bridget came over and placed a hand on my shoulder. "Why don't you go clean up, Brody? Ava is inside, I'm sure she wants to see you."

"I doubt it." I looked at the others for a second. "We should still go over there and gather together what we can from his store before others loot it."

"Great, so now you don't want to kill someone, you

just want to commit theft," Jason muttered before shaking his head and striding away.

Twenty Three – Malcolm

Von's Supermarket was a complete disaster, a charred mess that was still smoldering.

The Jeep rumbled to a standstill as we soaked in the sight of what remained of the west side. Someone had seriously gone to work overnight lighting fires all over the town. The few police officers we passed on our way over glanced at us but made no attempt to pull us over. Blackened by smoke, their weary faces painted a picture of the previous night. Now as they looked on, they squinted, and then continued cycling. It was if their orders had changed, or perhaps they had given up like the two officers who committed suicide in the aftermath of Katrina.

I still recalled reading the article in the paper; the words of the police chief were burned into my mind.

We had no food, no water, no ammunition, no vehicles, no gas; we had to scrounge equipment to fight this battle.

In many ways that was exactly what they were facing now, except there were only fifteen officers and not all of them would be on shift at any given time. No one could stay up for forty-eight hours straight, which meant fewer officers were on the streets maintaining order. And with the town spread wide, it was virtually impossible to cover it without a vehicle. The odds were stacked against emergency services and I imagined it wouldn't be long before the chief would give the order for officers to return home and protect themselves.

Whatever supplies remained in stores would soon be stolen as people came to the realization of what had happened. Word would have begun to spread, panic would set in as people tried to grapple with what a nuclear attack meant. Most wouldn't know what to do, so they would act out of fear and ignorance assuming the worst, and figuring that it was over.

"We should have killed that thieving bastard the moment we had hold of him," Marlin said.

"Your state of mind worries me," Chase said. "It's only

the second day after the attack and you are looking to start murdering people? Are you completely out of your mind?"

"Wake up and smell the coffee, Chase. We are at war. Troops might not be bearing down on us right now but it will only be a matter of time. Then what? You going to sit by and complain like a pussy? Tiffany has really done a number on you, hasn't she?"

"Careful."

"Or what?"

"I'm just saying. Be careful what you say, Marlin. You're walking on thin ice."

He snorted. "What month after you got married did she book the appointment to get your balls chopped off?"

Chase lunged forward from the rear seat and grabbed a hold of him. Todd tried to intervene and got an elbow in the face.

"Guys!" Kai shouted. They wouldn't listen so he grabbed a hold of Chase by a pressure point at the back of his neck. It immediately caused him to squirm and holler in pain.

"Okay, okay," Chase said, tossing up his hands. Marlin shook his jacket out; there was a slight tear. Kai released him and momentarily he sat back, I say momentarily as it lasted all of three seconds before he lunged forward again and started laying into Marlin.

"Oh for God's sake, Chase." I pushed him back. "Quit it."

"Yeah, stop being a bitch," Marlin said.

"I'm warning you," Chase yelled. "I'll fucking get out and walk if he keeps talking shit."

"You should, you could use the exercise," Marlin shot back. He really didn't have an off switch. I immediately leaned between the two of them, then asked Kai to come up front so Chase couldn't get at him. It was like dealing with two teenagers.

"Why did you bring us here, anyway?" Chase asked.

"I had to see it for my own eyes."

In reality I just wanted to get a better handle on who we were dealing with. Was it them? More than likely.

Who else in their right mind would have set a grocery store on fire? It was a vindictive act. Senseless and perhaps a personal jab at me.

"Well now you've seen it, can we go?" Chase said in a demanding tone.

"What is up with you, man?" Todd asked. He was the only one besides Kai that was all chilled out. He sat in the back puffing on a cigarette as though we were just going for a country drive.

"I just want to get back to the shelter."

"Where's Tiffany?"

And there it was. The question all of us had been meaning to ask him since he returned. We kind of had an idea, but we wanted to hear it from him.

"She wouldn't come back. Told me that I was talking shit about a nuclear bomb. She didn't believe me. Said this was just another attempt to control her. I mean control her? She's the only one that does the controlling. I have bent over backwards to please that woman and not once has she shown any sense of gratitude. It's never been enough. Do more, Chase. You are in the wrong, Chase. You make me feel this way, Chase. I mean I never enlisted because she was pregnant with Sofia; I turned down some well-paid jobs that came up in Seattle because she wanted us to stay local. Heck, I even took a shitty job as a TSA agent at Mammoth Yosemite Airport just so I could please her old man."

"Please her old man?"

"He works there, holds a managing position and whatnot. Anyway, you know, her choosing to not come to the shelter is one thing, but denying our children. That's where I draw the line. We had this huge fight. She told me it was over. She wants a divorce. Apparently I couldn't give her the life she wanted. As if it's all on me to give her the life? What about my life? I've literally given up my life for that woman."

Chase punched the back of the driver's seat and I jerked forward.

"Not everyone is going to believe it, Chase," Kai said. "It's just the way it is."

"Oh that's easy for you to say, you don't have any kids."

"No I don't but I understand what it's like to have a complicated marriage," Kai muttered and returned to staring at the scorched building

"Ditto," I said.

There was silence for a few minutes. It was crazy to think that thirty years later we were all struggling with the challenges and responsibility of our decisions. Life hadn't turned out exactly the way we wanted, that was for sure. And this, well, this attack was like the straw the broke the camel's back.

"If it's any consolation, Chase, I never enlisted either," Marlin said.

"Yeah but you have a thriving business."

"Yeah and no. It's not doing as well as it looks. However, I did join the reserves for a while but got kicked out."

Chase let out a laugh then screwed up his face. "Why?"

"Disobeying orders. Why do you think I work for

myself?"

"Because you're a dick," Chase said, casting a smile. We broke into laughter. That was one thing that hadn't changed in all the time we'd known each other. One moment we could be at each other's throats but the next we'd press on without giving it another thought. I think it was because knew each other well. We understood when one of us was being a jerk even if it was bad timing.

"Brody, what about Jen Lawson? You not going to swing by and pick her up?"

"She flew back to San Francisco to tie up a few loose ends the day we headed out on the camping trip."

All of us went quiet. Had she made it? Finally someone good had come into my life and I didn't know if she was dead or alive.

"We should go," I said giving the engine some gas and turning the Jeep around to head back to Jim's place. Along the way we heard gunfire, it would be a sound that would become all too familiar as folks took matters into their own hands.

As we rounded the corner that led down to his store, I swerved in behind a minivan and killed the engine.

"What's up?"

I made a gesture with my head. From behind the vehicle we could see the truck had returned. Two guys stood by it holding what appeared to be AR-15's while another was going back and forth and dumping boxes in the back.

"I bet they think they hit the mother lode."

"Well that's that. Let's head back," Chase said.

Marlin swiveled in his seat. "You can't be serious."

"There are cops to handle stuff like this."

I turned to him. "You saw them yourself. You think they're ready to deal with this? They are exhausted and aren't able to respond fast enough. This is down to us. Now I'm not going to tell you guys what to do here. If you think we should go back, we'll go but maybe we should vote on it."

"Vote? Are you kidding? Screw that shit," Marlin went to get out, gripping his Springfield M1A. All of us were kitted out in tactical vests and fatigues, even though I didn't expect them to return this fast, I figured if they did we would at least be ready.

"Marlin, I don't agree with this," Chase spat.

"Then you stay here."

"Marlin," I hollered. "Hold up." I hopped out of the vehicle then looked back inside as Kai and Todd crawled over Chase to get out. "You want to stay here and keep an eye on the vehicle?"

"Brody. We did not agree to this. What happened to voting?"

I shrugged as he attempted to plead with me. "We have enough back at the shelter to weather this out. C'mon, let's not do this."

"For now we do but what happens after? Marlin is right. What happens when they show up on our doorstep fully armed, kitted out and more prepared than we are? What happens if foreign troops arrive? We need what's in that store and right now they are cleaning it out. You want to help, help, otherwise stay out of the way."

I slammed the door shut, and we darted from one vehicle to the next trying to remain out of view. There were only a few ways we could catch them off guard. One was to cause a distraction and lure away the two standing out front, then slip in; the other was to approach from the rear. We were going to do both.

I gave a signal "Kai, Todd, circle around back. Stay out of view."

They nodded and dashed across the street, staying low and out of sight.

"And what do you have in mind?" Marlin asked peering around the corner of a Honda Accord.

"You'll see."

I shifted position and moved down, and as I came up alongside each vehicle, I checked the handle to see if it was unlocked. A few were locked but there was a small hatchback open. I stuck it in neutral, popped the trunk and moved around to check if there was a gas canister in the back. There wasn't. Just a bunch of bags of clothes that smelled like they'd been soiled. I winced and dropped down and pointed to the vehicle behind us. "Anything?"

Marlin shook his head. I went back to the vehicle and withdrew a hunting knife and used it to cut off a long strip of cloth from the seats. I opened the gas cap and stuck it inside and kept pushing it down until a small amount dropped out.

"Listen up. As soon as those guys turn to assist the one coming out with the boxes. We're going to roll this sucker out and…"

Before I could finish, I heard the Jeep start up. I shuffled back to see Chase pulling out. "What the hell is he doing?"

He flashed me a wink as he drove by and pulled up slowly in front of the truck.

"Hey fellas!"

From behind all I could see was a raised hand, and then the crack of a gunshot as he fired out the open passenger window. The round struck the truck's windshield and shattered it. Startled, the two guys dropped to the ground. Before they could do anything, Chase hit the accelerator, tires spun and smoke filled the air as he tore out of there. The men rushed out into the middle of the street and unloaded a few rapid bursts but it was too late, Chase veered around the corner out of sight.

Distracted, they didn't hear us come up behind them. I placed the barrel at the base of the tallest guy's skull.

"Don't even breathe!"

Marlin took their rifles. I clamped my forearm around the guy's neck and we dragged them out of view and then used the butt of our guns to knock them unconscious. Moving quickly, we hurried across the street before the other guy could return with more boxes. I shouldered my AR-15 and advanced towards the gate, my finger hovering near the trigger.

Before we even entered the backyard, shots were fired twice, then four times, and we pressed our backs against the stone wall and waited. I raised a fist and signaled for Marlin to take the other side and see if he could determine what was going on while I slung my rifle over my shoulder and climbed up onto the top of the wooden fence and peered over.

There was no one in the backyard. I dropped down, brought my rifle up and pressed on, hugging the wall close. As I dashed past a window, glass shattered and several more gunshots rang out. Both of us stayed low and looked up to see the barrel of a gun pointing out and firing towards the back area of the yard.

In the distance were Kai and Todd. Before I could suggest an idea, Marlin jumped up, grabbed the end of the rifle sticking out and yanked it forward, while bringing up a handgun and shoving it into the window.

"Flinch and you are going to be pushing up daisies."

Another gunshot echoed, and a man dropped near the gate. It was one of theirs. He'd sneaked up from behind. He must have exited from the front and doubled around. Now he was lying on the ground, a pool of blood slowly forming near his chest.

Kai and Todd came rushing up to join us. Todd's hands were shaking.

"Is he dead?"

I went over and checked to make sure that there was no one else coming before I flipped the guy over. He was average height and build, white, and his neck and arms were heavily tattooed. I ran a hand over my face. He couldn't have been more than seventeen years of age. It seemed pretty obvious from the get-go that he was dead. The bullet was lodged on the left of his chest. I placed two fingers against his neck, even though I knew there would be no pulse.

I shook my head.

"Shit, shit," Todd kept repeating over and over again as a hand came up to the back of his head.

"You had to do it," Kai said slapping him on the chest. "If you didn't he would have fired on them."

"Shit! Oh my god." Todd dropped to his knees and then vomited. Meanwhile Marlin hadn't taken his eyes off the guy inside the window. While Todd threw up his breakfast, Kai and I entered the house and cleared the rooms. We found the guy in the kitchen leaning forward against the counter. He couldn't have been more than nineteen years of age. He was tall, lean and fair-haired, and his eyes were wild as if he was on drugs. I grabbed him by the back of the collar and forced him down to the ground.

"Where are you taking this gear?"

He said nothing but sneered and looked down. Kai gave him a slap. "Answer him."

"He's going to kill you," he muttered in a low tone, his lips drawing together and his nostrils flaring.

"Who?"

The guy looked up and snorted. I glanced at Kai, then pulled the guy up and slammed him against the counter until his toes were barely touching the ground. "Who!" I yelled in his face, frustration taking over.

"Malcolm."

Twenty Four – Rising Storm

A clap of thunder startled us. Flashes of lightning followed it as more dark clouds rolled in and squeezed out what remained of ocean blue sky. Our nerves were fried as we gathered together the three survivors and pressed them up against the wall in the backyard. The two we'd overwhelmed were in their late twenties. They stared at the body of the kid and murmured between themselves.

I swallowed hard, and we grouped together just out of earshot.

"What do we do?" Todd asked. Naturally he was in shock and scared. Until now, none of us had killed anyone. Regardless who had killed him, it was affecting us all.

"I say we take their weapons and cut 'em loose."

Marlin coughed. "And let them run back to this Malcolm character? No, I say we execute 'em."

"Okay, you need to step away from the gun. No

wonder they kicked you out of the reserves," Chase said before Marlin squared up to him.

"At least I had the balls to join something."

"Stop it. This isn't a pissing match. Put your dicks away. I say we take the truck and what's left and get back to Mack's. It will be dark soon and I've got Ava to think about, and Amanda is probably wondering…"

"Yeah, you've got Ava, he's got Amanda, what about me?" Kai asked.

"You made your bed, now lie in it," Marlin barked.

Kai looked at me with a confused expression, maybe a little anger. He thumbed at him. "Did you tell him?" Kai said.

"No. Let's just load up the truck with what we have before the cops show up."

"Let's get out of here now. This is a fuck-up on an epic scale."

"What, because I killed someone who was about to kill these two?"

We all stared at each other blankly. Questions swirled

in our minds. Each of us wanting to find some way to justify what had happened but there was no easy way through this. What was done was done. The kid wasn't coming back, and neither was society by the looks of it.

"Whatever we are going to do, we need to act fast. That storm is heading this way and those clouds are dark. Which means black rain. Have we got the Geiger counter?"

I looked back at the three who were sneering at us.

There was hesitation by Todd. "It's in the Jeep."

Kai shot off to get it. While he was gone I went over to find out who this Malcolm guy was. Assessing the threat was critical right now. I loathed the idea of killing, the world was full of it, and yet when it came to survival, some would say the weak would die first. Perhaps they were right but did that mean society no longer had a choice in the matter? What made us human or animals? External forces pressing in against us, or the thought that we could get away with killing and no one would be the wiser? Truth be told we didn't know what would happen if we let them go. There was a fifty-fifty chance they were just as scared as we were.

"Please, just let us go," a guy with a goatee said. "We don't want any trouble."

"Shut up, you pussy," another said before spitting a wad of phlegm near my foot. "Fuck them. You want to kill us, go ahead. Either way he'll find you. This is just the beginning."

The other one was quiet and looked despondent.

"Who is Malcolm?"

At first they said nothing.

"Who is Malcolm?" I yelled even louder. Chase came over and pulled at my jacket. "We need to go. Now!"

"I'm not leaving until I find out."

I turned my attention back to the men.

"It doesn't matter. That was his little brother Dwayne you killed. You are so fucked!"

"Shut the hell up!" Marlin smashed him in the face with the butt of his gun before I could stop him. I dragged him off to one side. "You better reel that anger in fast or I'll put a bullet in you."

"You won't do shit, Brody." He jabbed his finger into my chest. "Just like you never had the balls to join the army. You don't have it in you to do what's needed."

In that moment I think the stress and frustration of what was taking place took over, and I lashed out and clobbered him across the jaw. Marlin jerked back and wiped blood from his lips, looked at it before returning his gaze to me. I returned to the men and pulled up the tattooed one that was mouthy and grabbed him by the throat.

"Who the fuck is he?"

"If you don't know that, you should get out of town now."

I was about to lose my own cool when the guy who was still staring at the body spoke.

"You never heard of the Devil's Reapers?"

"Outlaw motorcycle gang," Marlin muttered. "Had a few come into my business a couple of years back. Called the cops."

"Then you know," he said before looking back at the dead kid. Todd walked back across the yard to a shed and returned with a wet tarp and draped it over him. We regrouped again to discuss what to do.

"I'm telling you. If we kill them, they aren't going to know. Gunfire has been going off all over this town. Anyone could have done it."

"Of course they are going to know," Chase said. "How the hell do you think they found this place? Since that run-in with Markus, they've been eyeing our Jeep. That's how they knew about Crestwood Hills."

"So we put a bullet in them."

"We're not doing that," Todd said.

Marlin scoffed. "Says the guy who just killed a kid."

Todd lunged forward and pushed back. "Enough. We're not killing them."

"Then you are signing our death warrant."

"There is a fifty-fifty chance they won't say anything. Think about it. If you fuck up a job, how quick are you to go tell your manager? If you screw up in a motorcycle club, there are repercussions. They are just as screwed as we are, if not more."

Marlin shrugged. "So you just want to let them walk out of here?" he scoffed. "What part of we are at war don't you understand?"

"We are not at war with people in this town," I said.

"We are now."

Todd looked down. The guilt must have been crushing him. I placed a hand on his shoulder. "You did what you had to. There was no other choice. But right now we have a choice. Maybe tomorrow we have to kill, or the day after but today we don't. Not without good reason."

"Good reason? How's survival for a reason? Being proactive. Wasn't it you that was harping on about coming back here and getting justice for Jim's death? Huh? Or was that all hot air? Like the way you talked about joining the military."

"This is not about what we did with our lives, Marlin. Why does everything with you need to be a competition?

We are on the same side here."

"Are we, Brody? Because the way it seems to me, you want me to get on board with what you want. The way I see it. One is dead, three more isn't going to be an issue."

"Would you have made that call if none of this had happened?"

Marlin stared at me studying my face. "Don't twist this or try to make me out to be the bad guy here. What I'm suggesting is for the self-preservation of us all. Now if you all have a problem with squeezing the trigger, I'll do it." His eyes bounced between us. "I don't have a problem bearing that weight. But I'm not letting them walk."

"You don't get to choose."

He scoffed. "Of course I don't. It's always about what you want, Brody, isn't it? Even back when we were kids, you always had to lead the way."

"Mack chose me to take that position, I didn't volunteer for it."

"But you took it. You could have let me take that slot."

Chase pushed into the small gap that was between our chests. "Would you both shut the hell up! We need to leave now. I have to make another trip back to Bridgeport and get my kids. That's if Tiffany will let them go."

I nodded. "Let's get out of here."

We began walking back towards the gate when I heard a gun cocking. Marlin was still standing in the same spot though now he was holding up his S&W revolver. I darted into view with my hands up. "No! This is not what we do."

"The weak die, now it's either them or us."

I moved forward blocking his view of the three men. "Listen up, Marlin. What's happened here, happened but we are no better than them if we kill without reason."

"We have a reason. I just told you."

"What? So you want to kill every single person we come in contact with who you think is a threat? If that's the case, you need mental help."

Perhaps it was because I had worked in a job that required me to defuse situations, or maybe I just wasn't ready to take human life but there had to be another way. I didn't expect them to show mercy because we had. Whoever this Malcolm was, there was no doubt he would want revenge, but that was only if they told him. I looked back at their faces; except for the one in the middle, the rest had an expression of fear. No matter what kind of group they had fallen in with, they weren't prepared to die for it.

"Go ahead, shoot," the one with tattoos said. "He's going to kill us anyway."

I couldn't believe someone would go to that extreme, then again I understood what it meant to lose a brother. After losing Sam, I wanted to enlist simply to find an outlet for my anger. I wanted others to hurt. I wanted others to die and know what it felt like to feel my pain. That's why I was driven to ask Mack to train us. It wasn't pressure by Chase, as I had shot down his requests numerous times before. It was purely motivated by self-interest, and a desire to find a way to deal with my grief. But I saw what it had done to my parents. Few people in the world saw that side of death. Those who justified killing always painted a picture that it was the strong thing to do, the right thing, the just and unquestionably the American way. But that was just all bullshit masking as bravado. Any fool could squeeze a trigger and take a human life. It took courage to walk away. Maybe not in the midst of a war but this wasn't war. We were at war with North Korea, not each other.

And yet on a mini-scale this was exactly what was going on in the world.

Nations living in fear of each other.

Nations dividing over differences.

Nations ready to kill each other.

I shook my head. "Don't do it, Marlin. Put the gun down."

His eyes drifted from the three men to mine. He exhaled hard and put his weapon away.

"Coward!" the man said behind me.

I could tell Marlin wanted to react. I shook my head. Weak people only knew how to use their words as weapons. It was a weak attempt at positioning themselves as being right and yet it failed to harm those who could see through it. We finished loading up the truck and Jeep with what remained inside Jim's store, which wasn't much as they had already done the heavy lifting. There was an arsenal of weapons, ammo and survival gear that would see us through the coming months.

"Hey guys, check this out."

Kai had got an even higher CPM. It was too dangerous to stay outside. There was a chance it was another spike and it would drop but with all the clouds rolling in, and the echo of thunder I was pretty certain that black rain was on its way. A dark, greasy mixture of radioactive dust and ash that would contaminate everything and make structures glisten like oil.

I slapped the truck on the side and told Marlin to head straight back. Kai and Chase went with him while I jumped in the Jeep with Todd. He was still shaking and overcome by having taken a life. As the engine growled, and we peeled away, I tried my best to reassure him that

that what he'd done, had saved lives. Unless he focused on that it was going to tear him apart.

As soon as we returned to Crestwood Hills, several of the neighbors came out and followed us over to Mack's. The first order of business was getting everything inside, the next was to distribute out to others what we didn't need and then secure the roadway. There was only one road in and out unless of course we exited via the back of the houses and traveled down a steep incline and across to Juniper Springs Drive.

I put Todd in charge of distributing out to those in the community. It would keep his mind off the death for a short while. Bridget and Jason came out to meet us.

"How did it go?" Bridget asked.

"Yeah, what's it feel like to be a criminal?" Jason interjected with his self-righteous attitude. After what we had just been through, I wanted to drop him there. There was no thanks to be found in the risk we'd taken. Like many others who preferred to sit inside their ivory towers, point fingers and spout an opinion, that's all they were good at.

But it was those willing to make the tough decisions that would ultimately survive. Those who would take risks, roll the dice and weather the outcome. Tactically sound or not, it didn't matter. All that mattered was that we were standing at the end of the day.

A splatter of dark rain landed on my hand. More droplets began to fall. I gazed up at the storm that was rising and rolling over us like death itself. A mass of darkness, a menacing presence casting its shadow over the neighborhood. I yelled to everyone to hurry and seek shelter indoors. With trouble upon us we didn't even have time to secure a perimeter.

The wolf was at our door, ready to consume all that stepped out into its line of sight.

Twenty Five – Black Rain

Inside, I barked out orders asking someone to check that the vents had been sealed. We were closing in on forty-eight hours since the attack and according to Kai, the fallout intensity would have dropped to 1 percent. How dangerous that was still depended on the blast and how close it was to us. All I could be sure about was that remaining outside would lead to some form of contamination. The rainstorm was both a blessing and a curse. The storm would carry fallout but at the same time clear it out, eventually.

I dashed around the house double-checking the vents and windows, paranoid that someone had forgot. Sure enough, in the basement the dryer was still attached. I wrenched the tubing off the wall and searched around for some duct tape to seal up the hole. On my knees wrapping the silver tape tightly around the area, I hollered upstairs, "Bridget, where's Ava?"

"She's in the fallout shelter," she yelled back.

I nodded. "Good, I'm going to help the guys bring in the rest of the supplies and then we'll close the hatch and wait this out until the storm passes."

I hurried upstairs and along the corridor and ducked back into the garage. Todd, Marlin and Jason had formed a line and were tossing supplies to each other and setting them down inside the corridor. Chase brushed past me lugging in armfuls of clothing, some of which were CBRN suits.

"How many of those do we have?"

"Four here, but there were a couple more on the truck which is with Tracey and Matt Harper. I just let them take it. We have enough."

Marlin tossed a box of MREs my way. We worked fast and in silence, each of us mindful of the danger we faced. It was one thing to learn the theory from Mack, another to experience it. It didn't matter how prepared we were, doubt ate away at the back of my mind. Had we forgotten something? What if the shelter didn't suffice? Then there was the guilt that came with knowing that not everyone would know how to survive or be as prepared as us. Some would venture out and gaze up at the rain, wondering what anomaly they were witnessing.

Once the Jeep was unloaded, we made our way down to the basement and one by one entered the fallout shelter. I closed the steel hatch and locked it into place. I was the last one to enter the shelter. I clamped the locks and breathed a sigh of relief, though my mind hadn't stopped racing.

Each of us entered the decontamination area, stripped and took a shower before changing into fresh clothes. All of our clothes were carefully sealed inside plastic bags and kept in a storage locker. We weren't taking chances even with the small amount of drizzle that had fallen.

How you cleaned yourself mattered.

The key was not to scrub or scratch the skin, but to wash the hair with shampoo or soap and then cover up any cuts or abrasions to prevent any radioactive particles from entering open wounds.

The generator kicked in as warm water rushed over me and for a few seconds I closed my eyes and pushed the thought of that kid's dead body from my mind. How many more would I see over the coming days, weeks and months as violence erupted and how long would it be before I was forced to kill?

I felt like a new man after slipping into fresh clothes. A few chuckles came from farther inside, and Bridget asked if I wanted a hot drink. I muttered some reply then asked her to check if Ava wanted one. I was still doing up the belt on my jeans when I heard her panicked voice.

"Ava. Ava?"

I glanced up from navel gazing and poked my head around the corner. The expression on Bridget's face alerted me before her words did.

"She's not here. I told her to go to the shelter. I saw her go, Brody, I swear."

"Okay, don't panic," Chase said. Everyone began moving through the long shelter calling out her name and looking for her. They all knew that she had wanted to go home since the second she arrived. Her outburst at the house, and another here had made that painfully obvious.

"Ava!" I yelled but there was no response. I didn't wait another second; I was up the ladder and popped the hatch open. The others followed, and we went room by room.

"When did you last see her?" I asked Bridget grabbing hold of her.

"Maybe five minutes before you all returned. She said she wanted to head over to the Harpers' and hang out with Skylar but I told her she had to stay indoors."

I rushed to where we'd stored the CBRN suits and went about slipping into one.

"Wait, Brody," Chase said clasping my arm.

"My daughter is out there."

"But…" He pulled back the curtain and a heavy downpour of black rain fell. I continued suiting up unfazed by it. "Look," he yelled again. Though it was the middle of the afternoon, it looked like night outside. It descended in a torrent of black fluid, flowing and wiggling like worms down the face of the windowpane.

"I don't care, I'm not leaving her out there."

"She's probably inside the Harpers' house. You heard Bridget."

"And if she's not?"

Chase stared back at me as I covered my face with the hood and respiratory protector. I slung a rifle over my shoulder, pocketed ammo and took a Glock with me as I headed towards the door.

He hooked my arm before I turned the handle that led into the garage.

"Then I'm coming with you."

My perspiration began to fog up the mask as I nodded and pressed on. We would use the Jeep to get across to their home and hopefully reduce the amount of exposure to the rain. When Chase hopped in the passenger side, Todd and Jason were with him. I rolled the window down and told Marlin to pull up the garage door and then seal it closed as soon as we were out. Kai shouted that he would watch from the upper windows for our return.

The Jeep rumbled to life, and I eased it out and veered down the street towards the Harpers' home. My eyes roved side to side before pulling out. The streets were empty. A hard wind blew against the windshield and water pounded so hard that the wipers could barely clear it in time. The road before us was already being turned into a small stream of shiny black oil. It took less than two minutes to arrive at their home. I pulled in as far as I could before hopping out and sprinting to the door. I banged hard on the door but there was no response. They'd already experienced one home invasion, and they weren't expecting us to visit. I yelled loudly.

"Matt Harper, it's Brody. Can you hear me?"

Chase circled around back to try and get their attention, as we didn't know where they were, in the front or back of the basement. For all we knew they could have been locked inside a fallout shelter, in which case they might not even have heard us.

Chase reappeared and waved me over. "Brody!"

Jason stayed with the vehicle. Todd and I followed

him and found the sliding doors under the porch were open and Matt motioned us in. But we didn't enter. I didn't want to contaminate his house. My voice broke from behind the mask.

"Is Ava in there?"

A frown and headshake might have been enough to have me high-tailing it back to the Jeep, but I had to be certain so Matt called for his daughter, Skylar. She couldn't have been much older than Ava. A blond, doe-eyed and nervous-looking girl appeared, she looked past us to the dark rain splattering against the ground.

"Have you seen Ava?" Matt asked.

"She came over for about ten minutes but when you came back she left. She said she had to get home."

"What direction did she go, hon?" I asked.

She pointed haphazardly as if she was unsure. "Back up the street."

"Is everything okay?" Matt asked.

Now the street looped around like the eye of a needle and then stretched out at the end. We had come in on the left side so it was possible that she had traveled on the opposite side. I immediately turned and sprinted back to the Jeep.

"Brody," Jason called out.

"I know where she's going."

We hopped in and I backed out the Jeep so fast and without looking over my shoulder that I slammed into one of the stalled vehicles. It spun out, and the Jeep spluttered and died. Meanwhile rain continued to beat relentlessly against the vehicle, like small black stones drumming out a beat against a tin roof.

I turned the key, and it coughed. "C'mon!" I yelled trying again but it wouldn't start. I beat my fists against the steering wheel in frustration and then tried again. It spluttered, this time catching a little before it went silent. The fourth time it caught, and I revved the engine, shifted it in gear and gunned it. We jerked forward as it shot up the road, my heart pounding against my chest. My mind was a complete mess. Losing my daughter was all that I could think about even as Chase tried to tell me it was going to be okay.

The tires spun, and gravel spat against the sides of the Jeep as I hung a right onto Lake Mary Road. Through the torrential downpour, and wipers whipping back and forth, I scanned the area ahead searching for her. Condensation formed, and my vision became clouded by the damn mask. I wanted to tear it off.

I eased off the gas as the small silhouette of Ava came into view on the right side of the road. She had a tarp pulled over the top of her and was wearing a rain jacket and tall black rubber boots and running as fast as she could away from the neighborhood. Giving the accelerator a bit more pressure, I veered the Jeep about twenty feet in front of her to cut her off and jumped out. The very second she saw me she changed direction and rushed down an embankment.

"Ava!" I yelled but my voice was lost in the harsh weather. I took off after her, and slipped on the grass, landing hard on my side. I scrambled to my feet and gave chase, my thighs protesting with every stride. She ran into the thick pine trees that hedged in the road on either side. A few seconds later, the bag slipped from her hand, she turned to collect it only to see me closing the gap. I caught sight of her face, an expression of anguish. Tears streaked her cheeks as she bolted, though now losing the tarp that once covered her small frame. All that was protecting her now from the rain was the rain jacket, and that wasn't sufficient. Terror tore through me. Even though her head was down, she was breathing in the air. Air that was contaminated. I scooped up the tarp as I rushed by and within a matter of a minute I caught her around the waist. Like a fish on a hook, she struggled to free herself from my grasp.

I dropped to a knee and slung the tarp back over her, black droplets dripped off the end. "Let me go. Let go."

"Enough. Ava. Stop," I yelled.

"I just want to go home."

I started at her blankly.

"I want mom."

"I know, hon, but it's not safe to be out here."

"I don't care. I just want to go. I'm not going back."

She tried to pull away.

"Ava."

"You're not my father," she screamed in my face.

It was like a knife had been jammed into my heart. I felt my stomach catch in my throat. There was a break as she tried to catch her breath. "That's what mom says."

"Listen, I know you think I'm to blame for the break up. I'm not going to be able to change your mind on that. But I am your father. Maybe not the one you wished you had but I'm all you've got. And you are all I've got." I studied her face as I held her tightly. "One day you'll understand." I sighed. "I never stopped sending you cards, gifts or attempting to see you. I don't know what she did with them. Your mother didn't allow me…" I trailed off realizing this wasn't helping. Passing the blame only added fuel to the fire. This wasn't the time or place to have the conversation. I stared at her beneath the tarp. She looked like a scared, penned-in critter.

I was about to continue when I heard a single gunshot.

It echoed loudly. My head jerked to the side. "We need to go."

"I'm not."

I lost it in that moment. "If I have to throw you over my shoulder, you are going!"

She pulled again, and that's what I did, I hauled her up over my shoulder in a fireman's lift and trudged back to the roadway. More gunfire. What the hell was going on? As I got closer, I could see Todd and Chase outside of the vehicle, their rifles shouldered. Jason was on the ground, gripping his stomach. My eyes widened. They were taking cover behind the rear and every few seconds returning fire. My eyes darted farther up the road and that's when the pieces fell into place. *Shit!*

Keeping low to the ground, I placed Ava down and told her to stay out of sight. "Don't run." I stared right into her eyes and pleaded with her. "Please." She gave a nod. "Wait here."

I pulled my rifle off my shoulder and hurried along the tree line heading in the direction of the men. As I got closer, I counted heads. There were four armed men, kitted out in CBRN suits. We needed to get inside, not spend the next hour having a shootout. I only had one goal in mind, and that was to take out a tire. I kept away from the edge of the road and kept the truck in my line of sight. I placed my back against the tree, checked the magazine in the AR-15, chambered a round and brought it around. One shot. That's all it would take. I pressed the scope against my eye and squeezed the trigger.

The round echoed, the tire hissed and the four men who'd been taking cover turned my way and unleashed a flurry of rounds. I shifted position; my foot caught on a hidden tree root, and I slid down the side of a steep embankment. Thick brown soil mixed with the oily rain covered the suit. Gasping for air, I rolled out of view at the sound of men's voices and pressed myself into a thicket of mud and brambles. I gave it a minute or so before I peered out and shifted into a new spot that would have me behind them. Over the rise of earth and bushes, I could see Chase and Todd were still sporadically firing rounds. As my eyes drifted back to the men, I noticed that there were only three of them now. *Where'd you go?* I scanned the tree line. The sound of rain, and the heat of the day were making it hard to see. I ran a hand over the mask and a thick blur of dirt and black soil covered it, making it even worse. *Shit.*

With low visibility and the pummeling of rain and gunfire, I didn't hear the guy as he suddenly came into view and unloaded a round. It struck me in the chest and I reeled back and crumpled to the ground. My body rolled down the steep embankment disappearing into the brush. Searing pain gripped me. It hadn't penetrated the protective vest beneath my suit but it was going to leave one hell of a welt. It was the shock more than anything that caused me to gasp for air. The sound of boots trudging towards me pushed me back into action. I staggered to my feet and then dropped to a knee as I clawed at the ground to get beneath an uprooted tree. As I pressed myself into the soil to stay out of view I could hear his labored breathing, and the sound of his rifle as he chambered another round.

I peered around and spotted it. Damn! I'd dropped my rifle farther up the embankment. I reached for the Glock and held it against my chest as I pressed into the dirt beneath the overhang. The guy was right above me. His shadow cast before me. I didn't dare move a muscle. Not even an inch. Holding my breath I waited until he moved away before I exhaled. Not wasting a second, I rolled out, and scrambled up just in time to see him heading parallel to the tree line. If he continued on his way, he would run right into Ava. After that, he would easily be able to take out Chase and Todd.

I had a clear shot of his back.

He strode forward keeping his rifle low.

I raised the Glock. I knew this was it. My heart thumped hard, my pulse raced. I squeezed my eyes closed as I dropped to a knee. As it hit the earth and loose twigs and debris crunched, the man before me twisted. Everything seemed to slow in that moment. My breathing, his movement and my finger as it squeezed the trigger.

I fired two bullets, one round punched his chest, and the other struck him in the gut sending him backward. Knowing the gunfire would likely draw the others, I hurried forward scooping up my rifle, and moved back into position to get a view of the land.

Back at the truck one of the men was on the ground; only two remained. Divided, and feeling the pinch, they unleashed a flurry of rounds as they retreated back.

If we cut them loose, others will come, Marlin's words echoed in my mind.

Now I don't know at what point I crossed the line. Whether it was when I learned the truth about our country coming under attack, when the other man dropped, or when I made a decision to end those two men's lives, but I knew in that moment, life would never be the same again.

I raised my rifle, brought the first man's torso into the crosshair and didn't hesitate even for a second. The crack of the rifle split the air as the man crumpled. In one sweeping motion I focused in on the next. He tore off his mask to reveal the face of Markus. The same youngster that had tried to steel the Jeep in the beginning. He dropped his weapon and his hands shot up. Words spilled from his mouth as he dropped to his knees in an attempt to gain sympathy. A raw expression of fear masked his face. I was about to squeeze the trigger when a gunshot rang out. It was like witnessing Kennedy get shot in the back of the head. A portion of his scalp flipped up, and he fell face first against the wet asphalt.

Behind, jogging into view came Chase.

It felt like I'd been holding my breath for minutes when I exhaled. Drenched in sweat, my hands still shaking from adrenaline pumping through me, I climbed over the lip of the embankment. Chase gave a nod and went over to check that the men were dead; I gave a half-hearted sign of acknowledgement and then made my way down to collect Ava.

When I returned she was still in the same spot I'd placed her in, huddled under a canopy of branches that were dripping with oily black water. I extended a hand, and she crawled out from underneath, keeping the tarp tightly wrapped around her.

Back at the Jeep, I kept her behind me to shield her eyes from the bloody aftermath, including Jason' s body which now lay motionless against the back of the vehicle.

"Go hop inside, I'll be there in a second."

I closed the passenger door and went around to where Jason lay.

"They uh…" Todd began to say. "He tried to speak to them. Reason with them." He paused, shaking his head slowly. "They shot him in cold blood."

I crouched, removed Jason's mask and placed my glove over his eyelids. After, Todd helped lift his body into the back of the Jeep. The thought of telling Bridget overwhelmed me. It was going to be hard enough telling her, but being locked in that shelter over the coming days to bear witness to her grief, that would be unbearable. When Chase joined us, he said he'd checked the bodies for ID, to see if Malcolm had been among those seeking revenge.

"And?"

"Nothing." He shrugged. "Who knows? Maybe it was just a nickname for one of them." He paused for a second to glance at Jason. "We should head back," he said moving towards the passenger side.

"You took the shot," I said.

"So did you."

"What changed?"

Chase cast a glance over his shoulder. "There was a reason."

"Which was?" I knew but wanted to hear it from his mouth. Out of all of us he had been the one so adamant against any form of violence.

Without missing a beat he replied, "Our survival."

I slowly nodded. "And you can live with that?"

"Yeah." He then shrugged. "Maybe not, but it's what had to be done."

Todd slammed the back closed, and I gazed one last time at Jason's lifeless body through the window. Chase was right, but still, it should have never come to this, as our war wasn't with Americans and yet this was a new world we were entering.

A world in which one decision could have devastating repercussions.

Where appealing to someone's good nature could backfire.

And where hesitation could mean certain death.

I walked around to the driver's side and paused to reflect.

Who knew what tomorrow would bring, or what violence would erupt. America was at war, and only time would tell what that would mean for us. But one thing was certain, until it was over, we'd stand shoulder to shoulder, not as soldiers or brothers but old friends, ready to face the dangers of a nation on the verge of collapse.

* * *

THANK YOU FOR READING

War Buds: (Under Attack Book 1)

War Buds: On Alert Book 2 will be out in June 2017

A Plea

Thank you for reading War Buds: Under Attack. If you enjoyed the book, I would really appreciate it if you would consider leaving a review. Without reviews, an author's books are virtually invisible on the retail sites. It also lets me know what you liked. You can leave a review by visiting the book's page. I would greatly appreciate it. It only takes a couple of seconds.

Thank you — **Jack Hunt**

Newsletter

Thank you for buying War Buds: Under Attack, published by Direct Response Publishing.

Click here to receive special offers, bonus content, and news about new Jack Hunt's books. Sign up for the newsletter. http://www.jackhuntbooks.com/signup/

About the Author

Jack Hunt is the author of horror, sci-fi and post-apocalyptic novels. He currently has three books out in the Camp Zero series, five books out in the Renegades series, three books in the Agora Virus series, one out in the Armada series, a time travel book called Killing Time and another called Mavericks: Hunters Moon. Jack lives on the East coast of North America.

67872410R00255